The Wildflower Gazebo

Sarah Norkus

The Wildflower Gazebo

Published by West Alden Publishing, LLC

First printing 2018

ISBN 978-0-9976002-4-7 (Trade Paperback)

Cover design by Bonnie Watson. All rights reserved.

Published in the United States of America

In memory of my mother

Sophie

Chapter One

Summer 2012

Rain pounded Interstate 94's six lanes of traffic. Sophie Madison, along with other early morning commuters, hit the brakes as the visibility hovered near zero percent. The windshield wipers, whipping across the drenched glass, were of little help since her eyes were awash with tears.

A white truck swerved into Sophie's lane. Her hands trembled from the close call. If she had braked, she would have skidded into the concrete barrier skimming by on the right. Traffic halted within a few yards of an exit ramp. Sophie jerked the steering wheel and the SUV crossed on to the shoulder. She sped down the ramp, which dumped her out into more traffic.

She grabbed a tissue from the floral cardboard box on the console and ran it back and forth beneath her nose. When another ramp loomed up through the rain, she veered toward it, barely slowing in time behind a compact car.

An hour later, dry eyed and feeling as hollowed out as a dead tree stump, Sophie studied her surroundings. The rain had stopped, and she was almost to La Grange. Her mouth dropped open. What? *How did I get here?* Her slim fingers turned the wheel and she left WI-20 onto Territorial Road. This was a stretch of road she could have driven blind-folded, despite the fact she hadn't been back in the area for fourteen years. Her heart was beating a rapid tattoo in her chest. *No, no, no, I can't go back. Turn around!* But her foot continued to apply steady pressure to the gas pedal.

The odometer had clicked over another two miles by the time Sophie turned onto a heavily cracked asphalt driveway. The gray metal mail box lay rusting in the chickweed beside the warped weathered stake that had been hammered in the ground decades ago. Sophie's silver SUV bumped along, corn ripening to her left. The car slowed to a stop. As beads of perspiration appeared on her forehead, Sophie eyed the scene through the passenger window. Weeds and grass grew waist-high amongst the charred remains of the farmhouse. Sophie turned the key in the ignition and silence engulfed her.

Waves of nausea struck with a vengeance. Sophie fumbled with the door handle and then threw open the door. She lurched two feet before vomiting in the unkempt grass, heaving until nothing was left. She stumbled back to the car and reached over the driver's seat for the tissues. Sophie wiped her watery eyes and snotty nose, dropping the tissue on the ground. She grabbed her water bottle out of the cup holder, took in a mouthful and then spit it out in the weeds. She straightened and looked around at the landscape as she screwed the cap back on the bottle.

The large barn was missing half of its roof. Water and wind had taken a toll on the decades-old structure. The four walls still stood upright, barely. Sophie shuddered. What creatures now called it home? The silo had stood the passage of time better. The sun, peeping through the clouds, glinted off the metal of the circular building.

The lease manager mailed her a check once a month that barely covered the land taxes and insurance. She had given up trying to sell the farmland five years ago. No one had wanted to buy it except the neighbor to the right of the property to enlarge his acreage. But his counter offer was an insult. The farm was smaller than the properties that surrounded it, but her family had made a decent living in corn.

Sophie turned back to the remains of her home. A vision of a rambling, one-story clapboard structure, painted a pristine white, with a front porch and a brick-red tin roof, superimposed over the burned out dwelling. The shimmering front door opened and she was inside the farmhouse, gazing around the front parlor her mother had decorated with French country-styled furniture after Sophie's paternal grandmother had died. The sofa and chair cushions had been cream colored. A champagne and cream damask rug had covered the worn wooden floorboards.

Her virtual tour continued out of the parlor and down a hallway, past two bedrooms and a bathroom on the right, another bedroom, dining room and kitchen on the left. At the end of the hall was the den. Brown leather furniture sat upon an oriental rug in gold and brown hues.

A dog barked and the image vaporized. Sophie rubbed a clammy hand down the side of her workout pants and shoved the car door shut. Water bottle in hand, she crossed the uneven asphalt. Seed-topped blades of wet grass brushed her thighs as she made her way to the front of the foundation. She halted a foot shy of the porch swing's black skeleton. She closed her eyes. Her mother's voice had carried over the steady creak of the slight swaying.

"Sophie, ma petite, have you ever seen so many stars twinkling in the night sky?"

Sophie turned her head slightly on her Mama's shoulder and looked up at the multitude of blinking white dots. "No, Mama, never."

Her mama's arm tightened around her nine-year-old shoulders. "We are truly blessed to witness God's glory in the sky each and every night.

Sophie drowsily murmured, "We truly are, Mama."

Sophie opened her eyes, an ache shooting through her. She turned from the swing, walked to the right, and stepped around the corner of the foundation. She paused at the spot where her bedroom window used to be. Icy tentacles squeezed her chest before Sophie swiftly turned. A majestic oak stood a mere three yards away, a dry-rotted tire peeking through the tall mixture of grass and weeds.

Sophie's laughter filled the air as the tire swing swung high into an impossibly blue sky, her long dark hair flowing back from her face. "Higher, Aaron."

The young man laughed as his muscled arms pushed her ever higher. "Hold on tight."

Sophie's lips quivered as she turned away, walking to the rear edge of the foundation. A musical tinkling carried on the light breeze. The clothesline was made of two metal T bars, with four strands of rusted wire strung between them. Still tied to one of the bars, by nylon string, was an angel wind chime swaying gently. Her mama's face had glowed with delight when she pulled apart the tissue paper and discovered the angels nestled there in the silver box.

Sophie had taken only a few steps when she stopped at the crunch under her shoe. A broken beer bottle lay among the weeds. She shook her head and continued to make a path through the overgrowth to the clothesline. She touched one of the celestial figurines. Corrosion made the metal rough beneath her fingers. She dropped her hand and glanced up. Beyond the clothesline was the small grape arbor. Or what was left of it. The wooden posts and lattice lay on the ground, rotting, riddled with worm holes. But the grape vine had managed to survive, its grasping fingers twisting around the trunk and branches of a nearby pine tree. The fruit would be hardly bigger than a mustard seed at this time of the season. Sophie let go a whisper of a sigh as two figures from the past wavered beside the ghostly image of the intact arbor.

Sophie and her mother stood side by side on a cool September morning, picking the clusters of blue-black grapes.

"What kind of grapes are these, Mama?"

"They're called Worden grapes."

"They make the best-tasting jelly in the whole world." Sophie's earnest face looked up at her mother.

Mama smiled. "Can't argue with that, sugar plum."

Sophie's small forehead furrowed. "Why do you call me sugar plum sometimes, Mama?"

Mama shifted the basket on her arm to a more comfortable position. "Because of the Christmas story, of course. 'The children all snuggled, asleep in their beds, while visions of sugar plums danced in their heads.' That was my favorite story and I asked my papa one time what a sugar plum was. He said it's the sweetest thing you would ever come across in your lifetime."

A sad look crossed her mama's face for a moment and was gone.

She set her hand under Sophie's chin. "And he was right."

Sophie drew a finger across her wet lashes. She took a deep breath. She had to leave...*now*. Reliving memories best left buried had drained her and if she stayed any longer, the *other* memories might...

Sophie turned in the direction of her car and took three steps before pausing. Something winked at her from the corner of her left eye. She looked around. There. A shiny gold object between the tall blades of grass by the foundation. She walked onto a moss-covered patch of ground and looked down. The object was a crumpled, gold beer can with a black label. Her eyes widened as the ground shifted beneath her feet and started to give way, but before she could even blink the ground gave way completely and Sophie fell in a yawning hole.

Chapter Two

Bryan Taylor was late. The weather was terrible and he had been stuck in traffic for over an hour. His long legs strode into the operations section of the motorcycle manufacturing building in Milwaukee. He murmured a greeting to his secretary as he pushed open the door to his office.

Bryan stared out the large plate-glass window as Ms. Carter recited his schedule for the day and the latest crisis that had popped up on one of the manufacturing lines. His secretary's words slowed to a halt.

"Are you okay, Mr. Taylor?"

Bryan turned to face his secretary. "What? Oh…fine. There was an accident on the interstate."

But his thoughts weren't on the accident as his forefinger tapped a manila folder atop the desk. *Maybe he should call her.* As his secretary left the office with a worried glance in his direction, Bryan thought back to the conversation fraught with emotion that had taken place in his kitchen that morning.

Sophie had shown up at his condo dressed in black spandex workout pants, a bright pink t-shirt, and matching pink running shoes. Her long, gleaming, dark hair was pulled back in a tight ponytail. The aroma of hazelnut from the mug in his hand had risen to his nostrils as the breath caught in his throat. His fiancée simply was the most beautiful woman he had ever encountered. The type of beauty the troubadours wrote ballads for in medieval times. His gut had clenched.

She had accepted the mug of coffee, her gaze curious as he led the way into the kitchen area and the onyx-topped table. As soon as they were settled in chairs, Bryan spoke.

"I know you're wondering why I called and asked you to meet me here so early in the morning."

When Sophie didn't comment, Bryan gave a heaving sigh. "I can't do this anymore, Sophie. When you told me on Friday that you were pushing back the date of the wedding for the third time…it opened my eyes. You may not have consciously acknowledged it yet, but subconsciously you have. For some reason…you don't want to marry me."

Sophie's aquamarine eyes widened. "No, Bryan, that's not true. I told you my friend, Erica, is a bridesmaid and her boss gave her a promotion which comes with a special assignment. I need to postpone the wedding for only two more months."

"The first time you postponed, for your aunt's passing, was understandable—but not for three months. And then you postponed again because you had a story you had to cover for your newspaper for two months…and now a third excuse so you don't have to marry me."

Sophie's fingers gripping the mug turned white. "Bryan, it's not my fault that these circumstances…"

He placed a hand over Sophie's free hand. "The truth, Sophie. You owe me that."

Sophie's eyes welled up. "I love you… I do. I don't know if…" Sophie's bottom lip trembled. "…if I can marry…"

Bryan gripped her hand tighter. "Me?"

The tears spilled over. "It's not you."

Bryan whispered, "Talk to me."

Sophie shook her head. "I can't. And even if I could, it wouldn't change the fact that you're right. I *have* been looking for excuses...because deep down I know I can't marry you... or anyone else."

"Why?" A vise squeezed his heart.

Sophie's voice, barely a whisper, ignored the question, "You don't want to marry me."

She had pulled her hand from his, removed the engagement ring from the third finger of her left hand and set it on the table, the gold and diamond glinting against the black stone.

"I'm sorry, Bryan. Please forgive me." Starting to cry in earnest, Sophie had fled the condo.

Bryan's thoughts returned to the present as he walked around his burnished steel desk and sat down in the plush leather chair. He pulled his cell phone out of the holster on his belt. His finger hovered above the screen. *No, calling would make things worse.* She had made it clear. She didn't want to marry him. He was going to have to accept it and move on even though the pain in his gut said otherwise. The phone on his desk buzzed. Bryan set down his cell and lifted the receiver.

Chapter Three

Sophie's left ankle rammed onto the packed earth and she screamed, crumpling on her side. Groaning in pain, she pushed herself upright, onto her rear end. She took a deep breath and a spasm of coughing overtook her. The air was thick with the odor of mold and rotting wood. Sophie gritted her teeth and pivoted on to her knees. Leveraging her right foot against the ground and hands on the rough wall of the enclosure, she pushed up to a standing position.

Balancing on one foot, a wave of racking coughs took her breath away. Once it passed, Sophie raised her hand above her head and grabbed the ragged end of a moss-covered board. She yanked and it gave way without a struggle, letting a little more light in the dank circular hole. She took mincing steps, methodically pulling on the rest of the spongy boards, dropping them at her feet.

Sophie lifted her face towards the fresh air, struggling to take breaths between coughs. After a few minutes, her lungs filled with enough untainted oxygen and the coughing stopped. She wiped her filth-encrusted hands on the black spandex covering her legs and scrutinized the curved walls lined with old bricks. If it was a square, it would be about five feet by five feet.

Moisture from the recent rain oozed out of the soil near the top of the hole and trickled down the face of the bricks. Directly across from her, a cast iron pipe jutted out from between the bricks a few inches below ground level. Sophie grimaced with disgust. She had forgotten about the old dry well...once used as a depository for the dirty water from the sinks, bathtub, and washing machine of the farmhouse. The good news, if there was any to be had, was that she hadn't fallen in the old drinking well, with a depth of sixty-three feet. Her mama hadn't wanted to take the chance of her daughter falling in that well. It had been filled in before her birth.

She limped closer to a portion of the curving wall that faced the driveway. The bricks had been cemented together. Sophie pressed a finger against the cement above one of the bricks; it was firm. Her gaze roamed over the wall, pausing at a section two feet from the floor. A nugget of cement was missing. Sophie slipped two fingernails in the hole and tried to pry away a bigger chunk. She squealed when a nail ripped. She lifted the offended finger towards her mouth, but the tickle of blood was mixing with dirt. *Gross.* She pressed the finger against her t-shirt, trying to staunch the wound. She would need something to pry out the cement and brick if she wanted a foothold in the wall.

Sophie winced as she turned. She picked up a chunk of the wet wood. It had the consistency of the roast she cooked all day in her crock pot. She raised her arm and chucked it out of the hole. She spied her water bottle partially buried under another chunk of wood. She tossed the soggy wood aside and reached for the plastic bottle. Her hand froze in midair and her body tensed.

The bone was the color of parchment. Sophie's heart started beating like a trip hammer. She backed up until she was flush against the opposite wall. Sensing danger, her body was struggling with 'fight or flight' not realizing neither choice was an option. *Is it a human bone?* The stomach juices left in her gut started to churn.

Sophie clamped the back of her left hand over her mouth as the bile rose in her esophagus. She turned towards the wall, swallowing hard. *I won't throw up...again.* She shut her eyes and tried taking deep breaths. Her breathing slowed, the urge to vomit passing. She opened her eyes, blinked and tried an experimental swallow. *Get a grip, Sophie! You've seen worse than this. You're a reporter. Think like a reporter.* Sophie stiffened her spine and hopped the four steps back to the bone.

Her mouth formed a grim line as she gingerly lifted the rest of the rotted boards to reveal a full skeleton. It lay on its side, pressed against the curving wall that faced the back of the burned out house. The skull was not attached—the empty eye sockets facing the opposite wall. For the second time in less than fifteen minutes, something gold winked at her. She bent down and picked up a delicate gold necklace. A one-inch 'A' hung from the tiny links. A crow cawed. Sophie jerked, and fresh pain exploded in her ankle. She took deep breaths and eased down on to her buttocks, drawing up her knees as she stared at the necklace cupped in her palm. Raising her head, she studied the skeleton.

Nature's tiniest creatures had done a thorough job. There was no flesh on the bones. Tiny bits of fabric were attached to a zipper lying on the ground near the torso. Near the bones of the feet were two dark gray rubber objects shaped like the soles of shoes. She was no expert on the human body; she hadn't even taken an anatomy class in college. But it was likely the skeleton was female, based on the necklace. *Someone's daughter, sister, mother.*

"What is she doing in the dry well?" Sophie murmured. "I know she wasn't an idiot and fell in like I did. Those old boards have been covering this well for years, since before I left the farm."

A chill climbed her spine. Sophie pushed away from the bones. The hand holding the necklace started to tremble. *Could her father have...?* For the first time in fourteen years, her father's face rose up in her mind.

Sophie squeezed her eyes together, trying to force the image from her mind. But the image remained, and then was joined by others as memories flooded her mind like a disjointed slide show...pieces of recollections flashing rapidly, one after another. *The blades of her bedroom ceiling fan lazily circling above her as her eyes opened...the shattering of a water glass...the corn stalks so achingly green as she raced toward them in desperation...the sun suddenly blinding her as she lay in the dirt.*

A loud thrumming filled Sophie's ears and her breathing quickened.

The screen door slammed shut behind her... and Sophie jerked in the well, the sound so vivid. More sounds melded with the images. *The rustling of the corn...the pounding of her feet...her labored breathing.*

Sophie clasped her hands over her ears. The terrifying slide show abruptly stopped and her father's angry, confused face loomed impossibly large, followed almost immediately by Aaron's beloved face twisted in a mask of horror.

A scream erupted from the well. Crows perching in the old oak took flight, cawing and screeching. Sophie's grimy hands covered her face as she sobbed the child's anguish hidden so long in her adult body.

Sophie pulled the hem of her shirt up to her face and wiped her eyes and nose. Dropping the hem, she looked up at the clouds drifting above her and sighed. She felt lighter, like her mind had expunged a cancerous piece of tissue. The summer of her seventeenth year, Sophie had done the only thing she could to hold on to her sanity: she had locked away the trauma she had suffered in a mental safe. She hadn't listened to the therapist, the one and only time she made an appointment, who told her she needed to face her demons, bring them into the light of day and not let them consume her.

The mental safe had proven to be an illusion. The memory had been lurking, waiting for the crack in her mental defenses to occur so it could flood her mind. The therapist had been right. Sophie unclenched her hand and gazed at the necklace laying on her palm. She turned her head towards the bones. Absently, she shoved the gold necklace in the small pocket of her spandex capris, where she placed her car key when she jogged at the park. *Could her father be responsible for…?* She shook her head. *No, it wasn't him.*

Sophie leaned back and groaned. A painful pressure was building in her left ankle. She glanced at her foot. Her ankle was swollen. She untied her running shoe, grimacing as she removed her shoe and ankle sock. Definitely swollen, and there was a large scrape barely visible beneath the grime from the floor of the well. Looking at it seemed to cause it to start stinging. *Great, just great.*

Sophie eased across the floor of the well and retrieved her water bottle. She unscrewed the top and started to pour water on the cut. *Wait.* She didn't know how long she'd be stuck in the well and she didn't want to get dehydrated. Sophie recapped the bottle and scooted back to the wall.

As she stared down at her foot again, heaviness filled her body. She was tired. She blinked her eyes, and then blinked them again. When the lids dropped the third time she had no will to lift them, and fell asleep propped upright against the damp brick wall.

The absence of movement and sound encouraged a diversity of insects to emerge from the tiny cracks and crevices imbedded throughout the well. They had scattered and hidden when their habitat exploded with noise. A centipede crawled around one of the skeletal feet. Carpenter ants marched over the rotted boards. Pill bugs unrolled, but stayed stationary, waiting. A small spider chased another up the clammy bricks close to Sophie's head. Breathing evenly, she slept on oblivious until—Sophie's eyes snapped opened, her heart pounding in her chest. Her head snapped back and forth as her eyes darted around the well. *What...what?*

Her eyes widened and her lips quivered. A dream...about her mother. A family outing to the lake...one of many before her twelfth birthday. In the dream, she had been sitting on an old patchwork quilt, wearing her favorite yellow one-piece bathing suit. Her father had been fishing on the pier and her mother reclining on the beach lounge chair in a one-piece bathing suit and large brimmed white hat, looking like one of the beautiful Hollywood actresses of the nineteen forties.

A dark shadow had fallen across the blanket and Sophie had looked up. Angry clouds had formed and a strong wind ruffled the dark bangs across her brow. The temperature had dropped and she had started to shiver. Her gazed had lowered to her mother. But she had disappeared and her father was shouting…demanding to know why God had taken her away.

Sophie's eyes glistened as she whispered, "Mama." She stiffened and pain shot through her ankle as her gaze fell on the bones. She averted her eyes from the skeleton and glanced down at her ankle. It needed to be elevated and iced.

Using her arms as leverage, Sophie pushed herself on her butt over to the pile of rotted boards. Heedless of any bugs making the wet timber their new home, Sophie grabbed an armful and inched back up against the wall. She dropped the boards as a coughing fit erupted. The spasm passed. How many mold spores had she inhaled since her unexpected drop in the well? Sophie arranged the boards under her swollen foot. The boards only elevated her foot by a few inches, but it would have to do. When she raised her head, white spots danced briefly in her vision and she felt lightheaded. She grasped the water bottle and twisted off the top. She only took a small swallow. She paused in the act of screwing on the top and tilted her head back an inch. She held her breath. Someone was moving through the grass.

Sophie shouted, "Hey! Can you hear me? I need help! Hey, is someone there?"

She paused to listen.

The rustling grew louder. "Hey, I need…"

The grinning face of a yellow Labrador retriever loomed over her head. Sophie's shoulders sagged.

"I don't suppose your master's with you?"

The lab's mouth opened and he started to pant, saliva dripping off his elongated tongue.

"You're a good boy. Or girl. Go get your master. Okay? Do you understand me? Go home. Get help."

The lab continued to pant.

"Great, English must not be your first language. How about French? Au secours!"

The lab stopped panting and cocked his head. Laughter bubbled up from Sophie's chest.

"You understand French."

The Lab cocked his head in the other direction and Sophie laughed out loud.

"Now you're bilingual."

The dog let out a loud bark and Sophie jerked as the sound echoed around the well.

"Don't bark, okay? It hurts my ears."

The Lab's head snapped to the right and then he was gone. Sophie lowered her head. *How am I going to get out of here?* Her eyes started to well up again. *No. Stop feeling sorry for yourself.* Sophie squared her shoulders. *I need to concentrate on something else.* She stared at the skeleton.

It had been ridiculous to think that her father had in any way been responsible for this girl's death. It had only crossed her mind because it was his well. No, her father absolutely couldn't be the one who dumped the body in the well. It would have begun to stink to high heaven after a day or two and she would have smelled it. Someone put the body in the dry well after the farm was abandoned fourteen years ago.

Sophie addressed the detached head. "If I ever…correction, when I get out of here I'm going to find out who put you here. And you can take that to the bank because I'm a bloodhound when it comes to chasing down stories."

Her heart beat faster. There were many possibilities. *Was it a planned murder, a crime of passion, involuntary manslaughter?* She would check with her sources for missing persons and… Sophie grimaced then wiggled and squeezed her lower extremities.

"Come on, not here."

Her bladder ignored her plea and Sophie groaned.

A few minutes later, sweating profusely and ready to pass out, Sophie eased herself back onto her rear end and propped up her foot. Her speculations about the skeleton receded and remnants of her dream returned and, with it, her mama's voice as clear as if she sat beside her. *Pray for God's help, Sophie.*

Her mother's faith in God had been absolute. Genevieve's family in New Orleans had disowned her when she married Sophie's father, yet Genevieve had prayed for them every day. Sophie's lips formed a tight line. She had learned the hard way that God didn't give two flips for her. *You were wrong about God, mama. He won't help.*

Chapter Four

Allison Summers looked up from her computer screen and the headline she was crafting for an article on one of Milwaukee's small business success stories. Something felt—wrong. Her gaze traveled around the room. Reporters pecked away at their keyboards. Kirk's bespectacled face was intent on the copy in his hands. She glanced up at one of the ceiling fans circulating the frigid air. It didn't look like it was about to come loose and crash onto her desk, but that was the feeling plaguing her—like something bad was about to happen.

"Ridiculous," She muttered as she glanced at the wall clock.

In an hour, she could ditch her desk and head to *Paddy*'s for her lunch date with Sophie. A journalist like herself, Sophie had taken a well-deserved day off. Allison's upper teeth pulled on her lower lip as she thought about her best friend. To their co-workers here at the *Journal Sentinel*, Sophie was her usual cheerful, driven persona. But beneath the façade, something had been bothering Sophie for a while. Allison hadn't wanted to push, but she was worried. Maybe Sophie would confide what was going on with her at lunch.

"Ms. Summers."

Allison looked across the room at her boss, one of the editors of the paper, standing in the doorway to his office, arms crossed.

"Sir?"

"Where is the article on that bakery you promised me thirty minutes ago?"

"I'll send it to your computer in two minutes." Allison turned back to the computer, her fingers a blur of motion.

Allison squeezed the slice of lemon and then dropped it on the small plate beside her glass of ice water. She brushed a lock of her salon-dyed chestnut hair behind her ear as she leaned down to look at the time on her smartphone. *Paddy*'s was crowded, the loud buzz of multiple conversations swirling around her. She glanced over at the walnut door with the oval glass cutout as two women in their twenties pushed it open and strode in. *Where is she?* Sophie was twenty minutes late, and she was never late. Allison sent off a text and waited. She stared at the phone, willing it to beep. When no answering text was forthcoming, she tapped a button to dial Sophie. It rang five times before voice mail picked up. She left a message then sipped water as she continued to wait.

"Hey, new eyes, how's it going?" Ron Shank pulled out a chair from the table and sat, casually crossing one leg over the other.

"Not funny." Allison glared at the morning news anchor for the national affiliate, WTMJ.

"The glasses are gone and rumor has it you had laser eye surgery last week. Spill, cupcake."

No one got on her nerves more than her ex-boyfriend. "It's none of your business."

"Now, now, play nice. Three months ago, you played very nice." His handsome face gave her a knowing look.

Allison's face burned as the anger built. "Leave, Ron, now, before…"

"Before, what? You hurl your water glass at me?" His eyes narrowed. "You still owe me for the broken mirror."

"So sue me."

A leggy blonde with perfect features strode up to her table and spoke to Ron. "Here you are. I thought we were meeting on the patio."

Ron uncrossed his legs and rose to kiss the woman on the cheek. "Sorry, sweetie, I ran into an ex and stopped to say hi."

He cocked his head and studied Allison. "Really, if I were you I'd go back to the glasses; they gave you more of an… intellectual air."

Allison's hand closed around the cold glass, ready to follow through with Ron's suggestion—then sanity prevailed. She watched him walk toward the back door, one arm draped around the blondes' waist. *What goes around comes around, buddy.* Her anger evaporated as her mind turned back to Sophie. Something was wrong. It was the same feeling she had had back at the office. She picked up her phone and dialed another number.

"Bryan, it's Allison. Do you know where Sophie is?"

"I'm sorry, I don't." Bryan's voice was brusque.

"She was supposed to meet me for lunch, but she's thirty minutes late and I'm worried." Allison glanced up as the door opened again. It wasn't Sophie.

There was a pause, then Bryan spoke, discomfort clear in the tone. "I may know the reason. We broke off our engagement this morning. She was crying when she left my condo."

"Oh, no." Allison closed her eyes, her chest constricting.

Bryan cleared his throat. "I'm sorry. I don't know where she could be. She was dressed in her running outfit when she left."

Allison opened her eyes. "Okay. I'll keep trying to reach her. Thanks. Bye."

She pressed the disconnect on Bryan's goodbye then pulled two dollars out of her purse and dropped it on the table as the waiter walked towards her. She pushed her chair back.

"Sorry, my friend couldn't make it."

Allison elbowed the front door of the pub open and adjusted her sunglasses against the afternoon glare. She rushed to her vehicle. Nosing her car into traffic, she turned in the direction of Sophie's house instead of back to the office.

A traffic light turned green and Allison took a right, stepping on the gas. Tendrils of ice had wrapped around her chest, making it hard to breath. Sophie was your typical Type A personality, almost military in her organization, leadership skills, and sense of responsibility. No matter how upset Sophie was, she would have contacted Allison to cancel lunch...unless something had happened to prevent her from doing so.

Allison pulled into Sophie's driveway and slammed on the brakes. As she ran to the front door, she said a quick prayer. *God, please don't let my worst fear be true. Please tell me Sophie didn't do anything stupid.*

Allison banged on the front door of the small house, shouting her friend's name. She waited a few seconds then raced around the corner of the house to the back screened-in porch. She opened the screen door then pounded on the back door. No sound of feet approaching. Allison twisted the knob—locked. Her heart jumped into her throat. The hand gripping the knob trembled. She let go of the knob and took a step back...*Allison, get a grip!* She mentally slapped herself and took a couple of deep breaths. Logic began to seep into her brain. *Sophie wouldn't commit suicide over the breakup of her engagement.* She had to think. Allison closed her eyes then, two seconds later, snapped them open. *Her car.* She rushed to the garage and looked through the window. It was gone.

Allison strode to her ten-year-old compact vehicle as she went over the facts. Sophie was upset. She was in her running clothes. *Okay, the breakup of her engagement wipes everything else from her mind. Maybe she ran ten miles then came home, still upset, felt the house closing in and went shopping or something. Maybe she left her cell at home and forgot about our lunch date. There is a first time for everything.*

Allison nodded her head as she turned the ignition. Sophie would call as soon as she got her message. But as she looked over her shoulder and backed down the driveway, her stomach gave a nauseating flip.

Chapter Five

Identical twins Ryan and Kevin Peterman sauntered down the gravel strip beside the asphalt of Territorial Road ignoring the cars whizzing by. A few heads turned in their direction. Large headphones covered the boys' ears, blasting their favorite tunes and deafening them to any other sounds. Neither boy was in a good mood. Both teens were grounded until the end of the month. No cell phones, videos, driving privileges (car or boat), hanging out with friends, and a curfew of nine o'clock every night.

Two weeks before, they had taken their parent's boat to the lake with a few friends to throw back beers away from prying eyes. Kevin had cranked the speed too high when he drove the boat onto the boat trailer and the front of the boat crashed into the tailgate of the truck. Their father had been furious about the damage and the beer can the boys had missed while cleaning up the boat. The hammer had come down, with a thud, on them and their friends. Ryan and Kevin's parents had torn their bedrooms apart looking for more beer. But they didn't find any alcohol because the teens didn't hide it at home. The twins stashed it at an abandoned barn a quarter mile down the road. They had waited until today, when both of their parents were gone, to head for the barn and get a buzz on.

Ryan and Kevin's identical hands gripped the hard muffs of their headphones as their heads of unkempt brown hair bobbed to the music. The teens turned onto the gray-white asphalt drive, their feet faltering to a stop. In the year that they had been coming to the abandoned barn, the only vehicle they had seen was the dilapidated truck of the old farmer that leased the fields. Kevin started to turn back the way they had come. Ryan shook his head. Kevin lifted the headphones and let them cradle his neck.

"Someone's here."

Ryan jerked his headphones off with his right hand. "I don't care. I haven't had a buzz in two weeks and I'm getting the beer. We can drink it somewhere else."

Kevin scrubbed at the light fuzz covering his chin. "What if whoever's here catches us?"

"We can say we were looking for our lost dog."

Kevin's eyes darted around nervously. "I don't know, Ryan."

Ryan's fingers swiped sweat off of his forehead. The early rain had turned the hot day irritatingly steamy. "So go home. I'm going in the barn."

Kevin's Adam's apple moved up and down as he swallowed. "No...I'll stay and be lookout."

The boys approached the vehicle on silent feet and peeked inside. The SUV was empty.

"Do you see what I see?" Ryan whispered.

Kevin's eyes were darting around the landscape. "What?" He whispered back.

Ryan pointed at the ignition. Keys were dangling from it. Kevin's eyes widened.

"No, Ryan. Are you crazy?"

Ryan looked around the abandoned property. "I just want to drive to Milwaukee and hang out for a couple of hours. We'll dump it somewhere before curfew and walk home."

"But..."

Ryan's eyes grew steely. "Get in or go home."

Ryan was the older twin by six minutes and tended towards aggression and domination. Kevin generally deferred to him on all issues. He walked to the passenger door, opening it as quietly as possible, and slid in. Ryan opened the driver door, tossing his headphones onto the back seat.

"Don't shut your door until I start the engine."

Adrenaline coursed through Ryan. He took a breath and turned the key in the ignition. The engine started, Ryan shut his door and punched the gear shift in reverse. He slammed his foot on the gas and the SUV shot backwards, bouncing wildly over the ruts and cracked mounds to Territorial Road.

Kevin stared out the windshield, his grip on the dashboard draining his fingers of blood. His butt repeatedly jumped off the seat as he waited for the owner to appear and chase them. The car skidded backwards onto the road. Ryan shifted gears and pressed the gas pedal to the floor.

As Ryan whooped and pumped his fist in the air, Kevin looked back at the driveway. Why hadn't anyone appeared to stop them?

Sophie had started to doze off again when she heard a car engine start up. The engine roared, and then the sound receded and was gone. Her sea green eyes widened. *That was my car!*

She started to get up and then eased back down, sucking in quick little breaths. Tears welled and she slammed an impotent fist against the damp floor. She raised her fist again but stopped the motion halfway to the floor. *Someone stole my car.* Her jaw dropped open. *Who would steal my car?* Her heart started pounding and she broke out in a cold sweat. The odds weren't good that anyone would think to look for her at the farm, but at least a local might have seen the car and maybe be curious enough to check out a strange vehicle. But now the chances of someone finding her were about nil to none.

Sophie's body shook and her breathing hitched. This time Sophie didn't even try to stop the tears. As she wept, she wasn't conscious of uttering a petition to a God she no longer believed in. "Oh, God, no...Oh, God, no..."

A goose honked overhead as Sophie took a shuttering breath, her mind wandering back to her dream.

"Mama, I'm in trouble," Sophie whispered.

Her gaze settled on the human bones and an icy hand squeezed her heart. If no one found her here soon, there would be two skeletons to discover.

Sophie crossed her arms across her belly and squeezed. "Mama, I need you. I wish you were here."

Her eyes lost focus as her mind leapt back to the last time she had seen her mother. It was a bitterly cold morning in January—music was drifting into her bedroom from the kitchen...

Chapter Six

Winter 1993

The twelve-year-old girl leaned into the mirror on her dresser and applied pink gloss to her lips. Pulling back, she rubbed her lips together as she had seen her mother do countless times. She stared at her eyelashes. If only she could wear mascara. But her mama said not until she was thirteen. Her mother had used a curling iron on her long dark hair, the curls cascading to her waist. She picked up the hair spray and closed her eyes, lightly spraying her bangs.

Sophie set the can down and picked up a pink scrunchy, slipping it over her wrist. She stepped back and, with a critical eye, reviewed her outfit. She wore a white turtleneck under her pink sweater. Her jeans, tapering down at the ankle, were tucked in her half boots.

"What do you guys think?"

Every inch of Sophie's walls was covered in posters. Madonna, Amy Grant, Mariah Carey, Justin Timberlake, and the rest of the gang kept their opinions to themselves.

Sophie, breakfast is ready." Her mother's voice called from the kitchen.

Sophie paused in the doorway to the kitchen. Her father was sneaking up on her mother. Jimmy grabbed Genevieve around the waist and twirled her around to face him.

He tilted her back and grabbed an invisible microphone. "Oh, let me be... your Teddy Bear."

Many of mama's friends had said that her papa could have been Elvis Presley's twin. They talked about his full lips, white teeth, and wide smile. His hair was that same blue-black color... although her mama told her Elvis had dyed his hair. They said Jimmy had dark eyebrows and brooding eyes just like the rock and roll king. Whatever 'brooding' meant. She just knew that her papa was handsome. She smiled at their antics.

Genevieve pushed on Jimmy's broad chest. "Let me go. I don't have time for your foolishness."

But her pink cheeks said otherwise. Genevieve never tired of his playfulness.

Jimmy pulled her upright. "Yes, ma'am, but payment in advance for the shoveling I will be doing in the bitter, bitter cold."

Genevieve's toes, incased in their pale-yellow slippers, pushed up and gave Jimmy a warm kiss on the mouth.

Jimmy eased his arms from around his wife's waist. "Now that should warm me for a couple of hours."

He pulled on his boots and winter coat and opened the kitchen door.

Frigid air blew into the kitchen. Genevieve pulled the terry bathrobe tighter and turned back to the faded kitchen counter. Sophie went up to her mama and gave her a hug.

"Morning, sugar plum." Genevieve kissed the top of Sophie's head.

"Mama, please, I'm not six years old."

Her mama laughed as she lifted the top of the waffle iron and snatched the hot four-square waffle with thumb and forefinger, dropping it onto a large plate. She cut into the squares, stacking one atop the other. Genevieve added two slices of bacon and turned toward the small wooden table where Sophie had taken a seat, sipping her grape juice.

Genevieve frowned at Sophie's footwear. "You should wear your snow boots."

"Please, Mama, I want to wear my new boots. It's the first day back after Christmas break. All the kids will be wearing their new stuff."

Genevieve shook her head, but there was a twinkle in her eye. "I guess I should let you make your own decision. No crying if you get blisters from wet shoes."

"No, mama, I promise."

Genevieve turned back to the counter and ladled batter out of a large ceramic bowl. On the digital clock radio plugged in the wall beside her, Amy Grant sang, "Baby, Baby."

Thirty minutes later, Sophie fidgeted at the edge of the driveway, bundled in her heavy coat, earmuffs, and gloves, waiting for the school bus. The radio said the temperature was hovering around 20 degrees.

"Sophie."

Sophie turned at the sound of her mother's voice. Genevieve, in her snow boots, stepped carefully down the shoveled right side of the drive, clenching her coat together with one hand. The other hand held a brown bag. Her breath frosted in the morning air.

Sophie's tone was subdued as she received the bag from her mother. "Sorry, mama."

Genevieve's generous mouth curved up as she rubbed her daughter's cheek with a cold hand. "I love you, Sophie." The rumbling of a strong engine rent the winter silence as Sophie reached her arms around her mother's waist and hugged her. "I love you, too, Mama."

With a loud screeching of the brakes, the school bus halted at the end of the driveway and Sophie climbed aboard. She found a seat and looked out the window. Genevieve lifted her hand and Sophie waved back as the bus driver retracted the stop sign and pulled forward.

"Wow, a cop car." Dean Taylor's face was pressed up against the glass of the bus window. Twenty adolescent heads, including Sophie's, turned as the bus slowed to a stop at her driveway. A brown Walworth County sheriff's car sat in the driveway.

"Sophie, why is the sheriff at your house?" Erica stood up to let Sophie squeeze past her.

Sophie shook her head. "I don't know."

"Call me when you find out."

"Okay," Sophie said as she left the bus.

As she started up the drive, her father raced down the front porch steps, followed by a deputy in a tan uniform.

"Quick, Sophie, get in the deputy's car, we have to go to the hospital."

Sophie froze in her tracks. "What...why?"

Jimmy yanked open the back-seat door. "Your mama's been in an accident."

Terror got her moving. She jumped into the back seat, her heart pounding in her chest.

"Papa, what happened?" She grabbed the seat in front of her as the deputy reversed down the slippery drive.

"Buckle your seat belt. An elderly driver at the grocery lost control and hit your mama." Jimmy yanked the belt across his chest.

"But how did it..?"

"That's all I know!" Jimmy snapped.

Sophie's eyes welled with tears as she hooked the seat belt and turned to look through the car window at snow-covered fields. She heard her father shift in the seat in front of her and then his strong fingers gripped her hand.

"I'm sorry."

She blinked her wet eyes and continued to stare out the window.

Although she had been warned by Dr. Tripp, Sophie still froze in shock at the multitude of tubes running from beeping machines into her mother's body. Since arriving at Lackland Hospital, she and her father had been waiting for several hours to see her mother. One of those hours had been spent in the small hospital chapel. There were a few wooden benches and a large, ornate Bible on an altar. Sophie had never seen such a massive Bible. Sitting uncomfortably on the bench, Sophie had prayed hard for God to help her mom get well. She had absolute faith that he would answer her prayer.

Jimmy stopped at the head of the bed. Sophie forced her frozen feet to take the few steps necessary to the side of the bed. Her eyebrows drew together. The doctors had made a mistake. The face was swollen twice its normal size, with scrapes, abrasions and two black eyes.

"Papa, this isn't mama," Sophie whispered.

Jimmy didn't answer. Tears ran down his cheeks as he gently kissed the woman's forehead. His right hand reached down to fingers...small and pale. They blended with the white sheet draped across her body. He rubbed a finger across the gold band on her ring finger.

"Papa?"

Jimmy wiped his eyes with his sleeve and turned wearily to his daughter. "It is your mother."

Sophie gasped and looked back at the unrecognizable features of her mother face.

"But..."

Her father shook his head, walked over to a vinyl chair and fell onto the cushioned seat. He covered his face with his hands and started to sob. Her eyes widened. Papa had never cried before. Sophie tore her gaze from her father and looked down at her mother. Her breathing started to hitch and her eyes welled with tears.

Sophie crossed the threshold of her mother's hospital room twelve days later with a cassette of her mama's favorite music.

Mama's face was more recognizable now that the swelling had disappeared and the wounds were healing. She was still in a coma, but the doctor's said she might be able to hear sounds and voices. Sophie pressed a button on the cassette player that sat on the table by the window and slid in the tape. She pressed play and Amy Grant's voice filled the room.

"Hello, Genevieve," Jimmy placed a new vase of flowers on the same table as the cassette player. He stepped over to the bed and gently kissed his wife's lips.

"Mr. Madison?"

Jimmy looked over at Genevieve's doctor standing in the doorway.

"Could you come with me for a moment?"

He followed Dr. Tripp from the room. Sophie walked over to her mother.

"Hi, Mama. Tomorrow's Sunday and there will be a special prayer for you to get better. I saw Mrs. Cox from your Sunday school class today and she said they are missing your croissants and homemade jam."

"And they miss you, too," Sophie added.

Sophie stroked her mom's alabaster cheek. "I really need you to wake up soon. My hair is always a mess in the morning. I can't do anything special with it like you do. Okay, mama? Please wake up."

Her father stepped back in the room. His face was pale, his eyes focusing on her mama's face.

"What's wrong, Papa?"

He turned towards his daughter. "Your Mama, she...she's going to be taken off of life support. There isn't any sign of brain activity and..."

Jimmy tried to take a breath and then another. He doubled over, hands clenched at his mid-section. "Can't... breathe, can't... breathe."

Dr. Tripp, who had been standing in the doorway of the room, yelled down the hallway. "Oxygen!"

Sophie stood frozen beside the bed. "Papa, what's wrong? What do you mean?"

"Shut...off...the...music."

Sophie jumped to do her father's bidding and pressed the stop button as a nurse rushed in with a portable oxygen tank and mask. The nurse eased Jimmy onto the vinyl chair and placed the mask over his face and told him to take slow, easy breaths. Sophie looked up at the doctor.

"What does 'no brain activity' mean?"

Dr. Tripp cleared his throat. "Your father can explain it to you when his breathing is better."

Sophie's twelve-year-old face hardened. "No, I want to know, now."

The doctor turned his gray whiskered face to Jimmy and Sophie saw her father nod his head. Dr. Tripp led Sophie over to the small couch and sat down with her.

"No brain activity means your mother isn't going to wake up from the coma. The injury to her head damaged her brain beyond repair."

The doctor's brown eyes softened. "I'm sorry."

Sophie shook her head. "No, you're wrong. She will wake up. If you can't heal her, God will. Right, Papa?"

The nurse removed the mask and Jimmy slowly rose to his feet. "Can it wait until tomorrow?"

"Of course." The doctor said.

"Right, Papa?"

But Jimmy had turned away, her question addressed to his retreating figure.

Sophie opened the door of the truck and jumped onto the frozen ground. She ran to the end of the driveway and then veered off onto the snow-covered lawn. Her heartbeats pounded in her ears as she trudged through a foot of snow, past the clothesline and the naked branches of the grape arbor. She kept going.

"Sophie!"

She wanted to run and run and never stop. The snow was the enemy. Not allowing her to break free and out-run the truth.

"Sophie!"

Her father's voice was closer. Someone was screaming. She tried harder to run and tripped on something buried beneath the snow, slamming her face on the ice-glazed crust. A thousand pinpricks burned.

Arms pulled her onto her knees then wrapped around her and pulled tight. Sophie fought the arms with all that was in her.

"Let me go! Let me go! Let me go!"

"No." The sound was muffled in her back.

Sophie dropped her head and great heaving sobs filled the still cold air. The arms shifted, lifted and carried her back to the farmhouse.

Jimmy laid his daughter's trembling, weeping body on her bed and removed her boots. He gently swept tangled locks of her hair away from her face. Sophie shut her eyes tight and turned on her side, crying out her anguish. Jimmy bent down and kissed her exposed cheek then left the room.

Shadows were deepening inside the kitchen as the sun moved low in the sky. Jimmy sat at the old wooden table with a framed picture of Genevieve clutched in his hands. Sophie crossed through the doorway, her cheeks pink from the ice burn.

"What will happen when they unhook the tubes, Papa?" Her voice trembled.

Jimmy struggled to raise his head as if gravity was too much of a burden. His eyes were stark with grief.

Sophie stepped to her father's side, her red rimmed eyes bleak with the impending loss of her mother. He stroked the picture with his finger. It was a snapshot of her mama on the tire swing, her hands on the rope, leaning back and laughing at the camera. It had been taken last summer.

"She will stop breathing and then her heart will stop."

Sophie covered her face with her hands and choked out a sob. Her father lifted a hand and rubbed his daughter's small arm distractedly. "I'm sorry, pumpkin. She loved you so much."

Sophie looked at the photo of her mother. "But her soul will go to Heaven, right, Papa?"

Jimmy pulled his eyes away from the picture. "Yes, she will definitely go to Heaven and sing with the angels..." He paused and let his eyes be drawn back to Genevieve's smiling face. "...because she was already an angel in this world."

Sophie sighed in reassurance at her papa's words, though the ache in her heart remained.

The sun was low on the horizon and the shadows deepening in the well as Sophie whipped a tear away. The memories of her mother's death faded as she gazed at the skeleton...the throbbing of her ankle matching the throbbing of her heart. She leaned her head back against the rough bricks and closed her eyes.

42   Sarah Norkus

Chapter Seven

Summer 2012

Allison paced back and forth across the black and white geometric patterned rug covering her living room floor. Her steps came to an abrupt halt. She stared at the sunset through the small window of her apartment. Her lips formed a grim line as she turned on her heel and marched over to her latest flea market find, a fifty-year-old dented and scratched pine wood table and four chairs that she had spray painted black with Sophie's help. Allison ripped open the zipper on her purse and yanked out her smartphone. She tapped in the numbers, hit speaker and laid the phone on the table. Her hands pulled at each other in agitation.

"Allison?" said the male voice.

"Something's happened to Sophie."

"What? What happened to her?"

There was fear in Bryan's voice. Good, he needed to take her seriously.

"She never texted me back and it's getting dark."

Anger crept into his tone when he answered back. "You scared me to death. What's wrong with you? I thought she was in an accident."

"That's what I'm telling you. Something is wrong. Maybe you wouldn't hear from her since you broke up, but I'm telling you she would have called me!" Allison's breathing sped up. "What time was it when she left this morning?"

"Around eight." The anger had faded.

"That's twelve hours, Bryan, without a call or text. And I have been doing both all day." Allison could hear her heart thudding in her chest.

She waited, letting the obvious sink in.

"Okay, you're right. She would have called you."

Allison plunged in, "You have to call the police. She could have been in a car accident. She could be injured or..."

"I will, but they may not take me seriously because of what happened this morning, you should call, too."

Allison collapsed on one of the wooden chairs. "You're right."

"Wait a minute. I just thought of something."

"What?"

"The 'Find Friends' app on my iPhone can locate her. Hold on."

Allison held her breath as she waited.

"This is weird. She's on the WI-20 headed towards La Grange."

"La Grange?"

"That's where she grew up."

Allison's tone was desperate. "Please, Bryan... I know you broke up, but something's wrong...I know it. Can you go after her? Just make sure she's all right?"

There was a slight hesitation. "I don't know what kind of reception I'll get, but, I'll go. I'll call you when I know anything."

"Thank you."

Allison stared down at her cell phone in disgust. If she had an iPhone like Sophie's, she might have saved herself hours of worry. She breathed a sigh of relief as the tension left her body. At least they knew where she was, even if they didn't know why. She looked out of her window as the last of the light faded into twilight.

"Ryan, slow down! You're going to get us killed." Kevin jerked on his seat belt and clicked it in place.

"If we're not home in twenty minutes, our grounding is going to get extended another month." Ryan's high-top sneaker pressed down on the gas pedal sending the needle of the speedometer close to ninety.

"I told you we should have left an hour earlier than we did." Kevin's eyes were wide with fear. He hit the button to lower his window. The stale smell from the fast food bags, combined with the acrid fog of cigarette smoke and his own stink of fear made him want to gag.

Ryan hit the horn as he pulled around a slow car on the highway, passing illegally over the solid line. The light was fading fast. Kevin saw Ryan's left hand fumble around until the headlights came on. He sped up.

Kevin sucked in a terror-filled breath. "Slow down or let me out! I'd rather be grounded another month than dead."

"You are such a p…"

"Stop the car now!"

Ryan turned to Kevin. "Suck it up. I'm not stopping the car or getting gr…"

"Look out!"

Ryan whipped his head back towards the front of the car in time to see the headlights shine on a huge doe as she froze in her stroll across the highway. He turned the wheel hard to the left as he slammed on the brakes. Kevin felt Ryan's side of the car rise off the two tires and knew the flip could not be avoided. He screamed as the passenger door smashed into the deer. He had the sensation of weightlessness—and then nothing.

The impact knocked the deer twenty feet into a cornfield—the vehicle flipping several times in the same direction before slamming to a stop upright across two rows of corn. Lying in the corn field a few feet away from the wreckage was an iPhone, dirt sprinkled across its shattered screen.

Allison rushed to her ringing phone. "Bryan, thank God. I've been going stir crazy waiting to hear from you. Did you find Sophie? Is she all right?"

"I don't know."

"What do you mean you don't know?" Allison shrieked.

Bryan gave a heavy sigh. "The signal disappeared fifteen minutes after I left my house. I drove to the approximate location on my phone before the signal died, but there was nothing there, just fields on either side of the road. I drove twenty miles further and didn't see anything. It's pitch black on that road. I can't be certain where the signal stopped."

"But why would the signal disappear?"

"I have no idea."

The fear and tension were back, consuming Allison. "We have to call the police."

"I already did. I had to tell them about the breakup because they asked if she had been upset about anything."

Allison gripped the phone hard in her right hand. "What did they say?"

"They said they had to wait twenty-fours before issuing a missing person alert. But…"

"Oh, no! I know that's procedure, but…"

"Allison!" Bryan's voice rose an octave.

Allison clamped her lips shut.

"I called in a favor. The mayor's assistant is a good friend. I've met the mayor at a few social gatherings. I called Doug and he talked to the mayor who…never mind. Anyway, they put out a BOLO or ATL on her car. What that means…"

"I know what it means, I'm a journalist. But it's not enough. We should be out there looking…doing something." Allison looked out the window at the inky blackness.

"I know, but it's too dark."

"Bryan, I'm scared."

There was a hitch to Bryan's voice. "Me, too."

Allison hit the end button, too upset to say goodbye. She laid the phone on the table, bowed her head and gripped the table edge with both hands. *God, please help us to find Sophie.* Her head jerked up. She grabbed her phone and punched in a number.

"Don't say anything, just listen." After ten minutes, she ended the call and punched in another number.

Allison's eyes thinned into slits. "Hello, scumbag."

Chapter Eight

Sophie awoke in darkness so complete, her heart started to pound and her body shivered in the tepid blackness. She lifted her head like a drowning man seeking air. No visible moon, a few stars twinkling amidst the clouds in the indigo sky. She shivered harder, her teeth clicking together in a rapid tattoo. She dropped her head and crossed her arms, digging her fingers into her waist, trying to stop the shaking. She didn't need a doctor to tell her she was going into shock. *Come on Sophie, you're stronger than this. You have to get a grip. Someone will find you.*

Sophie took a breath, and then blew it out…another breath, blew it out. After five minutes, the shivering lessened, but the panic brought on by being trapped in a well, in the dark…remained. She needed to shut out her surroundings before she completely lost it. She closed her eyes, but when she emptied her mind, a face filled the void. She shook her head, but the face solidified eyes full of love. *Aaron.* The pain was almost too much to bear, but with nothing to distract her she couldn't stop the memory that flooded her mind…

Chapter Nine

Spring 1998

Sophie sat in Aaron's jeep silently staring out of the windshield. Aaron cleared his throat and repeated, "Where...where would you like to go?"

Silence.

"Hey, I'm cool...with just sitting in your driveway if... that's what you want to do."

Sophie gave a nervous giggle. "Years from now when I look back on this day, our first date, I want the memory to bring a smile to my lips and warmth to my heart."

Aaron's forefinger stopped nervously tapping on the steering wheel. "You should be a writer. You have a way of phrasing a thought that makes it clear in my mind."

Sophie shifted in the passenger seat to look at Aaron. "I am going to be a writer...a journalist."

Aaron shifted, too. "Writing the sports articles for the high school paper isn't just a hobby?"

"No."

Aaron reached out a hand and brushed light fingers across the knuckles of Sophie's right hand. "When did you know you wanted to be a writer?"

"I started writing in a journal after my mother died. It helped me deal with the grief. I wrote down special moments with Mama, stories she told me, or how I was dealing with her loss on a particular day. Papa came into my bedroom one day and saw me writing in it. He asked me if I would read one of the pages to him. I was going to say it was private, but he had such a forlorn look on his face, I couldn't say no.

"I read him a memory I had written down about picking grapes off the arbor with Mama. Tears ran down his cheeks as he told me that my words had made the memory come alive for him and he thought I might make a good writer one day. I was twelve at the time."

"If it's not too painful, I'd like to know more about your mother."

The screen door slammed and both teens jerked. Sophie's father stood on the stoop. A stray lock of ebony hair waved over his left eyebrow. He walked over to the jeep and leaned in the open passenger side window.

"Let me explain how this dating thing works. After getting in the vehicle you start the engine, back down the drive and head for—as an example—Whitewater. You may go get something to eat and then take in a movie or bowling…"

"Bowling?" Aaron and Sophie said in unison.

"Sure, your mom and I liked to bowl. We went every Friday night, for a while, after we were married."

"Okay, Papa." Sophie gently pushed his head out the window.

Jimmy stepped back and mimed turning the key in the lock. Sophie turned to Aaron. "I want to show you something—a way to know my mother."

The look on her papa's face was comical as Aaron turned the key in the ignition and pulled forward instead of backwards, according to Sophie's instructions. They passed the barn on the left as the jeep followed a rutted dirt and weed track. The tires pressed needles from the tall pines into the dirt. Aaron drove a quarter of a mile before coming to a stop.

Surrounding a pond on three sides was a riot of color. Flowering shrubs and trees intermingled a few feet from the water's edge: pink and white dogwoods, pink blossoms of the crabapple trees, bright yellow forsythia and the various shades of azaleas. A spreading carpet of wildflowers covered the ground in all directions.

"I am speechless."

Sophie's eyes were shinning with moisture. "My mama did this...even the wildflowers. The white-blossomed wildflowers are garlic mustard, cow parsnip, and trillium. The yellow ones are ragwort, and buttercups. The blue flowered ones are spiderwort, and Jacob's ladder. And the purple are phlox and dames rocket."

Aaron's ice blue eyes showed how impressed he was. "Are you sure you don't want to be a botanist?"

Sophie shrugged. "I spent a lot of time here with Mama."

She glanced over at Aaron. "Would you like to walk around the pond?"

Aaron smiled as he nodded his blonde head. They opened the jeep's doors and climbed out. It was a beautiful spring Saturday with temperatures hovering at sixty-five and an azure sky overhead.

As they strolled toward the pond, Sophie trailed her fingers across the tops of the flowering wildflowers with longer stems.

"Mama loved flowers, even the weeds—like dandelion. Sometimes she would stop on the shoulder of the highway and dig up wildflowers to transplant by the pond."

A sweet smile appeared. "She would ask my opinion first. She said it had to have Sophie's stamp of approval."

Aaron returned the smile. "Your mother must have been an amazing woman. I saw the picture of her on the tire swing in the den. She was beautiful...and you look just like her."

Sophie turned her head to hide the heat flooding her face. A few moments later she stopped by a forsythia bush. "Okay, let's test your knowledge of trees." She pointed to a tree next to the bush, with white blossoms.

Aaron put a hand on his chin and studied the tree. "Some kind of fruit tree. But not apple, I know what they look like."

He pointed to a tree across the pond.

Sophie grinned. "Right, it's a wild plum. I pick the plums and make plum sauce like Mama used to."

"I don't think I've told you that you are an amazing cook. The pot roast you made while I was helping your dad with the corn harvest was the best I've ever tasted."

To hide her embarrassment, Sophie pointed to another tree, the branches giving the illusion of a pink waterfall. "What about that one?"

"Some kind of willow, the way the branches bend over."

Sophie nodded her head and beamed as if Aaron was a particularly bright student in her classroom. "It's a weeping cherry tree."

Aaron's voice took on a British accent as he held out his hand. "Milady, take my hand, as I am eager to be off and learn more of thy mother's botany skills."

She hesitated for only a second before reaching out her hand and laying it in his larger one. The touch of his fingers sent a jolt though her midsection. She looked into those amazing ice-blue eyes and sucked in a breath. Aaron tugged gently on her hand and they set off together around the pond. Every few feet, Sophie would stop and point out a tree or shrub. She calculated that he got four out of twenty right. Not too bad, since she knew he was usually too busy thinking about baseball season to notice the trees blossoming in the spring.

They took their time circling the pond. Too soon, they reached the place where they had started their trip around the pond. As they approached the jeep Sophie felt a tug on her hand. Aaron was staring at a small gazebo with peeling white paint; its exposed wood was the color of dull pewter.

"Would you like to sit for a minute, Sophie? I'm kind of tired."

Sophie angled her head and smiled. "Doubtful."

Aaron put his free hand over his heart. "You wound me, my lady."

"You can't fool me I've seen you play nine innings of baseball."

Aaron's grin was sheepish. "Okay. I'm not tired. I just don't want to leave and let go of the moment …or your hand."

Sophie whispered, "Me either."

The bench inside the gazebo creaked just a bit when they sat down. She tilted her head to look up at the inside of the cupola. Above her head was a large spider web, but not the occupant. "This gazebo has been here for at least twenty-some years. My papa built it for my mama after the first time he brought her to the pond. She had told him there was a pond on her family's plantation with a pretty white gazebo where she used to spend the milder spring and fall days reading."

There was a honking overhead and Sophie and Aaron turned and leaned over the side wall to watch a grouping of Canadian geese fly by.

Aaron turned to Sophie. "Your dad told me your mom grew up on a plantation outside of New Orleans."

"Yes, a sugar cane plantation. Her family has owned it for generations, over two hundred years."

Aaron gave her a quizzical look. "Her family? Aren't they your family, too?"

"No." Sophie leaned back against the weathered wood and sighed. "My mother's family disowned her when she married my father."

His eyes widened. "Whoa. That seems a bit harsh. What happened?"

Sophie chewed on her lip.

"Hey, you don't have to tell me."

"No, it's okay. They met the summer after they both graduated from high school. Papa went with a friend to New Orleans for two weeks. His friend's grandfather owned a restaurant on Bourbon Street. Mama was staying with an aunt while shopping for new clothes to take with her to Tulane as a freshman in the fall. They met in a bar and it was love at first sight."

"They met in a bar? Did they use fake IDs?

"I asked Papa the same thing, but he said the drinking age was eighteen back in the seventies."

Aaron smile was sad. "I think I see where this story is going. Rich aristocrat's daughter falls for poor farmer. Daddy Warbucks wasn't happy."

"Papa said that Mama told him there was a 'row to end all rows.' No way was their beautiful daughter, whom they had groomed to marry a senator, going to marry a farmer from

Wisconsin. Of course, Mama pointed out that her parents were also farmers."

"I bet that didn't go over well."

Sophie sighed. "Mama told Papa that her papa's face turned purple. And then he ordered her gone...and told her never to contact them."

Her voice held a tinge of sadness. "I don't know how they could do that to her."

Aaron squeezed Sophie's hand. "They loved their status and their reputation in the community more than they loved their daughter. I'm also betting your mother had never defied her father before. What did her mother have to say about them marrying?"

"Mama told Papa that her mama just stood there stone-faced."

He squeezed her hand again. "Your mother must have loved your father very much to turn her back on her family like that."

"Papa said he felt guilty about causing her to lose her family, but Mama told him she never regretted her decision."

A single tear fell from the corner of Sophie's eye. "I asked Papa a couple of years ago why he didn't start dating again. He told me that no one could ever replace Genevieve. He wasn't capable of loving anyone but her."

She inhaled and let out the breath on a long sigh. "He said that they had a special bond that even death couldn't break. And that I was the only reason that he stayed on Earth instead of joining her in Heaven."

Aaron's eyebrows rose. "Wow. My mom and dad love each other, but not like that."

"It was an awesome thing to experience growing up."

Sophie pulled a little on Aaron's hand and stood up. "I'm ready now for the traditional part of this date."

Aaron stood up beside her. "Bowling it is."

Sophie's tinkling laughter was left behind in the gazebo as they walked to the jeep.

Tears slid down Sophie's cheeks as the spring of 1998 faded into the recesses of her mind. She closed her eyes and allowed exhaustion to take her to a realm beyond the misery of her circular prison.

Chapter Ten

Summer 2012

Allison flung the covers off of her and climbed out of bed before dawn. She had tossed and turned all night worrying about Sophie and was exhausted as she stumbled to the bathroom in the dark. After flushing the toilet, she walked through her living room, flipping on a light as she entered the kitchen. Her stomach rolled queasily. She grabbed a filter out of a cabinet and shoved it into the top of her ancient coffee machine. She filled the machine with water and spooned in the coffee. She pushed the "on" button harder than necessary and then walked back into the living room to grab the remote control to the television. Allison flopped back on the throw pillows of the couch and set the channel to a local news affiliate.

Allison glared at the set. "He'd better come through. He really doesn't want me airing his dirty little secrets."

Coffee mug in hand and body rigid, Allison watched as the scumbag's handsome face zoomed into view.

Ron had his serious persona plastered on as he began to talk. "We start this morning with a news alert. Sophie Madison, an award-winning journalist with the *Journal Sentinel*, has been missing since early yesterday morning. Ms Madison…"

Allison jerked, spilling coffee on her extra-large Milwaukee Brewers blue and gold T-shirt, when her cell rang. Ignoring the mess, she set the mug on the coffee table and rushed to her bedroom. She looked at the screen. It was Bryan.

"Bryan, have you heard something?"

"Yes, but it's not good news."

Allison's fingers turned white as she gripped the phone. "Oh, no, is she dead?"

"No…not as far as I know. Her car was in an accident on WI-20 last night."

Allison gasped.

"But she wasn't in it. Two teenage boys were discovered in the wreckage. The driver is dead and the passenger is in the hospital in a coma. They're putting his chances of survival at 50-50."

Allison looked over at the television, where Ron was wrapping up the segment on Sophie. "But I don't understand. Why would two…"

Bryan interrupted. "The speculation is that the boys stole the car. The police have to wait to see if the boy that was in the passenger seat wakes up in order to question him."

Allison shouted into the phone, "This makes no sense! If someone stole her car, why didn't Sophie call one of us or the cops?"

Bryan's voice was flat on the other end. "Her phone was found near the wrecked car. That was the signal I was getting on the highway. And now I know why it suddenly disappeared."

Allison could form no words.

"I'm sorry, Allison, but I have to go. I'll call if I hearing anything."

Allison slowly lowered the phone and looked blankly at the television as her ex-boyfriend voiced a new segment. Her feet dragged as she walked back towards the couch, reached down and clicked the power button on the remote. Her hopes that Sophie had just gone into hiding and would emerge once she saw herself on television and on the front page of their newspaper...had now been crushed. Numb with shock, she looked towards her bedroom. She might as well get dressed, go to work, and clean out her desk. After what she pulled last night, the editor was sure to fire her...big time.

Something tickled Sophie's cheek. She lifted her hand and brushed at the skin. She felt a sting on her finger and jerked her hand away. Her eyes popped opened and she froze as her gaze fell on the skeleton. It took a few seconds to remember everything... again. *Not a vision I wanted to wake up to.*

By the angle of the light in the well, it must be about eight in the morning. She had been in the well for almost twenty-four hours. She shivered. *Allison must be going nuts. But she won't be able to find me, even if she remembers me mentioning that I grew up on a farm outside of Milwaukee.* Sophie's eyes widened. But Bryan knew she grew up in La Grange. Maybe he'd think to check out the farm. But then her shoulders sagged. With her car gone, he wouldn't search the property.

A sudden sneeze caused Sophie's legs to jerk and she groaned in pain. Her swollen ankle was now an angry red and the slightest movement caused agony. Was it broken? Tears welled in her eyes. *It's bad enough I'm stuck in this well, but I can't even pace off my anger and fear. If I...*

A noise sent Sophie's thoughts scurrying to the back of her mind as she heard movement up above. She craned her head back.

"Hey, is someone there? I need help!"

The huge head of the yellow lab appeared to her left over the rim of the well. She sighed. "Oh, it's you again."

The Lab's long pink tongue hung out of the side of his mouth as he panted.

"God, why a dog and not a human? This is so…"

She paused. She had called out to God for the first time in over fifteen years. Her lips pressed together. *Remember, he's not there. He let Mama die and he didn't do anything when ….No! I can't go there.*

Tears squeezed beneath her lashes as she shut her eyes and shook her head. The Lab gave a sharp bark above her and Sophie winced. She opened her eyes and looked up as the dog barked at her again. Maybe the dog didn't think she belonged in the well and was telling her to get out.

"Trust me, if I could get out, I would. But see, I can't get up." Sophie put both hands on the dirt beneath her and pushed up a few inches.

The Lab's barks came shorter and faster. She eased herself back down.

"That's all I got, buddy."

His shrill barking became more frantic. Sophie's eyes widened. *Maybe someone will be able to hear the barking from the road.* She needed to keep him barking. She pushed up again on her hands. The dog kept barking. Within five minutes, spots appeared in her vision and her head started to spin. She eased back down. After a minute, the Lab stopped barking. When she craned her neck up, he dipped his head and whined. The dog lowered his body to the ground and placed his head on the edge of the well, watching over her now in silent vigil. More spots appeared behind her eyelids as she shut her eyes and lowered her chin onto her chest.

Phones were ringing all around her as Allison sat at her desk, hair mussed, staring at the picture of Sophie on the front page of the newspaper. Mr. McNair, her editor, walked in, a copy of the paper jammed under his armpit.

"Noah, my office, now."

A short man in his mid-thirties jumped up and rushed to the office, closing the door behind him. *This is it. When Mr. McNair finds out I lied to Noah about getting permission to run Sophie on the front page...* She sighed and picked up the front page again.

"Ms. Summer." Allison looked up as her insides clinched.

"Join me, please." Mr. McNair turned on his heel.

So this is what it feels like to be a prisoner summoned to the warden's office. Allison stood in front of the editor's gray metal desk, awaiting her punishment. She twisted her hands and bit down on her lower lip as the seconds went by and her boss just stared at her. The smell of his overpowering cologne was making her sick to her stomach.

Finally, he spoke. "You have got some b…"

Allison bit down a smile. He must have realized he was addressing a woman, which was surprising, considering he generally didn't notice his staff in a gender-specific way.

"You lied to Noah and told him I gave permission to run the front page about Sophie."

The top of his bald head was turning pink, matching his face. Red would follow and then the fun would really begin.

"Sir, there is nothing I can say to excuse my behavior. I will clean out my desk and go."

"Shut the door."

Allison obeyed, steeling her body for the chewing out.

"You're not fired."

Allison's mouth dropped opened. She quickly shut it and remained silent.

"Don't get me wrong, you deserve to be fired, but there are two reasons why I have decided not to fire you."

He folded his right hand into a fist, extending his index finger. "One... I may seem like a hard a..." He cleared his throat. "But I want Sophie found just as much as you do. And taking the initiative and jumping on this right away might make a difference."

His face hardened. "But you should have called me, not Noah."

"I don't know your..."

"And two." He held up his middle finger alongside the index finger. "On a more pragmatic note, the phones have been ringing off the hook and...well, that's not as important as finding Sophie."

His eyebrows rose. "Why are you still in my office?"

The door crashed into her large bosom as Allison hastened to leave his office. She sat at her desk, hugging her aching breasts, as she tried to wrap her brain around what had not happened. *I wasn't fired.*

Knowing she still had a job didn't raise her spirits—Sophie was missing. She picked up the paper again and stared at her friend's face. *Where are you?*

Bryan sat at his desk, rubbing his forehead with the fingers on his right hand. His head throbbed despite the pill he had swallowed. His love for Sophie hadn't suddenly evaporated when she gave him his ring back. It wasn't like flipping a light switch—relationship over, love gone. *If anything had happened to her...*

He ran the fingers of both hands through his thick blond hair. What could have happened? *Did she still go for a run or was she too upset?* Bryan's fingers gripped his skull. *Could she have been kidnapped?* He needed to concentrate on where she could have gone after leaving his condo. A place that made a kidnapping easy and just as easy for two teens to just walk up and steal the car...somewhere isolated where no one would have heard her scream. *If she had been able to scream.*

He rubbed a hand over his face and looked up at the ceiling. *One of the many parks—Riverside, Washington? The Monarch Nature Trail? A favorite place from her childhood? Maybe the lake she had mentioned near the farm she grew up on.*

Bryan stilled. *The farm.* She still owned it. *And hadn't her car been found on the highway that leads to La Grange?* He shook his head. That was the one place she wouldn't go. The couple of times he suggested they go and check on the property, she had told him in a steel-laden voice she was never going back. He had wanted to ask why, but her face had closed down. She wasn't going to share that information with him. He had let the subject drop.

"Mr. Taylor?"

Bryan looked up at his secretary in the doorway.

"A Sergeant Beckley is on line one."

He grabbed the phone receiver and punched a button. "This is Bryan Taylor."

He listened to the voice on the other end, then said thank you and hung up. Finally, good news. The kid from the accident had woken up from his coma.

It was mid-afternoon when Sophie woke from a fitful doze her heart in her throat...something was wrong. Her eyes darted back and forth around the drying brick walls of the well. She craned her head and saw the Lab asleep above her. The tension in her body eased... nothing was wrong. She rolled her eyes. That is, if you didn't count her present situation. She just needed to stay positive. The human body could go days without food and even water. Sophie looked down at her ankle. *Maybe the swelling would go down in a couple of days and then...* Sophie's forehead furrowed. A red streak was starting to snake its way up from her ankle. Her eyes widened. She had less time than she thought...a lot less.

Aaron

Chapter Eleven

Summer 2012

As soon as Aaron threw off the comforter, his muscular chest and arms pimpled from the blast of cold air that blew out of the vent above his head. Clad only in striped pajama bottoms, he crossed over to the thermostat and raised the temperature in the master suite. He needed the bedroom cold to sleep comfortably.

He left his bedroom, walking across the polished wood floor, down the hallway and into the spacious living room with a large bay window and a spectacular view of Lake Michigan. His feet padded onto the tiled floor of the kitchen area and up to the large polished steel refrigerator.

Aaron pulled open the freezer door and was enveloped by a cold mist as he shoved aside a package of steaks and grabbed an ice pack. He shut the door and strode back into the living room, settling into an overstuffed black leather recliner and raising the foot rest. He molded the ice pack around his knee and reached for the remote in the holder near his right hand.

As Aaron flipped through the channels, he thought about his future. The doctor said he needed to have surgery on the knee. But Aaron wanted to hold off until the season was over. Once he had the surgery, he was looking at missing half of the next season for a full recovery. But there was no guarantee that the knee would go back to performing at hundred percent, and most likely wouldn't.

The "R" word loomed large and he was only thirty-one years-old. As much of an asset as he was to the Chicago Cubs, it was still all about being at the top of your game. If he didn't recover the speed and agility he had before the injury…

Aaron tried moving the traitorous appendage twenty minutes later. Better—the pain was gone. The ice pack had done its job. He sighed as he lifted off the pack. He loved baseball and wasn't ready to give it up. He laid his blond head back against the soft leather of the head rest. His father had told him that anytime he was ready he could join him as a partner at the brewery. And he would…one day. But right now he still wanted to play ball. And the money he made from endorsements was very lucrative.

He sighed again as he pushed up from the chair and headed for the kitchen, returning the ice pack to the freezer. He switched doors and reached in for the bag of coffee. While the coffee brewed, he popped two frozen waffles in the toaster. He was buttering the waffles when a faint ring tone came from his bedroom. He walked down the hallway. The tone was his mom's. He picked up his cell phone from the nightstand.

"Hey, Mom."

"I hope I didn't wake you. I know you had a late game that went into extra innings."

By the tone of her voice, this wasn't a causal call. "What's going on?"

The pause on the other end caused the muscles in Aaron's shoulders to tense up. There had been another time, two years ago, when a pause on the phone had been followed by the news that his grandfather had passed.

"Is it Dad? Did something happen?"

"No, it's not your father. I debated about whether I should even call and tell you when I saw it on the news, but…" There was another pause.

Aaron's gut clinched. "What…who…Mom?"

A sigh came through the cell like a whisper. "It's Sophie."

The air left his lungs as if he had been sucker-punched. He had not heard that name out loud in fourteen years, yet it still evoked many emotions—mind numbing pain, crushing grief, an all-consuming love.

"Aaron?"

He cleared his throat. "What happened?"

"She's missing."

Aaron was braced for 'dead' or 'in the hospital,' 'missing' simply did not compute. His head felt like it was full of cotton instead of a brain.

"Aaron?" Her voice was tinged with worry.

"Um…can…can…" The anxiety was twisting his tongue, not allowing him to get the words out. His disability had not reared its ugly head since he had graduated college. *Concentrate! Let go of emotion.*

"Can …you…you… tell…me what the report said?"

"This is upsetting you, I shouldn't have called."

Aaron took in a deep breath, sat down on the edge of the king-size bed and lied to his mother. "No, I'm okay. What happened?"

"She disappeared early yesterday morning. It was on the news this morning. There really wasn't much to the report, just that she didn't return home and her fiancée and best friend are asking the public to phone in anything they may have seen or heard." She sighed again. "I just thought it would be less of a shock coming from me."

"Her fiancée? She's engaged?"

"That's what the report said."

His mother was one of a handful of people who knew why he and Sophie had broken up.

Aaron rubbed his hand over his face. "Have the police been…"

"Hold on a minute, Aaron."

He heard the tapping of her shoes on the tile floor as she carried the phone with her. A soft voice grew louder, but he couldn't understand the words.

"Who's there, Mom?"

"Hush." There was mild irritation in her voice.

Aaron bent over, his elbows on his knees as he stared at the floor.

"Oh, no, oh, no."

Aaron's head snapped back up. "What…what's wrong?"

His heart started to pound.

"I've had the television on, and the noon news has an update on Sophie. They found her car wrecked out on the highway."

His heart jumped into his throat. "Is she…"

"No, she wasn't in the car. They found two teenage boys in it. They suspect the kids stole her car. One is dead and the other is in the hospital. That's all that's being reported."

Aaron couldn't talk anymore. . "I've…I've got to go… Mom."

He pressed the red icon that ended the call. He eased back until he lay flat on the bed, breathing hard and staring at the ceiling. His breathing grew ragged. He bolted upright, slung his arm back, and threw his iPhone across the room. The phone bounced off the wall and landed with a rattle on the polished floorboards. He grabbed his head with both hands.

It had been many years since Aaron Reinhart had shed a tear. But there in his bedroom, rocking slowly back and forth, Aaron wept over Sophie. Sophie...and the tragedy that cost them...everything. There was no one on this earth who had loved each other more than Aaron and Sophie, except maybe for Sophie's mom and dad. And their love had also ended in tragedy. But not the Shakespearean tragedy that drove Sophie and Aaron apart forever.

Aaron rose from the bed and stumbled into the bathroom. He stared at his wet, red-rimmed eyes in the mirror over the bathroom sink and then turned on the faucet. He cupped his hands and splashed cold water over his face. Falling apart over a past that couldn't be changed wouldn't help him find Sophie. And he would find her. He wouldn't fail her again. His hands gripped the edge of the sink, his knuckles turning white. *It was my fault.* If he hadn't been twenty minutes late... He lifted his head back up to the mirror, water dripping off his face. A ghostly image of Sophie at seventeen wavered in the polished glass in front of him. He sucked in a breath and blinked. The image vanished.

Like a blind man, Aaron groped for the toilet lid, pulled it down and sat on it. He reached for the hand towel to wipe his face. His hand rubbed the towel across his face as his mind retreated into the past...

Chapter Twelve

Summer 1998

Darkness was coming when Aaron spread the blanket over the wildflowers by the edge of the pond. He and Sophie eased onto their backs clasping hands as they watched the lightening bugs flitter over their heads, their yellow tail lights winking on and off. For untold minutes, they lay silent listening to the creatures of the night—the croaking of the frogs, the buzzing of the cicadas, crickets chirping.

Aaron turned on his hip...his eyes traced the contours of Sophie's face.

"What?"

Aaron smiled.

"Why are you staring at me?"

Aaron leaned over and whispered in Sophie's ear, "Guess."

"There's a pimple the size of a grape on the end of my nose." Sophie's eyes danced.

Aaron laughed as he kissed the tip of her nose. "Nay, Milady…I but gaze in wonder at your fair beauty."

Sophie turned onto her side, laying a hand on the side of Aaron's face. "And your beauty is as equally fair."

"Oh, come on… beauty? How about ruggedly handsome?"

"Naw, you're too pretty with those china blue eyes and…"

Aaron grabbed Sophie by the waist and started to tickle her.

Sophie squealed. "No!"

Aaron tickled more. "Okay…okay!" Sophie said between gasps of laughter. "Ruggedly handsome."

Aaron pulled her into a seated position, grasping her hand again. He could barely see her face as stars appeared in the night sky. "Sophie, I'm in love with you. I have been since you bumped into me outside of our English class last fall. I know we've only been dating for two months, but I wanted you to know how strong…"

"Aaron…I love you, too." Sophie's hand was trembling in his hand.

"What…you do?" He heard the wonder in his voice.

Aaron stilled as Sophie leaned in and whispered in the seconds before her lips touched his, "Always and forever."

Chapter Thirteen

Summer 2012

The doorbell chimed and Aaron's head snapped up, the memories of the first time he had told Sophie he loved her receding. He pushed off the commode and replaced the hand towel, catching his reflection in the mirror. Aaron winced and turned away. He looked like he'd been on a bender. The bell chimed again. He left the bathroom and crossed to the front door, looking through the peephole. He drew back the bolt and opened the door.

A smile lit up the Irish mug of his best friend, Sean O'Connor, but faded quickly.

"Boyo, you look like hell...sorry... slipped out. Did you party last night without me?"

Aaron opened the door wider and turned back into the living room. "How many times have you seen me drink more than one beer, Sean?"

"Well…never." He shut the door. "But there's always a first time."

Aaron ignored him and walked into the kitchen. He picked up the plate of waffles and dumped the food into the trash. He reached into a cabinet for two coffee mugs.

Sean leaned up against the counter. "If you didn't go out drinking, why do you look like you lost your best friend? And I would have remembered if you lost me, boyo."

Aaron poured coffee into the mugs and handed one to Sean. "Not in the mood to discuss it with you. Why are you here? You were up as late as I was and you normally crash until mid-afternoon at the earliest."

Sean shook his head. "Whatever you're going through has to be really bad for you to forget the promotion spot for the new bat. You asked me to pick you up."

Aaron's hand holding the mug of coffee froze halfway to his mouth. "I did forget." He took a sip of the coffee and then lowered it to the counter. "How much time do I have to get ready?"

Sean pulled his cell phone out of his pocket. "Fifteen minutes."

Aaron pressed the palms of both hands against his temple then dropped them to his sides. "Ready in fourteen."

Sean's worried green eyes followed Aaron's abrupt departure as he sipped the hot brew. "Something's wrong with that boyo."

As Aaron shampooed his head and soaped his body, his mind chased possible scenarios for Sophie's disappearance. He exited the steaming shower and grabbed the towel with such force the metal bar rattled. Sophie was in serious trouble and he had to go shoot a commercial.

Sean plastered on a smile as Aaron returned to the kitchen dressed in jeans, polo shirt, and scuffed sneakers, grabbed his mug of coffee and finished off the contents in two large gulps. They left the condo. The corners of Sean's lips pulled downward as his vehicle turned left out of the parking garage. Aaron was staring out of the passenger window. It was one o'clock and the traffic in downtown Chicago was heavy with people returning to work from lunch.

Sean drew in a breath. "Come on, spill. Share the load. What's wrong?" He spared a quick glance at his friend.

Aaron adjusted the seat belt and leaned forward slightly. "A girl I knew in high school is missing."

"You look like death warmed over because a girl you knew has gone missing? I don't buy it. You wouldn't...wait a minute...is it the woman I read about in a Milwaukee paper when I stopped for a quick bite before picking you up? A journalist from Milwaukee?"

Aaron stared out the windshield. "Yeah, that's her."

Sean gave a low whistle and looked crossways at Aaron. "That is one gorgeous woman. You..."

Aaron's eyes widened. "Look out!"

A large dog, with a leash trailing behind him, dashed in front of the car. Sean hit the brakes, narrowly missing its hind quarters.

Heart thundering in his chest, Sean concentrated on driving and let Aaron's revelation go for the moment. Silence rode with them for the rest of the trip to the television station. As they neared the entrance, Aaron cleared his throat.

"She was my girlfriend...and we were in love." His voice was raw with emotion.

"Oh, man, I'm sorry that's..." Sean's brow wrinkled. "Wait a minute."

A memory popped out of the recesses of Sean's mind. It was late August of 1998. He and Aaron had just met and were busy unpacking in the two-person freshman dorm room at Ohio State. Aaron had pulled a well-used baseball glove out of a torn cardboard box and tossed it on the unmade mattress of his twin bed. Sean had sat a framed picture of his girlfriend, back in Pennsylvania, on his rickety nightstand. He had turned to Aaron and asked if he had a girlfriend.

Sean's thoughts returned to the present. "You told me you didn't have a girlfriend. That first day we meet in the dorm." Sean's tone was accusatory as he stopped the car.

"I couldn't talk about it then...and I still can't."

Sean swallowed his irritation. "Okay, boyo, but I'm here if you change your mind."

He pulled on the door handle and stepped onto the pavement. After the chill of the SUV, the hot air outside of the vehicle was suffocating. Sean waited for Aaron to emerge, then strode towards the back of the studio. The doors to three vehicles parked side-by-side in the parking lot opened and a dozen women between eighteen and twenty-five rushed toward the two men.

"Aaron, Aaron, can I have your autograph!" Eleven voices chorused together.

"Here we go." Sean muttered under his breath.

Sean loved Aaron like a brother, but he couldn't help the flash of envy as girls flocked around his friend. Aaron's rugged good looks drew the women like bees to honey. The blue eyes and sun streaked blonde hair didn't hurt either. He, on the other hand, did not garner that kind of attention with his flat face, a nose that had been broken by a bad pitch, and a scarred lip from a dog bite when he was fifteen. Sean shook off the envy as he reminded himself that it didn't matter, he was a happily married man.

"Sean, would you autograph my t-shirt?"

Sean turned towards the voice, staring at a rail-thin girl with a plain face and squinty eyes.

"Sure, darlin', turn around."

"I prefer the front." She winked at Sean.

"And I prefer to sleep with my wife and not by myself on the sofa."

With a harrumph, the girl turned around and presented her back. Sean had just finished signing her left shoulder blade with the marker she furnished when the back door to the studio opened and banged against the outside wall.

Sean and Aaron's agent charged towards them. "You're late. We have to get inside. No more autographs, girls. Shoo."

He stood only five foot-eight, but Jason Whitley's commanding voice had the girls backing up and dispersing to their vehicles.

The three men hurried to the studio's back door.

Aaron slammed the door of his condo. *Three hours!* Before the shoot was over he had been ready to strangle the director. They had to shoot the whole thing from the front, then the back. Side angles, close-ups, back-offs. The only angle they missed was upside down. His heart was beating an urgent tattoo…hurry up, hurry up. He had three days until his next game and he would spend every minute looking for Sophie.

He charged into the bedroom to retrieve his phone, praying it wasn't damaged. He leaned over and picked it off the floor. The black screen had a crack in the upper left corner. He heaved a sigh as the pass code was accepted and the bright icons appeared. He crossed over to his mahogany dresser and picked up his car keys. As he slipped the phone into his jeans pocket, he glanced over at the large bay window. The turmoil inside him drew him like a magnet to the calmness of Lake Michigan and the clouds drifting overhead. Placing his hands on the large pane of glass, he bowed his head.

"God, I need your help. I can't do this on my own. Please help me find Sophie." Aaron cleared his throat. "Alive." He squeezed his eyes shut, shook his head, and then turned, wiping an arm across his eyes. As he entered the living room his stomach started to rumble. He hadn't eaten all day. In the kitchen, he opened the door to the pantry and snatched a box of breakfast bars and two bottles of a sports drink off the shelf.

Aaron locked the door of the condo and rode the elevator down to the garage. As the doors slid open he pressed the unlock icon on the fob for his new black SUV. His footfalls were silent on the vast expanse of gray concrete as he crossed to the vehicle. He yanked on the door handle and slid into the driver's seat.

The driver of a fancy sedan honked and waved as Aaron set the drinks in the cup holders and used his fingers to rip open the cellophane on four of the breakfast bars, tossing them onto the cream-colored console. He loosened the caps on the bottles. Checking behind him, he backed out of his space and headed for the exit.

Now that he had a plan of action, the churning in his gut had disappeared. He would leave searching Milwaukee to Sophie's fiancée and friend. They would know about her habits and haunts there. But if she was in the La Grange area…nobody knew where Sophie would go in the area she grew up in more than he did. And it felt like more than a hunch that that was where she would be found. Her car had been wrecked close to La Grange. That couldn't be a coincidence. *But what had she been doing there? And what had happened to her?* Aaron shook his head. Those types of questions were counter-productive.

As the traffic started to thin out on the interstate, Aaron pressed his foot down on the gas pedal. He was two and a half hours from La Grange and the temptation to speed was strong—daylight would be fading fast when he arrived. But the fate of the dead teenager cautioned his race to save Sophie. He grabbed a granola bar, chewing while he wove around the slower traffic. After consuming four bars, he drained one of the bottles of sports drink. His hunger taken care of, Aaron gripped the wheel and flew down the interstate.

The audible swish of the glass door had customers shifting their eyes from their food or dinner companions to stare as Aaron walked into *Jessica's* restaurant. The atmosphere was in sharp contrast to the restaurants in Chicago he was invited to as a local celebrity. At those high-end places, most of the diners didn't pay attention to who walked through the door. They were totally absorbed with what was going on in their sphere of existence and couldn't have cared less about anyone outside that sphere. He preferred small town diners like *Jessica's.*

A middle-aged waitress hurried over to welcome him and then led him to a booth towards the back of the room, introducing herself as Pat.

"I need to ask you a couple of questions, if that's okay." Aaron's heart thrummed in his chest.

"Sure." Her smile encouraged him to speak whatever was on his mind.

"Did you work shifts here today and yesterday?"

"All day yesterday and today. We had two girls quit."

Aaron leaned in and placed his cupped hands on the table. "I'm looking for a woman about 5'7 with dark hair and green eyes."

"Honey, that describes half the women who came in. The hair, I mean. Don't notice women's eyes and height much."

"You would have noticed this woman's. Her eyes are aquamarine."

The waitress eyebrows drew together.

"Sea green," Aaron added hastily.

"Let me think on it while I place your order."

As much as Aaron wanted to get his answer and bolt out of there, he needed to eat something besides four granola bars. He ordered ice tea and a hamburger.

Pat was back ten minutes later. She set the plate with his order and a side of fries down in front of him. "Is this woman local?"

"She was fourteen years ago."

Pat shook her head. "I've only been here eleven years and the women with dark hair who came in to eat were all locals as far as I know."

Aaron's face fell. "Thanks for answering my questions."

Her voice was sympathetic. "I'm sorry. I don't think that was the answer you were looking for."

She turned as the booth in front of Aaron vied for her attention. Aaron ate his burger, ignored the fries, and drained the glass of tea. He threw a couple of bills on the table and strode out onto the sidewalk. Fists clenching and unclenching, Aaron stared at the peach hues on the drifting clouds.

"Aaron?"

Aaron's head swiveled as the glass door swung shut behind an elderly man with a shock of white hair.

Aaron smiled in recognition. "Mr. Wesley."

"I thought that was you." He shook his head. "I lost mighty fine neighbors when your folks moved back to Milwaukee after you left for college." He cocked his head slightly to the right. "What brings you back to Whitewater?"

Aaron squirmed, but Sophie was more important than what people might think about why he was personally looking for her.

"Do you remember my old girlfriend, Sophie?"

The old man's bright eyes sparkled. "Of course. I knew the whole family. And they might as well have hitched you and Sophie to a cart and been done with it. You two were glued at the hip that summer...1997 wasn't it?"

"1998. Unfortunately, Sophie is missing. I'm here trying to find her."

"Missing?"

"It was on the news this morning. I'm asking around town if anyone has seen her here."

The sparkle in Mr. Wesley's blue eyes dimmed. "I'll ask around and get other people to spread the word."

"Thank you, sir. I have to look around before I lose the light." Aaron strode down the sidewalk to the florist shop where Sophie had worked part-time the summer they were together.

An hour later, and the light all but gone, Aaron heaved a sigh. He would have to stop searching until the next day. None of the store owners he had talked to up and down Main Street had seen Sophie. There was no point checking the bowling lane or theater. If she had made a nostalgic trip back to Whitewater, it wasn't to take a trip down memory lane the summer of '98. Of that he was positive. Aaron rubbed at the bristles on his cheek. Whitewater was a bust.

Aaron pulled in the parking lot of the Baymont Inn and Suites on Main Street. He left the motel office, swiped the keycard in the slot, and opened the door to his room. He sighed when the frigid air cooled his sweaty face.

He tossed the key card on the nightstand and sank on the edge of the bed. Aaron dropped his hands between his knees and stared at the maroon carpet. Tomorrow he would go to all of the favorite places she and her mom had gone to together, like the lake and the farmers market.

He lay back on the bed. Maybe rushing here half-cocked wasn't the best of plans. He really had very little information to go on. He didn't know a thing about Sophie's life now. What was her emotional state when she left her home yesterday? Was she happy, sad, mad—exhilarated? If she had been angry, no telling what she would have done. The corners of his lips turned up at the memory of sneaking up on Sophie in the kitchen at the farm when she was washing dishes. He had whispered "boo" in her ear. She had jumped, whirled around, and thrown a plastic cup full of soapy water at him.

Aaron's eyes lost their focus as he looked at the ceiling. He let his mind drift to a memory of another time he had raised Sophie's ire…

Chapter Fourteen

Summer 1998

Aaron reclined on the steps of the gazebo, watching Sophie pick flowers at the edge of the pond. He reached down and removed his leather sandals. He stole through the flowering weeds without a sound. He stopped, bare inches from Sophie's bent form. Sneaking long arms around her waist, he leaned into her ear and whispered, "Gotcha."

Sophie jerked up, whacking her head against his nose.

"Ow!"

She started to whirl around when she lost her footing on the slippery bank. Her weight shifted towards the pond and he gripped her tighter. But his footing wasn't solid either.

With a huge splash Aaron and Sophie landed in the lukewarm water of the pond. Aaron scrambled to get his feet beneath him and pull Sophie upright. The bottom of the pond was slimy and squished between his toes. When they were both standing, he turned Sophie to face him. Her eyes glared daggers at him through dripping tendrils of her hair. He cautiously swept the soaked locks behind her ears.

"I'm sorry. I didn't…"

"…mean to scare me." Sophie's eyes narrowed. "Yes, you did."

"…mean for you to fall in the pond."

Aaron grasped her hands. "If I promise not to sneak up on you ever again, will you forgive me?"

Those beautiful aquamarine eyes softened as the anger ebbed away. Mesmerizing tiny droplets of water sparkled on her long eyelashes. The emotion filling his heart was indescribable as he lowered his head and placed his lips on Sophie's for the first time. Everything disappeared except the softness of her lips and the pounding of his heart.

But instead of her lips kissing him back, they retreated.

He lifted his head. Sophie stared at him, her cheeks pink and eyes wide.

He cringed. "I'm sorry. I didn't ask. You looked beautiful and…"

Sophie's eyes lit with amusement. "I look beautiful? More like a drowned rat."

And then she laughed.

Aaron turned toward the bank, his feet making sucking noises in the mud.

"You think my kissing you is funny?" His tone was sharp.

Sophie squished after him, still laughing. "No."

He stomped his muddy feet back to the gazebo. "Our first kiss and you think…"

Sophie grabbed his arm and yanked. "Stop being mad and look at me."

He crossed his arms and glared. He hadn't been mad, he had been hurt. Something that made time stand still for him had made her laugh.

"Aaron, I'm sorry I laughed. I wasn't laughing at you." She sighed and walked past him, up the two steps and into the gazebo, her clothes dripping water on the peeling paint of the floor. She backed onto the bench, sitting on her hands.

Aaron followed and stood in the gazebo doorway.

Sophie rocked slowly. "I imagined our first kiss to be…so romantic. Maybe we would spread a blanket on the sand by the lake after dark and look up at the stars and then you would lean over and kiss me. Or maybe we would go to the drive-in and watch a romantic movie in your jeep and you would lean over…" The rosy hue in Sophie's cheeks deepened. "You know what I mean."

She stilled, then squared her shoulders and looked up at Aaron. "It was such a shock when you kissed me. I wasn't expecting it. And it just struck me as funny because soaking wet and stinking of pond water was about as far away from my romantic vision as you could get."

Aaron's stance relaxed and he grinned. "We do stink, don't we?" He stepped in front of Sophie, placing his large hands on her shoulders. "How about I make you a promise? A romantic date you…we… will never forget."

And he had kept that promise. A week later, early in the evening, with Sophie's hand in his and permission from his best friend Jason, he had led her into a field of purple wildflowers on the Burbage farm for a blanket picnic. Later, with her hands softly folded around his neck, Sophie had whispered that his second kiss was better than all the romantic kisses she could have imagined.

Chapter Fifteen

Summer 2012

Aaron stood just shy of the lapping water that caressed the shore of Lake Geneva. The mid-morning sun beat warmth down on his shoulders. He should have arrived much earlier, but he hadn't fallen asleep until four in the morning and then overslept, awaking bleary-eyed. Where was his determination from yesterday? All he felt now was overwhelmed. It was a big lake, with homes on all sides. What did he think? That Sophie would be lounging here beside the condos, sipping tea? He shook his head and heaved a sigh.

A toddler rushed toward the water, chubby legs pumping and laughter bubbling all around him. Aaron watched a school of minnows dart away from the little boy's feet as he entered the water. *Lord, I need a miracle.* Sighing again, he turned and made his way back to the SUV.

Aaron started the engine and let it idle. Sophie *should* be in this area, because of her wrecked car. But he needed more information. And talking to Sophie's fiancé was the best way to get it. He pulled the iPhone out of his pocket and searched the internet for the news story. Her fiancé's name was Bryan Taylor and he worked at a motorcycle manufacturing plant. After getting the contact info, he tapped in the company's number. When the receptionist picked up, he asked for Mr. Taylor.

"Bryan Taylor."

Aaron took a breath. "Mr. Taylor, you don't know me. My name is Aaron Reinhart and…"

"…the baseball player for the Chicago Cubs?" There was obvious astonishment in his voice.

"Yes."

"This is a surprise." A puzzled tone replaced the astonishment. "What can I do for you?"

Aaron tapped his finger on the steering wheel. "I heard about Sophie's disappearance. And I'd like to help find her."

"You knew my fiancé?"

"We were friends in high school."

"Strange…she never mentioned knowing you. I mean, you're famous… I'm surprised she didn't."

Now was not the time to explain his relationship with Sophie to her fiancé. "It was a long time ago…anyway, I know the La Grange area like the back of my hand and on the news they said those kids were found in her wrecked car near the area…I thought I would look around…and, as her fiancé, I thought if you and I put our heads together…"

Aaron's words trailed off.

There was an awkward silence and then Bryan cleared his throat. "I'm afraid I don't have anything to add to the news report. The teen that survived the crash has no memory of taking Sophie's car."

Aaron's tone grew desperate. "You have no idea where she was headed that morning?

Bryan sighed. "No."

"What kind of mood was she in?"

"I'm sorry, but I'm not going to discuss that with you." Irritation came through the line.

Aaron gripped the phone tighter. "I don't mean to be personal but knowing her mood might help me know where she would have gone."

"How well did you know Sophie?"

Aaron chewed on his lip then took the plunge. "She was my girlfriend." He rushed on before Bryan could comment. "We were very close. I knew all her moods…where she might go when she was happy, sad, mad, contemplating life."

A soft chuckle came through the phone. "Contemplating life…I know what you mean."

There was a brief silence and then a heavy sigh. "I don't think it will help you, but Sophie was upset that morning. She broke off our engagement and then left my place in tears. I left for work and haven't seen her since."

Aaron should have felt sadness for the break-up of Sophie's engagement, but his heart gave a traitorous little leap followed by a quickening in the rhythm. "Wait a minute…that actually is a help. I think I know where she went if she came to La Grange."

"Where?"

"The old farm where she used to live."

"No, you're wrong. I tried to get her to go for a visit a couple of times and she said she was never going back."

Aaron could almost see Bryan shaking his head in denial.

"I know, after the fire and her father's…" Aaron paused. He was divulging information he shouldn't. "But there is a place on the farm that was one of her favorite spots. She would go there when she was sad or upset. It helped to calm her and made her feel closer to her mother. I'll go there now and let you know if I find anything."

"I should go."

Aaron cleared his throat. "I'm already in the area."

"Oh."

There was a pause. Bryan was probably wondering why Sophie's old high school boyfriend would rush out to try and find Sophie after all these years.

When Bryan spoke, his voice was tinged with emotion. "Even if she went there, I don't think she's there now. I think she's been kidnapped."

Aaron closed his eyes. Bryan had voiced his worst fear.

He took in a breath. "We need to stay positive. She's alive and we're going to find her."

"One last thing, please keep our broken engagement to yourself for now."

"I will...look, I don't know if you're a praying man..."

"Not usually. But I will keep that in mind. And...thank you for your help."

Aaron said goodbye and pressed the end button.

Bryan's logic had doused ice water on Aaron's efforts to stay positive. The odds were slim to none that Sophie would still be at the pond... had she gone there in the first place. But he had to go to be sure. He put the car in reverse and swung around to the exit. Finally, a gap opened in the traffic and he pressed his running shoe down on the gas and screeched onto the road.

The yellow Lab leaned his head over the edge of the well and whined softly. Moans were coming from the bottom of the well. The girl cried out and the dog rose up on his haunches and barked. She didn't respond. He barked again. He started to lie down again, and then stopped. His ears pricked up and he turned his head. He swiveled his head back to the well and whined again. At the bottom of the well, the girl shivered and moaned. He gave a sharp bark, then turned and rushed off in the direction of home.

Aaron slowed as he made the turn onto the badly damaged asphalt. His heart was pounding in his chest and he had started to sweat. He had the air conditioning on full blast, but it wasn't helping. Sophie wasn't the only one who had never wanted to see the farm again. At the first glimpse of the charred remains of the house, an unbidden memory played out.

Pulling into the driveway, Aaron heard a scream. He slammed on the brakes and jumped from the car, running for the back door. Another scream rent the humid air and Aaron turned, charging in the direction of the cornfields on his left. He rushed into the field, slamming stalks out of his way. The treads of his shoes left deep impressions as he skidded to a halt, his mind trying to comprehend the nightmare on the ground at his feet.

Aaron whipped his eyes to the front, breathing hard. *Forget the past. Concentrate on now.* He pressed on the gas and shot past the barn. The dirt road to the pond had completely disappeared. Aaron shifted into four-wheel drive and hoped he didn't take a wrong turn.

The grass and weeds brushed the sides of the car and the bottoms of the windows. He had to weave around young trees that had sprung up everywhere, their growth unchecked. But at least the tall pines were still here to help guide him. The pond came in view and he slowed to a stop.

The contrast was jarring. Since he had turned onto the property, except for the corn fields, everything his eyes gazed upon was in a heart-wrenching state of neglect. But the landscape around the pond was still as beautiful as the first day Sophie had shown it to him. He sucked in a quick breath. It looked impossibly the same as the last time they were here, in July of 1998 when he had surprised Sophie with a special gift.

Aaron had blindfolded Sophie and driven her to the pond. He had helped her walk a few feet from the jeep and removed the blindfold. Standing directly in front of her was the little gazebo, freshly repaired and painted. The pristine white paint shone in the sunlight. Sophie's gale of delighted laughter had washed over him as they walked around the structure. She continued to gasp and giggle with delight as she touched the satiny wood. Aaron's heart had been full of love and contentment. She had loved his gift.

Tears wet his cheeks as he walked towards the gazebo. It was still standing, but large sections of paint had blistered and peeled off. Some of the dark gray shingles were missing from the roof. He sat down on the water-damaged bench and gazed around carefully, but it did not feel as if she had been here. Wouldn't he have felt something?

He stood up slowly and his throat closed. Bryan was right. Sophie had been kidnapped. There was no other explanation. His anguished wail startled a group of napping birds. The branches under their feet shook as they took flight. Aaron pounded his fist into the nearest pillar. Pain shot through his arm. He grabbed the pillar with both hands and pressed his head against the peeling paint as he drew in ragged breaths.

A few minutes passed. Aaron whispered into the wood. "I won't give up, Sophie."

He walked to the SUV and got in. He made a sharp turn, chewing up clumps of flowering weeds. He grabbed his cell phone off the console and speed dialed a familiar number.

"Sean, it's me." The hand holding the phone bobbled as he traveled over the uneven ground.

"Aaron, boyo, how goes the search?"
"No sign. Look, I'm calling because I want to hire a private detective. Do you know a good one?"

"As a matter of fact, I do. I hired a guy for my sister, Colleen. The detective caught her lying, cheating, husband red-handed with his secretary in that classy joint on the shore. You know the one…forget the name…"

Aaron cut him off. "That's great. Can you get his name and number and text it to me?"

"Sure." Sean's tone sobered. "I'm sorry you haven't found anything."

Aaron swallowed hard. "I'll call when I get home."

He ended the call.

He slowed as he approached the weed encrusted foundation of the house. His heartbeats increased and he had the strongest urge to get out of the car. He stopped and put the gear shift into park. His hand reached for the door handle.

His phone beeped with a text message. It was the number for the PI. He put the car back into gear as he punched in the number. As the car rolled forward, a dog started barking.

"Lakeshore Investigations."

"Yes, I'm looking for a detective for…" The frantic barking was interfering with his thought process. It seemed to be coming from right behind him. He looked in the rearview mirror and saw a yellow Labrador Retriever barking at the ground by the foundation.

"Sir?"

Aaron's gaze dropped back to the windshield. "I'm sorry, I was distracted by this dog…never mind." He put his foot on the brake as he came to the end of the driveway. He put on his left turn signal.

"I want to make an appointment…"

A man shouted. Aaron glanced in the rearview mirror again. An elderly, darkly-tanned man in baggy pants and a tank top stepped out of the cornfield to the left of the driveway.

"When is the best day and time for you?"

"Huh… what?" Aaron watched the man cross the drive.

"I wanted to know…"

"I'm sorry. I have to call you back." Aaron punched the end button as he continued to watch the old man.

He had crossed over to the yellow Lab and was staring at the ground. The man dropped to his knees and looked down. *What is he looking…?* Aaron slammed the gear shift into park and shoved the vehicle door open. His heart beat loudly in his ears. All other sounds were obliterated. He had mind-numbing sense of déjà vu.

Aaron charged right at the old man, who looked up with wide eyes. Aaron's gaze searched through the high weeds for Sophie's body even as his mind refused to consider that she could be gone. He stopped a couple of feet away from the man and the dog. There was no body. He turned to the old man to ask what he was looking for when the yellow Lab moved and revealed a large hole in the ground. It was the old dry well.

"Do you have a cell phone? We need to call for help." Watery gray eyes gazed up at him.

The breath Aaron drew in caught in his throat as he forced his feet to the edge and dropped to his knees.

Chapter Sixteen

Sophie lay at the bottom of the dry well, curled in the fetal position. Her long ponytail lay across her shoulder. The yellow Lab whined at his shoulder.

Aaron jumped into the well, landing inches from Sophie's head. He squatted down and placed a shaking hand on her shoulder.

"Sophie, can you hear me? Please, Sophie...please answer me. Please don't be...please wake up." Tears coursed down his cheeks.

He moved his trembling right hand to her neck. As he placed two fingers on the side of her throat, Sophie jerked and moaned. Aaron yanked his hand back. *Alive! She's alive.* He twisted his head up.

"Call 911!"

"I don't have a cell phone."

"In my car at the end of the driveway. Call 911. Hurry!"

The dog bent his head over the edge of the hole and whined again.

Aaron wiped an arm across his eyes. "Good dog. You're a very good dog."

Aaron turned back to Sophie. He wanted to hold her, but he had no idea what injuries she might have, external or internal.

The old man was back. "I don't know how these new-fangled cell phones work."

Aaron stood up and grabbed the phone out of the gnarled hand. He quickly punched in the numbers.

"911, what is your emergency?"

"A woman has fallen into a dry well."

"What is the location, sir?"

Aaron gave her the address on Territorial Rd.

"And your name, sir?"

"Aaron."

"Do you know her name?"

"Sophie Madison."

"Okay. What is her condition, Aaron?"

"I don't know; I'm afraid to move her."

"Look her over carefully and describe what you see."

"Okay, buutttt… can you, you… tell me howwww… long until they get, get… here." Aaron shut his eyes and took a deep breath.

The woman spoke in a soothing tone. "Emergency services out of La Grange should be there within ten minutes."

The invisible weight pressing down on Aaron's shoulders dropped away. He shifted closer to Sophie. "Her face is flushed." Aaron reached down and placed the cool palm of his hand on Sophie's forehead. "Oh, myyyyy, God… she's burning uuuppp… with fever." The invisible weight settled back like a bag of wet sand across his shoulders. "Please hurry."

"Check the rest of her body."

Aaron studied Sophie's still form and then focused on her left foot. The ankle was horribly swollen.

"Her left, left… ankle is swollen."

"How swollen, Aaron?"

The dispatcher's professional tone helped Aaron to concentrate and lessened his panic. "About the size of a grapefruit."

"Can you examine it without moving her?"

Aaron stepped closer to her ankle. He leaned in and then gasped. Bright red lines snaked from her ankle up her leg and disappeared beneath her black Capri pants.

"Anything else, Aaron?"

"Red, red, red…" He clenched his fist in frustration.

"Aaron, take a deep breath for me and let it out slowly."

He did as she suggested. "Red streaks… going up her leg."

"Okay. Is she conscious?" Her tone was still professional, but a sense of urgency had crept in.

The dog's ears pricked up and he snapped his head to the right.

The old man's gnarled hands gripped the mossy edge of the well. "Son, the ambulance is almost here. I can hear the sirens. I'm going down to the road."

Aaron looked up at the old man and nodded and then his eyes widened. "Oh, no, my car's in the way."

"I'll take care of it."

Aaron had pulled the phone from his ear and the dispatcher's barely discernable voice was trying to get his attention. "Sorry, ambulance is almost here."

"Stay with me, Aaron. Is she conscious?"

"No."

"Okay, don't hang up until the EMT's take over."

Aaron's gaze strayed to the opposite wall and he gasped.

"Aaron? What's wrong?"

Seconds ticked by as the dispatcher repeated his name again. "There's a...it's a...skeleton."

"What!" The dispatcher's professional tone had disappeared. "Did you say skeleton?"

The loud blaring of the sirens broke Aaron's paralysis and he tore his gaze back to Sophie. She was moaning.

Aaron moved closer to her and squatted down again, setting the phone on the dirt. "Sophie, can you hear me?"

Sophie's eyes fluttered and then opened.

Aaron bent his head down close to her face. "Sophie, it's me, Aaron."

Sophie tilted her head up. "Aaron?"

Aaron laid his hand on her hot cheek and smiled. "Yeah, it's me."

A smile formed briefly on Sophie's mouth and then morphed into a grimace of pain.

"An ambulance is here, Sophie."

The blaring of the sirens stopped and doors slammed. The forgotten dispatcher repeated his name from the phone.

Aaron picked up the phone as four men encircled the hole in the ground. Two were firemen holding a ladder and another man held a transfer board to stabilize Sophie.

Aaron spoke into the phone. "EMT's are here."

"Tell them what you told me. Don't touch the skeleton. I'm going to contact the Walworth County Sheriff. Good luck."

The ladder dropped inches from where Aaron squatted. He looked up. One of the men dressed as an EMT spoke to him. "Quick, son, climb the ladder so we can get to her."

Aaron shoved the phone in his pocket and climbed out of the well. The older of the two EMTs descended.

"Watch out for the skeleton."

The man's head whipped around as his feet landed on the bottom of the well. He muttered, "Lord, have mercy," then bent down to check Sophie. He looked up at the other EMT, a young man in his early twenties, holding the transfer board. "That one won't fit down here. Get the pediatric board and ankle brace."

The young EMT tossed down the neck brace and raced to the van. He was back in seconds.

"Okay Jess, pull up the ladder. Trey, I'll secure her on the board and then you can come down and help me lift her to Rick and Jess."

Aaron crossed his arms and grabbed both of his biceps with his fingers, squeezing hard as he spoke down into the well. "She has a fever and I saw red streaks on her leg."

The EMT in the well carefully stabilized Sophie's ankle with the hard plastic brace and took her vitals. As he moved her onto the shorter board and strapped her down, one of the firemen spoke into his two-way radio. "…female in her…"

He glanced at Aaron.

"She's thirty-one."

He spoke into the radio, "thirty-one-year-old female."

"Temp 105, BP 180/90," a voice called from below.

The man relayed the information and added, "possible cellulitis."

The radio squawked. "Roger. ETA to Lackland?"

The man below shouted up, "ETA twenty minutes."

The fireman repeated the time.

"Roger, I will relay, out," the voice on the radio said.

The fireman dropped the radio into his holder.

Through the entire exchange Aaron's eyes never left Sophie. He watched as Trey dropped lightly into the hole and helped to lift the board with Sophie on it. One of the firemen grabbed a handle and pulled the board across the weeds as the men in the well kept it lifted. As soon as Sophie's legs passed the edge of the well the ladder was dropped in the hole and both men scrambled up.

Aaron looked down at Sophie's face.

"She passed out," the older EMT said. "Back up, son, we have to transfer her to the gurney."

Grass and weeds brushed his jeans as he moved backwards. "I'm going with her."

The elderly farmer spoke up. "I'll drive your SUV to the hospital, son."

The dog stood next to his owner, looking in Sophie's direction and whining.

Aaron acknowledged the kind gesture with a nod and a thank you. He patted the dog on his head. "What's his name?

"Cooper."

"I'll take care of her now, Cooper."

The Lab turned his head and licked Aaron's hand.

Aaron watched as they efficiently transferred Sophie to the gurney and loaded her into the ambulance. He jumped in after her, turning to face the firemen through the open doors.

"Walworth County Sheriff deputies should be on their way for the skeleton." He barely got the words out before the ambulance doors slammed shut.

He sat down next to the younger EMT on the vinyl-padded bench bolted to the side of the ambulance. He placed his hand over one of Sophie's still, white hands as the vehicle's engine started and the sirens blared. He started to weep silently.

The emergency medical tech gripped his shoulder. "She's going to be okay."

Aaron nodded his head and whispered, "She has to be. I can't lose her again."

The Walworth County vehicle braked to a stop in the tall weeds beside the fire truck. Sheriff Jim Cox heaved a sigh and opened the driver's door. There was no question he had to personally take the call, despite the fact that he had officially taken four days of vacation time; and he still had two left. His dark shoes pressed the matted weeds further into the unkempt lawn as he stepped away from his vehicle.

He ignored the two firefighters as he observed the crime scene through his sunglasses. His gaze settled on the burnt carcass of the Madison farmhouse and then shifted to the cornfields to the left. The last time he had stepped foot on this property had been fourteen years ago. He had been sheriff for a year, and thirty pounds lighter. In his fifteen years as sheriff, only one crime scene had him desperately trying to hold back his emotions.

The sheriff reached into the back pocket of his tan trousers and pulled out a handkerchief. He wiped the perspiration off his forehead as he tried to wrap his brain around the information the dispatcher had given him. Sophie Madison had come back to the farm and fallen in the well. His gaze drifted back to the cornfields. He shook his head and walked towards the firemen. He would have bet money that she would never return.

"Sheriff." One of the firemen, with coal-black corkscrew curls, nodded his head.

The sheriff acknowledged both men. "Rick… Jess. I hear we've got ourselves a skeleton."

"You heard right." Jess said.

The three men turned as one and looked toward the well.

"Either of you been down in the well?"

"Nope. Didn't want to mess up the evidence any more than necessary." Jess's face was shiny with sweat.

Sheriff Cox sighed. Their six-year streak without a homicide had probably been wiped out. "Show me the skeleton."

Jim followed the firefighters to the well and peered over the edge, scrutinizing the bones.

"Detectives should be here soon. I beat them here only because I was closer. Give me a hand taping off the crime scene."

After the yellow tape was in place, the men walked towards the fire truck.

Jess ran a hand over his slick scalp. "This humidity is kicking my butt."

"You two get going. You can come back for the ladder tomorrow."

Rick glanced towards the well. "You sure?"

"Nothing more the two of you can do here."

"Okay, sheriff. Wait in your car, run the air. I don't want to get a call that you've had heat stroke," Jess said.

"Yes, Ma."

Both Jess and Rick laughed as they climbed into the fire truck.

After the fire truck had backed onto Territorial Road, Jim's eyes again focused on the cornfield. The horror was as fresh as if it had happened yesterday. He closed his eyes to dispel the image, but it remained. He rubbed his hands hard over his face, took a deep breath and muttered, "In the past, let it go."

Sherriff Cox turned, with a purposeful stride, towards his vehicle. Once inside, he cranked on the air conditioning while he waited on the Walworth County detectives. He tried to concentrate on the reports that would need his attention when he got back to his desk in two days. Jim needed to flood his mind with any thought other than that poor, traumatized seventeen-year-old girl screaming in the cornfield, her father's still form on the ground, the dazed expression on her boyfriend's face, and the flames and black smoke shooting out of the windows and roof of the farmhouse.

Aaron

and Sophie

Chapter Seventeen

Aaron sat on the vinyl chair in the emergency waiting room of the Aurora Lackland Medical Center. His foot tapped a nervous tattoo on the light gray tile floor. It felt as if a stone was lodged in his gut, which grew heavier with each passing minute. He had been waiting for almost two hours with nothing to occupy his mind. His thoughts kept trying to drift to the last time Sophie had been brought here in an ambulance. But he refused to go there. Dredging up all that pain wasn't going to help Sophie now.

The automatic doors leading to the parking lot slid open and Aaron glanced over. Bryan should be here soon. He had called him right after Sophie's gurney had disappeared into the emergency treatment room, leaving a message for Bryan to call him back. Bryan had returned the call an hour ago. He was on his way. The thought of meeting Sophie's fiancé…no, ex-fiancé… made his insides clinch around the phantom stone.

Aaron's first glimpse of her in the well… and the last fourteen years of separation had dissolved as if they had never been apart. *Oh, Lord, what I wouldn't give to be able to go back and change the past.* Aaron laced his fingers, placed them on the back of his neck and squeezed…hard.

"Mr. Reinhart?"

Aaron jumped to his feet and looked toward the treatment room. A young man in casual clothes and a white hospital coat stood outside the double doors with a questioning look.

"I'm Mr. Reinhart." Aaron rushed up to the man.

"I'm Dr. Franklin." Aaron's eyes widened. He didn't look to be a day over eighteen.

"You came with Ms. Madison?"

"Yes, how is she?" Aaron held his breath.

"She's stable at the moment. She has a broken ankle that will need surgery after the swelling goes down. She's being given a strong antibiotic through an IV to combat the bacterial infection that developed through a scrape on her ankle."

Aaron held the doctor's gaze. "Is she going to be okay?"

"She's a very lucky lady. The bacteria hadn't traversed too far. Another day in the well and the odds for survival would have been against her. I'm optimistic that she will make a full recovery."

Aaron let out a relieved sigh. "Thank you."

"They'll be moving her to a room in about an hour and you can see her." Dr. Franklin gave Aaron a brief smile and returned to the treatment room.

That twenty-pound stone was gone from his gut. His stomach rumbled, reminding him that he hadn't eaten at all that day. He walked over to the reception desk.

"Can you tell me where the cafeteria is?"

An older woman, with short gray hair, smiled and gave him directions. He strode towards two double doors. He passed through the cafeteria doors to the food line. He picked up a tray and stepped in line behind an elderly man with a cane hooked over his elbow.

Aaron grabbed his silverware, set his tray on the metal bars, and slid it to the first choice. He chose a small garden salad and then moved on to the entrees.

"What can I get for you, sweetie?"

Aaron couldn't help but smile back at the jolly nut-brown face with twinkling eyes. He perused the selections. He was careful about his diet normally, but this meal called for some comfort food. "I'd like the fried chicken, mashed potatoes, and the carrots. Is that brown sugar in the carrots?"

"Butter and brown sugar." The server's face split into a wide-mouthed grin.

"Perfect."

Aaron reached the end of the metal bars, grabbed a glass of iced tea, and carried his tray to the cashier. He paid for the meal and then walked to a small round table by a window and set down his tray. He pulled out a chair and sat down. Stomach growling again, he picked up a fried chicken breast and bit off a huge chunk. His sigh was pure pleasure as he chewed.

Aaron took his last bite of carrots and suppressed a burp. He leaned back, reached into his pocket, and pulled out his iPhone, glancing at the time. He should be able to see Sophie in about thirty minutes. He slid the phone back into the pocket of his jeans.

"Excuse me, aren't you Aaron Reinhart?"

Aaron looked up into blue eyes set in a freckled face.

"Yes." Aaron's forehead creased. Did she look familiar?

"Jennifer Newton, Chicago Tribune."

Aaron groaned inwardly. For the past twenty-four hours he had actually forgotten that he was a celebrity.

"Can you tell me about the woman you came here with in the ambulance? Do you know her, or were you helping out a stranger?"

Bright hot anger filled him as he stood. "No comment."

He pushed past the woman, leaving his tray on the table.

She hurried after him, her smartphone clutched in one hand. "Please, Aaron, just answer a couple of questions for me."

He seethed as he hurried down the long corridor, ignoring the reporter. Had someone at the hospital called the newspaper? He better not find out who did it. If he did, they would...*no, let it go. Only Sophie matters.*

The reporter appeared to be getting desperate, trying to dart in front of him to force him to stop. As soon as he reached the emergency waiting room, she would have to back off or be thrown out. On a normal day, with advanced notice, he would have been glad to talk to her, but not today...and never about Sophie.

The reporter rushed to block the doors to the emergency waiting room. "Aaron, come on, just answer one question."

He reached above her and pushed open one of the double doors. She moved aside, shoulders slumping. He strode toward the reception desk.

He spoke to the same woman. "It's me again. Any word on when the room for Sophie Madison will be ready?"

"Soon."

Aaron turned towards the voice. A tall man in pressed khakis, an oxford shirt, and loafers stood a couple of feet away. The man shortened the distance between them and held out a hand.

"I'm Bryan Taylor."

Aaron took the proffered hand. "Aaron Reinhart."

"I can't tell you how grateful I am. What an amazing coincidence that you were there when she was found by that farmer." Bryan let go of Aaron's hand.

Aaron set his face to a mask of neutrality. "I think of it as more of a miracle. I believe God led me there and sent that dog to watch over Sophie."

Bryan gave a polite nod. "Whatever the reason, I'm grateful."

Aaron cringed. He needed to drop the aggressive attitude.

Bryan's cell phone beeped. He pulled it out of his trouser pocket and glanced at the text. He glanced back at Aaron. "It's Sophie's best friend. She'll be here in about an hour and a half. I appreciate what you've done and I know you have to get back to the Cubs, Allison and I can take over here."

Aaron gritted his teeth. Bryan wasn't going to get rid of him that easily. "I texted the manager about what happened and he told me to take the week off. Probably doesn't want my presence distracting the rest of the club when it gets into the news feed."

Bryan's lips tightened for a brief second. "Okay. I'm sure Sophie will want to thank you in person."

The phone on the desk beside them rang and the receptionist answered. She listened, said okay, and hung up. She looked at the two men standing in front of her. "That was the nurses' station. Ms. Madison is in room 230. You can go on up, but only one visitor at a time for now."

Bryan and Aaron turned and looked at each other. Aaron spoke first. "You go, you're her fian...ex-fia...you go ahead."

Bryan gave another tight-lipped smile and strode towards the elevator.

Detectives Hank Burke and Derek Mason gazed down into the dry well as Lloyd "Jonny" Johnson, a forensic anthropologist with the medical examiner's office in Waukesha, bagged the last of the bones—the skull. Jonny wasn't wearing the protective suit that covered you from head to toe for two reasons. One, it was too hot and, two, it was unnecessary. They were bones and the crime scene had already been compromised by multiple people. Finished with the last bag, Jonny hugged it close, grabbed a rung on the ladder, and started to climb. Near the top of the well, he handed the bag to Derek and pulled himself onto the solid ground. He stripped off his latex gloves and booties.

Despite not wearing the suit, sweat glistened on any area of exposed skin. His tee shirt was soaked. Jonny grabbed the ice-cold bottle of water Hank passed him from the ice chest and dumped half of it over his head. "Five more minutes and you could have scooped me up with a spoon."

He shook water droplets in a halo around his head. "Man, that feels good."

"Well?" Derek held the skull gingerly in his slender brown hands.

He and Hank had refrained from asking questions while Jonny worked, but now they wanted as many answers that the forensic anthropologist could give them.

Jonny's head was tilted back and he was guzzling water. He drained the last drop then tossed the empty plastic bottle into the back of the white van. He yanked his wet tee shirt over his head and reached for a towel hanging on the door of the van. He toweled off the sweat while he addressed the detectives.

"Now, this is a guess, but it looks like death came from a blow to the frontal lobe of the head. No way to tell right now if it was intentional or an accident."

Hank scoffed. "The body was hidden in the well."

Derek surveyed the vicinity. "Could have been an accident and the person responsible panicked."

"I'm leaning towards a homicide."

"Fair enough. I'll take accidental. Winner buys the beer for a month."

Hank shook his head as he looked back at the well. "She was murdered."

Derek's head swiveled towards the well. "She?"

Jonny tossed the towel back in the van and pulled a dry tee shirt over his head. "She."

"Your skeleton is female. A young female. Now, detectives, I need a shower and I still have to log and pack the evidence for transport."

Hank lost the bantering tone. "Anything else?"

Jonny shook his head. "The woman who fell in the well contaminated the site all around the bones. This one's going to the forensics lab in Milwaukee. Not much to go on. Glad it's out of my hands."

Jonny took the skull from Derek and placed it in an evidence box before slamming the back doors of the van shut and securing the latch. Flipping a backward wave, he climbed into the van's cab and drove off.

Derek removed his hat and wiped perspiration from his forehead and shaved head. "I feel a cold case coming on." He returned his hankie to his back pocket. "When do you think we should interview the woman from the well?"

Hank walked over to the county car. "We'll give her a couple of days. Let her heal up some. There's no hurry. Those bones have been in that well for a while. Not like this case needs solving tomorrow."

Derek followed. They entered their vehicle cranking up the air conditioning as they waited for a guy from the local hardware store to bring them a large piece of plywood to cover the dry well.

Chapter Eighteen

Sophie blinked at the bright light coming through the large window to her left. Her eyebrows drew together and she frowned. *Where am I?*

She started to turn her head to the right, away from the light.

"Sophie."

Sophie jerked at the sound and a dull pain shot upward from her ankle. A face loomed over her. She pushed her head deeper into the pillow.

"It's me...Bryan." He gently rubbed her hand.

Sophie blinked, trying to focus her eyes, but they seemed connected to a brain wrapped in cotton or a fog bank. She licked her dry lips.

"You've got a strong painkiller in your IV...you probably feel somewhat disorientated." He patted her hand. "I'll get the doctor."

In the second floor waiting area, Aaron watched Bryan leave Sophie's room and head in the direction of the nurse's station. He'd been cooling his heels for an hour. Taking advantage of this window of opportunity, Aaron sprinted up the hall and entered Sophie's room. He came to an abrupt halt. Memories flooded his brain of the last time he had seen Sophie laying on a hospital bed looking helpless.

She had been propped up in the bed, staring out the window when he paused on the threshold of her hospital room, the stems of her favorite flowers gripped tightly in his hand. Hearing his footsteps, she had turned her head and looked in his direction. Her face had flushed a deep red, her eyes broadcasting anguish. She had quickly turned her head back towards the window. He had turned back to the hallway as footsteps approached behind him.

"I'm sorry, Aaron. She doesn't want to see you." Sophie's aunt clutched a Styrofoam cup in her hand. With the fingers of her other hand, she squeezed Aaron's arm. "You have to give her time to come to grips with everything that's happened."

He had handed her aunt the flowers and walked away.

That had been fourteen years ago, the last time he had seen Sophie.

Aaron took in a calming breath and put his feet in motion, stepping to the side of her bed. She turned her head in his direction. A smile trembled on her lips.

"Aaron?"

Aaron smiled back, tears beginning to form. "Yes, it's me."

Sophie tried to lift her hand. Aaron reached down and grasped it. "I had a dream about you. You were looking down at me, and then you touched my cheek."

"It wasn't a dream, I did…"

"Sophie, I'm back." Did Bryan's cheery voice seem forced?

Aaron let go of Sophie's hand and stepped back. "I saw you leave. I decided to check on her."

"The doctor should be here any minute. I haven't had a chance to talk with Sophie. She just woke up."

Aaron took the hint. He winked at Sophie and left.

Bryan took Aaron's place, unlocking his jaw from the sight of him holding Sophie's hand.

"How are you feeling?"

"Confused. What happened to me?"

Bryan gave her a reassuring smile. "What do you remember?"

Sophie's eyes gazed at the ceiling. "Going to your condo and we talked about…"

She looked at Bryan, her lips pursed.

Bryan sighed. "You broke off our engagement."

Her eyes grew bleak and then seemed to look right through him. "It was raining on the interstate. I…" Her brows drew together. "I drove to…"

Sophie's eyes refocused and she stared at Bryan.

"I drove to the farm and fell in the well." She whispered.

Bryan squeezed her hand. "I'm sorry, honey."

Jonny looked over his row of evidence boxes with a critical eye. The bones had been securely packed for the short trip in the van to Milwaukee. He had identified, wrapped, and sealed the evidence by the book to avoid contamination…and a possible mistrial…if the victim was ever identified and a perpetrator was found. A couple of big ifs, in his opinion.

Smaller items, such as the zipper, had been packaged in a plastic bag. Each container had been labeled "EVIDENCE", Walworth County Sherriff's Office, and noted with a case number and item number. His property sheet with all the evidence listed was carefully logged, along with a lab analysis slip.

Delivering the containers personally would allow him to discuss the case with the forensic scientist. He had already phoned the crime lab and coordinated a time to meet in the morning. He pulled on the diamond stud in his earlobe. There wasn't much hope that there would be a DNA match with the national database.

Jonny shook his head and checked his work area. Everything was in its proper place. Time for that shower. He couldn't stand the rank odor coming off of his skin a minute longer. He crossed to the frosted glass door and flipped the light switch off. Closing the door, he turned the key in the lock and then pulled on the knob to be sure it was locked. Jingling the keys, he walked towards the exit.

Aaron pushed up from the chair he was sitting in and crossed to the window that looked out onto the parking lot. He rolled his shoulders back, then leaned his head over to the left and then to the right to stretch his neck. Another thirty minutes had passed. He turned and strode to the doorway, staring down the hall. Quick footsteps had him swiveling his head right. A young woman with brown hair hurried past him, paused at Sophie's room, and then entered.

Aaron turned back into the waiting room, his shoulders slumping. That must be the friend Bryan had mentioned earlier. He plopped back into a chair, resigned to at least another half-hour. Aaron leaned his head back and stared at the ceiling.

Allison wiped her eyes as she pulled back from Sophie. "Oh my goodness, Sophie, I was so worried. You have no idea."

Sophie's eyes glistened with tears. "I'm sorry. Such a stupid mistake. I should have remembered the dry well."

"What happened? How did you end up at the farm?"

Bryan shifted towards the door. "While you two talk, I'm going to get something to eat. I haven't eaten all day."

As soon as Bryan left, Allison turned back to Sophie. "What…"

"Allison, can you do me a favor?"

Allison's tone brightened. "Sure, anything, you got it."

"Go out to the waiting area and bring Aaron Reinhart to my room."

Allison's brows drew together. "Who?"

"He's…it's complicated. Could you just go get him? I'll explain later."

Allison's eyes searched Sophie's for a clue to this strange request. "Sure. Okay."

She walked down the hall and paused at the waiting room doorway. "Aaron Reinhart?"

Aaron jerked upright and turned. "Yes?"

It was the woman he had seen going into Sophie's room.

"Sophie wants to see you."

He jumped up and followed the woman into Sophie's room. Sophie was sitting up and there was a little color to her cheeks. Her sea-green eyes lit up and his heart gave a little lurch.

"Aaron, this is my best friend, Allison. Allison, this is Aaron."

Aaron reached a hand out and Allison's eyes narrowed as she grasped it. "It's nice to meet you, Allison."

He turned to Sophie. "Does Erica know she's been replaced? I bet she's not happy about it."

Sophie laughed. Allison had a puzzled look on her face.

"Erica was my best friend in high school."

Allison's face cleared. "Oh…your friend out in California." She paused. "But…wait, how does Aaron know about Erica?"

"Allison, could you give us a moment alone?"

"Sure." Allison's eyes darted between Sophie and Aaron before she exited the room.

Sophie's eyes turned to Aaron. "Why are you here? How did you know I was here?"

Aaron smiled. "I guess you don't remember me being in the well with you."

Sophie's eyes widened. "What?"

Aaron pulled the vinyl chair, which Bryan must have vacated, closer to the bed and sat down.

"Let me start at the beginning. My mother called and told me you were missing. That your car and been found wrecked near La Grange. I..."

Sophie's eyes widened further. "My car...was wrecked?"

"I don't have the details...I just knew I had to look for you." Aaron's lips tightened. "I just had to."

Sophie's face was unreadable as he cleared his throat and continued. "I went up to Whitewater and looked everywhere and then over to Lake Geneva. I was trying to think of where you would go if you were upset."

"Wait." Sophie looked at Aaron in confusion. "How did you know I was upset?"

"Bryan told me you had left his condo upset."

Sophie's voice rose in astonishment. "Bryan? You talked to my fiancé?"

"I was desperate. I needed to know your mood."

Sophie was staring at him like he had suddenly grown two heads.

Aaron ignored the look. "I thought you might have gone to the gazebo on the farm. Remember...I would find you sitting there sometimes when you were upset."

A ghost of a smile played across Sophie's lips. "I remember."

"I didn't find you there. I was driving down the driveway when I heard this dog barking and saw this old man looking down at the weeds near the foundation of the house. I stopped the car and ran over." Aaron took a breath. "And that's when I saw you in the well."

"Bryan said the farmer next door and his dog found me. He didn't mention you."

Aaron took the high road. "He probably didn't want to confuse you with too much info at once."

Sophie gazed into Aaron's eyes and whispered. "It wasn't a dream."

Allison pulled out a chair and sat down as Bryan looked up from his meal, his eyebrows raised.

"Who is Aaron Reinhart?"

Bryan swallowed a bite of chicken. "He's a baseball player with the Chicago Cubs."

"Very funny. Who is the Aaron Reinhart in Sophie's room right now? And don't you dare lie to me." Allison's eyes glared daggers at the man across the table. Bryan's mouth dropped open. "Is he what this broken engagement is all about? Don't you dare tell me you accused Sophie of fooling around on you...because she would *never* do that to you. Is that why she ran out of your condo upset? If you caused..."

Bryan finally found his voice. "She broke it off...not me. And of course I know Sophie would never cheat on me. That would never cross my mind even for a second."

Allison pulled back the claws. "Then why did you break up? You were perfect together. And who is Aaron Reinhart?"

Bryan sighed. "It's complicated..."

"Of course it is. At least you and Sophie are on the same page about things being complicated."

"What?"

Allison waved a hand. "Never mind."

Bryan shrugged. "You'll have to talk to Sophie. And Aaron Reinhart really is a baseball player with the Cubs."

"What is he doing here at the hospital?"

Bryan set his fork down on his plate. "He was her boyfriend in high school. He heard about her missing on the news and wanted to help find her. He was with the farmer when she was found." Bryan's right eyebrow rose a fraction of an inch. "Are you done interrogating me? I want to finish eating."

"Right… Sorry." Allison pushed up from the chair. *Why hadn't Sophie mentioned that she had a boyfriend in high school?*

Time crept by as Sophie took a deep breath and tried to calm the myriad of emotions rising inside her. She stared at the man across from her as she remembered the boy she had loved more than life itself. His features had matured; the soft lines of his face had hardened, giving him a more chiseled look. But his hair was the same blonde and the familiar crystal blue of his eyes stared at her with calmness and reassurance.

"You're suddenly quiet. Not like the Sophie I knew." He winked, teasing her.

The Sophie he used to know, before… Sophie's hands became clammy and beads of perspiration appeared on her forehead.

"Sophie, what's wrong? You're as white as your sheet. Should I get the nurse?" Aaron rose out of the chair.

Sophie gripped the sheet as a wave of nausea hit. "No, don't get the nurse… I think… I need to rest."

"Okay, I'll come back tonight."

Her heart thumped against her chest wall. "Could you wait until tomorrow morning?"

Aaron gave a nod.

He forced a smile. "I'll come by about ten o'clock."

Sophie gripped the sheet tighter as the queasiness increased. "Tomorrow."

She shut her eyes tight and took deep breaths. Gradually, the desire to vomit passed. Her ankle protested as she slid down in the bed, curled up into a fetal position, and wept.

The elevator doors opened and Allison flinched as Aaron loomed over her. He gave her a tight smile as he entered the elevator. She exited and hurried to Sophie's room. Her friend was curled up, shoulders shaking, tears running down her cheeks onto the pillow.

"Sophie! What happened? Did Aaron say something to upset you?" Allison fell into the chair and grabbed the hand without the IV drip.

Sophie vehemently shook her head as she took her hand from Allison's and reached for the tissue box.

Allison handed it to her. "What then? What's wrong?"

Sophie wiped her eyes and blew her nose as she pushed back up to a seated position. "It's me. It's my fault."

Allison leaned in. "No, it's not. You've been through a horrible ordeal. You're probably in shock…and you have three people hovering…with the best intentions, mind you, but it's too much. I'm leaving and you're going to rest. I'll tell Bryan to wait until tomorrow to see you again."

Sophie offered a weak smile. "Thank you."

Allison squeezed Sophie's hand. "You're welcome."

Chapter Nineteen

Aaron sat in his SUV, searching the internet on his iPhone for a motel in Elkhorn. His finger stopped scrolling through the options as he lifted his head and gazed through the windshield. Sophie's eyes had held a look of panic as he left her room. He looked down at the phone, his body going numb. Not just panic, her eyes had been...haunted. *Remembering*...Aaron sighed deeply as the guilt returned and washed over him. *He had killed her father. No matter the circumstances...it was his fault.* Aaron leaned his head against the headrest. If only he hadn't pushed him...

Sophie's screams had been tearing at his gut as he sensed, rather than heard, Jimmy gain his feet. Whipping his head around, Aaron jumped up from his knees. Cornstalks leaned at drunken angles around Jimmy and Aaron. The adrenaline pumping through Aaron's body had him tensed up like a coiled spring as he faced Jimmy. He had bare seconds to react when

Jimmy suddenly cursed and swung a right hook at his head. He had ducked and pushed on Jimmy's chest. His only intent, trying to protect Sophie. Jimmy had backpedaled, lost his balance and fallen.

Aaron leaned over and rested his forehead on the steering wheel. He had been frantic about Sophie, he hadn't given Jimmy another thought after he fell. He had tried to gather Sophie in his arms as she screamed and fought him. He had finally managed to pull her struggling body tight against his chest when he noticed the flames. The farmhouse was on fire. But there was nothing he could do. It had taken every ounce of his strength to hold on to his hysterical girlfriend.

Everything had become a blur after that, the sirens, the fire trucks, the sheriff and the ambulance. Aaron didn't find out until the next day that Jimmy had died from hitting his head against the ground hard enough to burst a weak blood vessel in his brain that caused major hemorrhaging. The autopsy showed that Jimmy had suffered two different strokes on the same day. At the hearing, the judge had ruled that Jimmy's death was an accident.

Aaron lifted his head off the wheel. The only people who knew what he had done were his parents, Sophie's aunt, Sophie, the sheriff, and those involved in the court case. His parents had immediately moved him back to Milwaukee. For the next month, before he started college, he had seen a therapist three times a week to deal with the guilt that consumed him. As far as he was concerned, the whole incident was his fault. If he hadn't been late picking Sophie up for their date...

Aaron wiped moisture from his eyes and heaved another sigh. He would die before he allowed the anguish he had seen in her eyes to return. He tilted his head up. *Please Lord, watch over*

Sophie. Aaron turned the key in the ignition and left the hospital parking lot. At the intersection he turned right, heading back to the highway, and beyond that, the interstate that would take him back to Chicago.

Chapter Twenty

Sophie opened her eyes and looked around the unfamiliar surroundings. It took a few moments before she remembered that she was in the hospital. Moving her legs under the sheet caused pain to return to her ankle. Hearing a pattering noise, she looked towards the window. It was raining. She pushed her head back into the pillow and closed her eyes, drifting on the calming waves of the vestiges of the sedative she had requested during the night.

Someone was calling her name. She turned her head on the pillow. She didn't want to answer.

"Sophie, time to wake up. Your breakfast is here." The voice was way too chipper.

Sophie groaned and shook her head.

"Come on, little darling. You have to get your strength up so you can go home."

Little darling?

Sophie turned her head and popped open her eyes. An Amazon was standing next to her bed...an Amazon who had chopped off her hair and dyed the one inch remaining —red. The woman was seven feet tall, if she was an inch, and had the muscled body of a warrior. *Why would she put down her spear and don a nurse's smock?*

"I know, I know, you've never seen such a beautiful sight in your life." The nurse ran a hand over her henna dyed hair and batted her lashes.

Sophie clamped down on the hysterical laughter threatening to burst between her lips.

"I know you're still a little groggy from the sedative they gave you, but it will wear off soon." She leaned down and helped Sophie to sit up. "My name is Cleo and I'm a giantess. A genetic disorder caused by a tumor on my pituitary gland." She winked. "And I'm also psychic. I know exactly what you were thinking."

Cleo closed her eyes and pressed three fingers to her forehead. "And your next question will be…how tall are you?"

She opened her eyes and rolled the tray with Sophie's breakfast into position over her lap. "Seven feet, four inches."

Sophie's eyes widened.

"I know…you're in awe at how impressive I am."

Sophie laughed as she reached for the apple juice on her tray.

Cleo grinned. "That's what I was looking for. Feeling better?"

Sophie smiled. "Actually, I am. Thank you."

"You're welcome. If you need anything, give me a buzz. I'll check back in an hour." Cleo practically folded her body in half as she ducked out the door.

Sophie had just finished her breakfast of scrambled eggs, bacon, and toast when Allison came through the door carrying a vase full of roses. Her eyebrows rose.

"From our boss. Who knew he was such a softy? He didn't even fire me."

Sophie's thoughts were still on Cleo and she only caught the word 'fired.'

Her eyebrows shot to her hairline. "You were fired?"

Allison set the vase on the table by the window. "Almost...hey, you wouldn't believe this nurse I just saw, she's..."

"A giantess and she's my nurse. Don't change the subject. How did you almost get fired?"

Allison pulled a chair over and told her.

Sophie wiggled her shoulders into the fluffed pillows on her bed and sighed as a young man in blue scrubs removed her lunch tray and exited her room. Bryan and Allison should be returning soon from the cafeteria. She gazed at the flowers that had been arriving all morning. At least twenty arrangements sat on tables and the window sill of the room. Their colorful blooms brightened the bland room and were a balm for her assaulted emotions. Her eyes grew moist. Her friends and acquaintances were so thoughtful! Sophie gave her head a sharp shake. *This has got to stop.* Sophie jerked a sleeve across her eyes. She hadn't cried for the last fourteen years, but for the last three days she'd been crying non-stop.

Her eyes were drawn to the door of her room. Her upper teeth bit down on her bottom lip. Aaron hadn't returned to see her at ten o'clock. He had clearly sensed something was off with her behavior before he left yesterday. He had probably seen the anxiety in her eyes, blamed himself, and decided he didn't want to upset her further.

What happened at the farm the summer they were seventeen was not his fault. She had never blamed him, not even for her father's death. But the emotions that had surfaced, when he inadvertently reminded her of the past, had almost suffocated her. It was too much all at once...her broken engagement, the trauma of the well, and seeing Aaron again.

Sophie wrapped her arms around her stomach and rocked.

"Sophie what's wrong?" Allison rushed to her bedside.

"Nothing...everything." *At least no tears.*

"Oh, Sophie." Allison wrapped her arms around Sophie and hugged her close.

"Please don't take this the wrong way, but your overly large bosom is very comforting."

As Allison laughed and pulled away, Bryan's face tinged with embarrassment. He cleared his throat.

"Sophie, the doctors told me you're out of danger and I just got a call from work ..."

"Go on Bryan, I'll be fine."

"I don't want to leave, but Andrew needs me to..."

Sophie smiled. "Seriously, Bryan, I'll be fine."

Bryan leaned down and gave her a kiss on the forehead.

Sophie reached for Bryan's hand. "Thank you for being here for me. After the way I behaved..."

"It's okay." He gently removed his hand and turned away.

As Bryan's footsteps faded away, Allison turned to Sophie. "How in the world could you break your engagement to that man? He's perfect."

Sophie sighed. "I know."

Allison cocked an eyebrow.

Sophie looked down and smoothed out a wrinkle on the sheet in her lap. "I had a lot of time to think while I was stuck in the well and here in the hospital…to think about things I haven't told a soul…but need to."

She looked up at Allison. "After I'm released, you and I will go out for a cup of coffee…"

"…or glass of wine."

The corners of Sophie's full lips turned up. "Or wine. And I will tell you what happened that has made me…"

Allison squeezed her hand. "It's a date."

Chapter Twenty-One

As Sophie pulled a lavender tee shirt over her head, there was a knock at her hospital door. "Come in."

Two law enforcement officers came across the threshold.

"Ma'am, I'm Detective Burke and this is Detective Mason. We're with the Walworth County Sheriff's office and would like to ask a few questions about the body…um, skeleton found in the well."

"That is, if you are up to it," Hank added.

Oh, the irony of the role reversal. She was the one usually peppering the police with questions in her role as journalist. She used the crutches to maneuver back to the bed and propped herself up against the pillows. "How can I help you?"

"Frankly ma'am, we need you to recall everything you can about the skeleton," Hank said.

Derek pulled the chair closest to the bed back a couple of feet, sat down, and flipped over the cover on his tablet computer.

Hank moved a chair located near the window closer to the bed. "How long after falling into the well did you notice the skeleton?"

Sophie's eyebrows drew together. "I'm not sure. Fifteen minutes?"

"Did you touch the skeleton?"

"No."

Hank's gaze was skeptical. "Are you sure?"

Sophie's answer was firm. "Yes."

The door Detective Mason had shut behind him, opened. Allison stepped in. "Sophie, I'm back to take you home. Oops…I'm sorry, I didn't…"

"Ma'am, if you could give us about forty minutes, Ms. Madison should be ready to leave."

Allison's face showed her chagrin. "Sure, sorry, I'll be in the waiting room."

Hank turned back to Sophie. "Okay, back to the skeleton..."

Sophie's ankle was throbbing by the time Hank asked his last question. She would wait until she returned home before taking another painkiller. She looked down at her foot. The orthopedist from Milwaukee, who had consulted with Dr. Franklin, had told her as long as she kept the ankle elevated the swelling should go down enough by the end of the week and he could operate and set the break.

Derek closed his tablet, which now contained notes on the interview. "Thank you for your help. If you think of anything else, give us a call."

He took a contact card out of his wallet, extending his arm towards her. Sunlight, shining through the window, glinted on Derek's gold watch band. Sophie's brows drew together and she frowned. *Something about...* Her eyebrows shot up. *The necklace!* She started to move off the bed to go get her workout pants and then groaned with the pain.

"I just thought of something, Detective Mason. I found a necklace in the well with an 'A' on it and put it in my workout pants pocket. The pants are in the cabinet."

Hank stepped over to the cabinet, opened the door and located the pants. He looked over at Derek.

Derek laid down the tablet and strode to the door. "I'll get an evidence bag."

Derek was back in no time, pulling on a pair of latex gloves. Hank looked around the room, obviously seeking a surface to lay the pants on. Finding none, he sat down and laid them across his knees. Derek handed him the see-through evidence bag and then reached in one of the tiny pockets. His fingers stilled. He pulled the necklace from the pocket, dropping it into the evidence bag, the gold chain settling into two small loops at the bottom.

Hank sealed the bag as Derek removed his gloves.

Sophie spoke, heat permeating her cheeks, "I'm sorry. I handled the evidence. I know better."

Hank's eyes were sympathetic. "Ma'am, thank you for your time. We'll be in touch."

Derek tossed the used gloves in the trash and picked up his tablet. "Hope you feel better soon."

Hank clicked the door shut behind him and headed down the hallway, Derek at his side. Derek looked over at Hank. "Is she a person of interest? She did say she handled the evidence even though she knew better."

Hank didn't answer until he had pushed the down arrow button for the elevator. "I doubt she's our perp. If she was the one to conceal the body, why would she go anywhere near the dry well? Not to mention practically falling right on top of her victim?"

"Good point." The elevator door slid open and the two men stepped inside.

Chapter Twenty-Two

Aaron nursed his beer in Johnny O'Hagan's Irish Pub. When he looked up, Sean and his wife, Brigid, were grinning down at him.

Sean and Brigid scooted onto the padded bench across from Aaron.

Sean smiled. "Eight years I've been coming here and this is the first time I come across you in my favorite pub."

"I've been here before *with* you."

Sean held up his right hand and then lowered two fingers and a thumb. "Twice."

"Not fond of Irish food," Aaron's mumbled words were swallowed by the din of conversation and laughter.

Brigid's large pale hand covered one of Aaron's. Her round, freckled face reflected her compassion. "I'm sorry for your friend. Sean said…"

Sean cleared his throat.

"I mean, it was on the news…what happened. Horrible. How is she doing?"

Aaron picked up the tall glass and took a long swallow.

"Never mind, I shouldn't have asked."

Aaron set the glass back on the cardboard coaster. "She's going to be alright."

A waitress in an emerald green polo shirt and khaki pants, her long brown hair pulled back in a French braid, arrived to get drink orders. Both Sean and Brigid ordered the same as Aaron and asked for menus.

Aaron started to protest. "I'm not..."

Sean gave him a look that brooked no opposition. "You've lost weight. I can tell you haven't been eating."

"I don't like..."

"So eat the fish and chips. That's English, not Irish."

Aaron grinned at Sean with his flattened nose and Brigid with her cloud of wiry pumpkin-colored hair haloing her face. The salt of the earth.

Sophie leaned the crutches against the side of the booth, carefully maneuvering her recently cast ankle under the table. "I finally made it to *Paddy's.*"

Allison placed her black leather clutch on the table and sat down across from Sophie. "Yeah, three weeks late." The levity faded from her face. "I'd rather not remember that day."

Sophie reached her hand across and gripped the hand Allison had laid on the table. "Me, either."

She released her hand and sat back.

Allison squared her shoulders. "I'm taking you home. I can't believe you insisted on taking a cab here when I could have picked you up."

"It's out of your way."

"End of discussion." Allison's tone was firm. The corners of her lips drew slightly downward. "Sophie, are you sure you want to have this conversation here? It's hardly private."

A waitress with cropped ebony hair sidled up to their table. "Hi, ladies, my name is Rachel. What can I get you to drink?"

Sophie smiled brightly at their server. "Ice water with lemon."

"And two glasses of wine."

Sophie watched their server leave then turned to Allison. "I don't need to drink to tell my story."

"Let me be the judge of that."

Sophie sighed. "Okay, you may be right. And to answer your question… I need this public atmosphere so I don't break down." She lowered her voice into a conspiratorial whisper. "That would be *sooooo* embarrassing."

Allison gave a weak smile as the waitress returned with their drinks. They gave their order, both knowing the menu by heart. After the waitress left, the friends fell silent as they sipped the wine.

Sophie took a deep breath and cleared her throat.

"Sophie, really, if this is too painful you don't have to…"

"No, I have to. Keeping it bottled up… pretending it didn't happen, has left me with a half-life…a false life."

Allison's eyes spoke volumes. She had been there for her many times, and would continue to support Sophie…no matter what was revealed.

"Before I tell you what happened, I have to tell you about Aaron." Sophie took a sip of her wine. "Aaron told me that he fell in love with me the first time he saw me, and, although I didn't admit it for a long time even to myself, I fell in love with him a couple of months after we met, while he was helping my papa with the corn harvest."

Sophie sighed. "From the time of our first date, Aaron was everything...the sun, the moon, and the stars. I know that sounds cliché, but he was. The summer after our senior year, we were in love, deliriously happy, making plans for college. We would snuggle together in the gazebo, on the farm where I grew up, and talk about Aaron's dream of becoming a professional baseball player and me being a journalist."

Allison leaned across the table. "Okay, I'm intrigued. How did you meet? And why didn't you want to admit to being in love with Aaron?"

Sophie's eyes danced with humor. "Because I disliked him intensely."

Allison's eyebrows shot up. "What...that makes no sense. You can't be in love and dislike someone *intensely* at the same time."

Sophie laughed and began to tell Allison about the new guy who moved to Whitewater from Milwaukee the beginning of her senior year. They had met the first day of classes in September. He was very good-looking. All the girls had a crush on him. But Aaron never said more than two words to any of them. His arrogance infuriated her for months, the way he laughed and joked with his baseball buddies and the rest of the guys, but ignored the girls...never even glancing her way.

But all that changed one day in April...

Chapter Twenty-Three

Spring 1998

The bleachers at the baseball field were packed. Whitewater High was up one run against Elkhorn High in the eighth inning. The pitcher wound up and threw a pitch dead center across home plate. The batter swung, connecting bat and ball with a loud crack, sending the ball high over the pitcher's head.

Erica moaned and gripped the seat beneath her. "Looks like a homerun."

Her eyes widened as she watched Aaron rush backward at incredible speed, suddenly stop and leap into the air with his glove raised. Erica's mouth opened. No one could jump that high. She gripped harder—it was going to be close.

Erica shot up from her seat. "Yeaaaaaaaah! He caught it! Sophie did you see that catch? Unbelievable."

"Great, superstar strikes again."

"Stop being sarcastic. This is one of our best seasons yet. You should be pumped."

Sophie swiveled her head around. "Oh, please, he's a show off."

Erica's nostrils flared. "Enough already. That's all I've heard for the last six months. Give it a…" Erica broke off as a baseball whacked Sophie on the right side of her head, knocking her backwards off the bleacher seat.

"Sophie!"

As Erica leaned over her friend, an adult male from two rows up leaped down to her side. "She's out cold, someone get the medics!" He cradled her head.

Four students leaped to the ground and ran over to the EMS vehicle idling by the front entrance to the field.

A crowd pressed in as Erica continued to call her friend's name. Someone leaned into her shoulder.

"How is she?"

Erica glanced over her shoulder. Aaron's worried blue eyes stared into her brown eyes. She opened her mouth to answer but was interrupted by the arrival of the medics, barking orders for everyone to move away. Aaron drew back as Erica turned her attention back to Sophie. The medics placed a neck collar on Sophie and transferred her to a hard plastic board. They slowly carried her down the bleacher steps and to the waiting ambulance. Erica refused to be left behind, jumping into the back and sitting on the bench. Tears started to fall as she held Sophie's hand and the ambulance started to move, sirens blaring.

The next afternoon, Erica walked through the door of Sophie's room with get well cards in her hands. Several bouquets of flowers sat on the night stand and the table under the window. Sophie was sitting up, with two pillows propped behind her head. Her hair looked clean and brushed.

"Wow, you look good. Much better than yesterday."

"So you're saying awake is a better look for me than unconsciousness?"

"Much better." Erica handed her the cards. "I see you've already read the other cards."

Sophie nodded her head and winced. "I can't believe all the flowers and cards people have sent me."

"Why not? Everyone likes you."

"Not everyone." Sophie turned to look out the window.

"You might be surprised. Aaron ran from the field and climbed the bleachers to ask if you were all right. And…"

"What?" Sophie's jaw dropped.

"Stop interrupting. And he came by to check on you yesterday while you were still out."

Before she could respond with another word of shock, the object of their discussion knocked on the open door. Sophie clamped her lips shut. Aaron stood just inside the door, a card clutched in his hand.

"Aaron! How nice of you to come by." Erica looked over at Sophie and raised an eyebrow.

Getting the hint, Sophie hesitated and then said, "Yes, thanks for stopping by."

Shoulders relaxing a bit, Aaron walked over to the bed and handed the card to Sophie. He cleared his throat before speaking. "I'm glad you're awake." He paused before continuing. "Has... anyone told you how you got hit?"

"Yeah, Mrs. Stillwell stopped by earlier. She was at the game and said it was a foul ball."

"I'm glad you're okay."

Sophie's eyes dropped to the card in her hands. She slipped a finger under the flap of the envelope. She pulled out the card and read the sentiment.

She looked up at Aaron. "It's really nice, thanks."

"You're welcome." Aaron smiled and took a step back. "Well, I…I should be going. See you at school."

He turned on his heel and left the room, Sophie staring after him. Erica pulled the card out of Sophie's fingers and read it.

"It is a nice card. Who would have thought that Aaron could be a nice guy?" Erica leaned her head to the right and folded her arms. Sophie stared at the card clutched in Erica's hand.

"I…don't…I'm totally confused."

"You were too busy being mad at him for imagined slights…"

"I was never mad at him!"

"You can try selling that line to someone who doesn't know you like I do."

Sophie opened her mouth then shut it as her papa came through the doorway. "Time to get dressed, Soph, you're going home."

A twelve-year-old truck pulled into a parking space at Whitewater High School on Friday morning, with Sophie in the driver's seat. Maybe she could catch Aaron before he walked into school. Her heart pounded in her chest and her palms were sweaty. She loosened her hands from the death grip she had on the steering wheel, took a couple of deep breaths and wiped her hands on her jeans. *Relax.*

Sophie rubbed her hands once again down her jeans and took in another deep breath when Aaron pulled into the parking lot in his jeep. She pulled on the door handle and stepped out of the truck onto the asphalt. She watched as Aaron exited his jeep and locked it.

"Aaron!" Sophie lifted her hand as she walked toward him.

Aaron turned in her direction, glanced briefly toward the school, and then turned back, his gaze neutral.

Sophie halted in front of him. "Could we...talk for a minute?"

Before he could answer, she spoke again. She had to get this out before she lost her nerve. "I owe you an apology. The way I've been treating you, especially when you were helping my papa at the farm, was inexcusable. I really don't know why I was acting that way. Some imagined slights, according to Erica. And then you came and visited me in the hospital and I felt bad...and..."

Sophie's words ground to a halt. She wasn't sure what else to say.

"Apology... accepted." Aaron looked over as a few more cars pulled into parking spaces and then turned back to Sophie with a sigh.

"Look, I...I owe you an explanation for not being...being more approachable. But not here." The slams of car doors reached them as students exited their vehicles.

"Hey, Sophie, how you feeling?"

Sophie looked over and waved at Jillian. "Great."

Aaron cleared his throat. "How about if...if I come by your place after practice?"

They were starting to get curious looks from some of the girls heading into school.

Sophie's heart started to flutter. "Yes, that would be great."

One of the long yellow school buses pulled into the lot. The doors opened and students jumped down the steps. Three of Aaron's buddies exited their vehicles and eyeballed them. Aaron's body tensed. "I should be...done by six."

He turned in the direction of his buddies and walked off before Sophie could utter an invitation for dinner. She sighed. Maybe he had a good explanation for his less than stellar people skills. She rushed back to the truck to retrieve her books.

The wall clock in the front parlor chimed six-thirty as her papa walked into the kitchen. "If he doesn't get here soon, I'm going to eat. It's already an hour past supper time."

Sophie had stopped by the barn after getting home from school and told her papa that she had apologized to Aaron and that he was stopping by. She had asked if he could stay for dinner. Jimmy had rubbed the bristles on his chin and smiled before heading for the house to shower.

Sophie's heart ratcheted up a notch at the sound of a car engine.

"Great, now we can eat." Jimmy pushed open the back door and went out to greet Aaron.

Sophie was pulling the pot roast out of the oven when the door reopened and Jimmy and Aaron walked through.

"It's nice to share a meal with you again, Aaron. And I'm glad to see that you and Sophie have settled your differences." Jimmy pulled out a chair to the table, missing the twin hues of pink that blossomed on Aaron and Sophie's cheeks.

Her father dominated the conversation during the meal. Sophie stole quick glances at Aaron, but mostly kept her head bent over her food. Each bite seemed to lodge in her throat and she had a hard time swallowing.

Jimmy belched. "Great meal, Soph. Aaron, would you like to join me in the den? Should be something interesting on the television."

"I would, sir, but…"

Sophie jumped in. "Actually, Papa, Aaron and I wanted to talk for a little bit."

Jimmy pushed his chair back and stood. "Okay, but when you get done jawing, come join me."

"Sounds good."

Jimmy winked at Sophie then left the kitchen.

Aaron watched as he disappeared into the hallway. "I like your dad, he's a fun guy. You should have heard some of the jokes he told when we were harvesting the corn."

"Oh, I can imagine," Sophie muttered.

Aaron cleared his throat, took a breath, and looked down at his hands folded together on top of the table. "This isn't easy to…to talk about and if you tell anyone, especially Erica, I really won't talk to you again." His voice was mock stern. "The only people who know are my family and my…my ex-girlfriend.

Sophie nodded.

"There is a reason you haven't seen me in conversations with the girls at…at school." Aaron took a breath.

"I had a pronounced speech impediment when I was younger. I stuttered—a lot. I…was teased by a couple of the girls when I started elementary school and because of it I developed a complex. I…I stopped talking all together for a year."

Aaron took a sip of his iced tea. "I worked with a speech therapist and, after a few years, learned how to control it—except for every time I tried to talk to a girl. It was a much milder form…" Aaron took a breath. "…but still embarrassing."

He shrugged his shoulders. "My old girlfriend said it…it was like planning a military campaign just to get me to ask her out on a date."

"That's why you limit answers to questions to: yes, no, or one sentence," Sophie mused.

"This is the longest conversation I've had with any girl since Kristen moved to Canada."

"That would be the ex-girlfriend?"

"Yes."

His body started to tense like it had in the parking lot. How could she reassure him?

"Your secret is safe with me. Erica couldn't get it out of me with a crow bar."

Aaron gave her a warm smile, causing her heartbeats to speed up.

She cleared her throat. "I never should have judged you. I'm sorry."

"And I'm sorry for the rude remarks I…I said to you."

"Cool." Sophie smiled. "Let's start over. But can I ask one question?"

It was clearly costing him, as he tensed again.

"Why did you come to the hospital after the way I treated you?"

He took a breath. "You can't guess?"

Sophie's brow furrowed. "No."

"I…I…I" Aaron pressed his lips together and closed his eyes.

Sophie reached across the table and placed her right hand firmly over Aaron's folded ones. The tingle zinged all the way up to her shoulder as she squeezed his hands. He looked up and Sophie sucked in a breath. His blues eyes spoke volumes and her heart skipped over fluttering and went straight to pounding. Her cheeks grew warm and she lifted her hand off of Aaron's. Before she could pull it back, he grabbed it in both of his.

Aaron's expression steeled. "I have …feelings for…for you that have been…been… hard for me to …express with words." He paused. "Literally."

Sophie's spontaneous laugh must have helped to ease Aaron's tension, because his shoulders relaxed. "I don't know if you feel the same, but I hope you do. If you haven't guessed, that's why I volunteered to help your dad with the harvest last fall." His lips turned up at the corners. "Not for the money…just to be near you."

He let go of Sophie's hands waiting for her reaction, hope clearly written on his face.

Sophie heart was a wild bird trying to escape her chest. She opened her mouth to say she did feel the same, but found her own tongue unwilling or unable to form words. She had never told any guy she had feelings for him, because she had never had these unsettling feelings before. She had been out on a few double dates, but no more than two dates with one guy. Aaron's face started to fall. Say something! But the words were stuck in her throat.

Aaron pushed back his chair and rose. "It's okay, I under…"

"No, don't go." She struggled to say what seemed to consume her entire being at that moment. Her cheeks burned with heat as she spoke. "I…I…I…do…feel the same."

Aaron's eyes crinkled in the corners as he sat back down. "You really should get that speech impediment checked out."

Sophie started giggling and couldn't have stopped if she had wanted to. Her shoulders started shaking and Aaron joined in with his own burst of laughter. Her heart returned to a normal beat and her cheeks cooled as her laughter melded with Aaron's, filling the room with their merriment.

Neither heard Jimmy enter the kitchen. "Hey, I want in on the joke."

Which only made them laugh harder.

Chapter Twenty-Four

Summer 2012

The uneaten portion of their dinner was congealing on their plates when Sophie's words describing her and Aaron's romance slowed to a halt. The waitress walked up to remove their plates and ask about dessert.

Sophie and Allison shook their heads and then Sophie spoke. "Could you give us about twenty minutes before bringing the check?"

"Sure." The waitress walked away with their dirty plates.

Sophie's hand whitened on the stem of her glass. "It was perfect… and then in an instant…everything changed."

Allison slid her arm across the table and grasped Sophie's left hand. "Sophie are you absolutely sure you want to talk about this in such a public place? We can go back to your house or my apartment." She leaned in and whispered, "I have a bottle of Irish Whiskey. I could brew us some coffee, pore in a shot…or two…of whiskey and add some whipped cream."

Sophie's smile trembled a bit at the corners. "No, it has to be now or it may be never."

"Okay." Allison squeezed her hand and let go.

Sophie breathed in deeply and slowly exhaled before speaking. "Aaron and I had a date. We were going to the lake, lie on the beach, soak op some sun and just...be together. I remember I had bought a new bathing suit. I spent at least three hours getting ready. I wanted to look perfect."

Sophie paused biting down on her trembling lip. She pulled in a shuttering breath before continuing her remembrances of the tragic events of a perfectly still July afternoon...

Chapter Twenty-Five

Summer 1998

The ceiling fan moved the air, sending the flame of the scented candle flickering around the wick. The aroma of ripened raspberries filled the room. Sophie opened her eyes and glanced at the digital clock. Aaron should be here any minute to take her to the lake. Her mesh beach bag was packed and lay against the footboard of the bed. She glanced down at her royal blue cover up. Underneath was a brand-new bathing suit, also royal blue.

Catching a glimpse as she emerged from the bedroom in her bikini, her papa had said that she would have Aaron's eyes popping out of his head. She had flushed with embarrassment and rushed back into the bedroom. He had continued to tease her until after lunch, when he went out to the barn.

A crash brought her straight up on the bed. She was swinging her legs over the side when there was a thud in the hallway. She stood up and was taking steps towards the door when her papa appeared in the doorway. Sweat glistened on his too-pale face.

Two locks of hair clung to the perspiration on his forehead. His eyes were unfocused, seeming to stare right through her.

"Papa?"

His head moved a fraction of an inch. Sophie could see his eyes trying to focus. "Papa, what's wrong?"

Awareness returned to his eyes, and a myriad of emotions chased each other across her papa's face –confusion, disbelief, astonishment, amazement, and, lastly, a joy that lit his face in radiance.

Her papa's lips moved and he whispered. "Genevieve."

It wasn't a question. It was a statement of fact. Sophie backed up, hitting her calves against the bed frame.

"Papa, its Sophie."

The words had barely left her lips when her papa rushed in and grabbed her. He pulled her against him so tight she thought he would break her ribs. He was heaving great wracking sobs.

Sophie tried to wiggle free, but he had her arms pinned down. "Stop, Papa!"

Jimmy pulled her tighter and suddenly Sophie couldn't breathe. She struggled in earnest, shouting at him to let her go. With no warning, he abruptly released her, causing her to fall back on the bed. Eyes awash with confusion stared at her.

Sophie's heart was racing, her limbs trembling. "I'm not Genevieve, Papa."

But she could tell the words held absolutely no meaning. "I've missed you so much. I've been in agony."

The confusion had vanished from Jimmy's eyes, replaced by adoration. He reached out his hand. Sophie scooted to the edge of the bed, out of reach, as her papa dropped his hand.

"I love you, Genevieve, and you love me. Why are you acting like this?" There was sorrow in his voice.

Sophie's fear was a living, breathing animal cornered in her mind. She lashed out. "Get out of my room, Papa! Now! I'm not Genevieve! She's dead!"

Jimmy's face flushed an alarming red. "Get out? You're telling me to get out of our bedroom." He roared like a wounded animal. "Where have you been for the last five years?!"

Two hands reached out, like claws, to grab Sophie. She lunged off the bed, hitting the nightstand and knocking over the candle. It rolled, coming to rest near the window curtains. Missing his target, Jimmy overbalanced, landing across the bed on his stomach. Sophie raced around the bed and out the bedroom door. Her heartbeats sounded like the booming of a bass drum in her ears. An enraged roar echoed behind her as she rushed headlong into the kitchen, banging her hip against the kitchen table and knocking over a water glass. Pain exploded beneath the flesh, but she ignored it as she slammed her hand against the screen door and fled towards the cornfield.

As she entered the corn, she could hear her papa hard on her heels. She screamed a name in her mind. *Aaron!*

Sophie's bare feet pounded in the dirt and her chest labored to breathe. She tried to veer to the left through two corn stalks, but was jerked backwards. Jimmy twisted her around to face him. His rage was terrible to see.

Jimmy roared. "Where have you been?"

Sophie could not speak. She couldn't breathe.

"Genevieve, answer me." He shook her.

Sophie tried to take a breath, couldn't. Bright spots danced across her vision.

Now there was alarm in her papa's voice. "Genevieve, I'm sorry, I love you. I didn't mean it."

Her legs grew weak. She collapsed to the ground, on her back. Her mind mentally slapped her. *Breathe. Breathe or you will die.*

Sophie struggled to find the precious air to fill her lungs. Her mouth finally opened. She pulled air in—deep, deep, again, and again. As the stars cleared from her vision, she gasped. Papa was tugging at her bikini bottom.

Sophie screamed.

"It's okay; I just want to show you how much I love you. I understand now. You've just forgotten me. But now you'll remember." Jimmy's voice was soothing.

Sophie tried to fight, but her flaying was weak and ineffectual. When he dropped down on top of her, all she could manage was a wail of pure anguish. 'No, Papa!'

The weight lifted and Aaron's face wavered in front of her. He was talking to her, but someone was screaming.

Chapter Twenty-Six

Summer 2012

Sophie took a sip of her wine. Good, her hand barely shook at all. "That's really all I recall…nothing after seeing Aaron's face. I learned the rest from my aunt."

"What was it?"

Sophie's brows drew together. "What was what?"

Allison laced her fingers around the stem of her glass and despite the churning in her gut managed to speak in a calm voice. "What caused your father to act like he did?"

"The autopsy revealed that he had had a stroke." Sophie took in a breath. "I was a month shy of my eighteenth birthday that July and the spitting image of my mother at the same age.

Allison's eyebrows reached for her hairline." Oh, blessed Jesus who died on the cross. I am sorry, Sophie." Allison took a quick sip of the wine, resisting the urge to down the contents like she wanted to do. "This explains everything."

Sophie gave a puzzled frown. "What do you mean?"

"All the questions about high school and boys that you avoided…or outright lied about, now that I think about it. You never dated when we were in college, always refusing to let me fix you up with anyone. All the times you pushed back the wedding." Allison's eyes widened. "Bryan! Are you going to tell him?"

"I don't know. It was hard enough telling you." She chewed her bottom lip. "And I thought once I told you I would feel lighter…freer. But I just feel drained."

Allison reached a hand across and squeezed Sophie's fingers. "Do you know how proud I am of you? How brave you are?"

"I don't feel very brave. I …I just hope this first step will lead to the next and eventually I can let go of …" She sighed.

"Of what?"

Sophie's eyes glistened. "…this terrible feeling of loss."

Allison's eyes widened. "Romeo and Juliet."

"What?"

Allison gripped her friend's fingers harder. "Sophie, you know how I feel about Bryan, but I think you should give your love for Aaron another chance. He still loves…"

Sophie gave her head a rapid shake back and forth. "No."

"Why not?"

Seconds dragged by before Sophie whispered, "Because he saw…saw what my papa did to me."

"Oh, Sophie, I don't think that matters to him."

Sophie's tone sharpened. "But it does to me!" Tears trembled on her lashes. "That image had to have been seared into his brain."

"Sophie…"

"Here's your check, ladies. Whenever you're ready." The server set the check on the table and left.

Sophie blinked back the tears as she pulled her fingers from Allison's hand. She picked up the check. "I'm paying for dinner. It's the least I can do after everything you've done for me."

"I know there is no use arguing…thanks. But about Aaron…"

"The subject of Aaron is closed. I won't change my mind."

Chapter Twenty-Seven

Hank poked his head into Derek's cluttered cubicle. Manila folders were stacked on top of the gray filing cabinet instead of in it. His softball cleats, bat, and uniform lay haphazardly across two metal chairs against the wall of the cubicle. Two cardboard boxes sat on the floor, waiting to be unpacked. Paper from various cases lay strewn on top of the metal desk.

"I think I found her."

Derek didn't look up from his computer. "Who?"

"The girl in the well."

Derek's eyes turned away from the notes he was typing into the computer on the McClellen case. "I'm impressed. It's only been…what…seven weeks…since they removed the bones from the well?"

Not considered a priority, they had only been allowed to work on 'the skeleton in the well' case when not working on other cases. Over eight hundred thousand people had gone missing in the United states thirteen to fourteen years ago, when the woman in the well had been killed—over twenty thousand had been Caucasian women in their early twenties—the approximate age and race of the victim, according to preliminary forensics.

"Ashley Keller." A triumphant grin spilt Hank's face.

"And you're sure it's her because…?"

"The necklace."

Seconds ticked by. "Hank, the suspense is killing me. Spill already, before I choke it out of you."

Hank laughed. "I finally had some spare time to work my half of the list. I concentrated on the girls missing in a three-hundred-mile radius of the well. I wasn't getting anywhere—dead-end. I widened my search and, bingo, found her. Ashley Keller lived in Columbus, Ohio. I talked to her mother and she wore a necklace with a gold 'A'. The police department in Columbus is sending her DNA…some hair strands…to the forensic lab for a comparison. But it's her. I know it."

Derek nodded and then slowly grinned. "Now we can do some real investigating and collar a murderer instead of chasing down information that will lead us to the perp who broke into the cemetery and shattered a headstone."

Hank turned to leave. "I'll get clearance for our road trip to Columbus."

Sophie walked gingerly to her desk at the newspaper, in her most comfortable workout shoes. The orthopedic doctor had told her yesterday that the broken bone in her ankle had knitted together well and she could remove the walking boot she had worn for the last couple of weeks.

Allison wouldn't be here yet. Her best friend would rush in a minute or two late, breathing hard. Noah was the only other early bird. He was usually the first to arrive and last to leave. Like her, Noah considered his career in journalism a top priority over anything else in his life. She glanced in his direction and he gave her a thumbs up.

"Madison…you planning on goofing off all day?"

Sophie whipped her head around. Why was her boss in the office early? "No, sir."

Mr. McNair stood in his office doorway. "I am relieved. The mayor's wife is giving a thank you speech to the Milwaukee Garden Club this morning for their beautification efforts all around the city. I want you to cover it."

Sophie groaned.

"Did you say something?"

"No, sir." Her eyes shifted away from her editor's intense stare.

Mr. McNair's voice softened the tiniest bit. "You and I both know you're not ready to go traipsing all over the city chasing hard stories on that ankle."

Sophie nodded. "Yes, sir."

Her boss started to turn away.

"Uh… Mr. McNair? I'd like to do some searches in the newspaper's database on missing girls. See if I can come up with any info on the …um…skeleton that was in the well…" She cleared her throat. "…with me."

Mr. McNair's gray eyes narrowed. "After the assignments I give you are complete and on my desk."

He returned to his office, his voice bellowing behind him. "Garden Club, ten o'clock."

Sophie plopped down on the chair at her desk, muttering about what the city could do with their flowers. She pushed the on button of her PC and waited for it to power up.

Chapter Twenty-Eight

Hank and Derek stepped out of Derek's black SUV at ten-thirty on a sun-drenched morning in September and walked up to the front door of the restaurant. Both wore faded jeans and long-sleeved button-down shirts. But that is where the similarities ended. Hank stood six feet-five inches and weighed two hundred and fifty pounds...Derek was six foot and one hundred and eighty pounds.

The building was nothing special. It was a one-story wooden structure painted a deep red on the outside with white trim around the four large windows and door. A large neon sign above the door announced that this was *Jack's Rib Shack*.

Derek gripped his tablet computer in one hand and opened the door with the other. Hank reached up with his right hand and removed his sunglasses. The sunlight streaming through the windows didn't do the inside of the restaurant any favors. The interior was a large open space with a bar to the right and the kitchen in the back. Dark paneling covered the walls and a medium grade burgundy commercial carpet, which had seen better days, covered the floors. Stains, that no amount of steam cleaning could remove, dotted throughout in a rambling pattern. Booths lined the left wall and dark wooden tables and chairs filled the middle space. The interior was empty except for a man with a shaved head and small goatee stacking glasses behind the bar.

Hank's nostrils flared. Despite the ban on cigarette smoking in restaurants years ago, the stench of stale cigarette smoke lingered, mixed with what smelled suspiciously like feces. He followed Derek to the bar.

Hank placed his hands on the polished surface. "Are you Jack Perry?"

Jack turned and eyeballed the two men. "Little early for a drink, gentlemen."

"I'm Detective Mason and this is Detective Burke." Both men showed their badges.

Jack gave a deferential nod. "Traffic must have been good. I expected you around lunchtime." He waved a hand towards the center of the room. "We can talk at one of the tables."

Jack came around the corner of the bar area, his stomach protruding to the point that it looked like someone had cut him open and inserted a basketball. "Sorry about the smell. Sewer pipe burst out back this morning. Guys are out there fixing it now." The three men drew out chairs. "You said you wanted to ask me about one of my employees?"

Derek opened the notes app as Hank answered. "She would have worked for you about thirteen years ago."

Jack leaned forward, his t-shirt covered gut bumping the table and sliding it forwards an inch. "You've got to be kidding. I can hardly remember who I hired last month. You wouldn't believe my turnover for waitresses. They tend to get in a huff when the men have one too many brewskies and make a grab."

Hank leaned back in his chair and reached into the pocket of his jeans. He removed the gold necklace encased in an evidence bag. "Mr. Perry, do you recognize this necklace?"

Jack's eyes tried to bug out of his head. "Where did you get that?"

Derek stopped typing and looked at Hank. "You recognize it?"

Jack's eyes welled with tears. "It belonged to Ashley…do you know where Ashley is?"

Hank's eyes narrowed. There was more than an employee/employer relationship going on here.

What reaction would he get if he hit hard? "She's dead."

Tears coursed down Jack's cheeks and then the tough-looking guy, with tattoos on both arms and a gold hoop in one ear, blubbered like a baby. Hank drew back in his chair again, his eyebrows rose. This was a first. He had seen many women cry while he was in the line of duty, a few men tear up at the loss of a loved one, but he had never seen a man sob like a child…not one.

Jack spoke through the sobs. "Oh, my, poor Ashley. I knew…when they found her… it wouldn't be good, but I kept…praying…she would be…found alive."

"Excuse me." Jack rose and walked back to the bar, struggling to get himself under control. He leaned over the shiny surface and emerged with a paper towel, wiping his eyes and blowing his nose.

He returned to the table. "I'm sorry I broke down like that, but I loved her. It's just hard."

Hanks eyebrows rose higher. Jack had to be in his mid-sixties. Ashley's mother had said earlier that morning that thirteen years ago Ashley had been twenty-three. Jack would have been about fifty. *Love scorned. Crime of passion?* Hank shook his head to clear it of that line of thought. His job was to gather information that would lead to an arrest, not speculate on who *might* be the perpetrator of this crime.

"You were in love with her?"

Jack looked at Hank as if he had lost his mind. "Not *in* love with her. I loved her like... a daughter. She worked for me for five years...since she turned eighteen." Jack's eyes dropped to his folded hands. "She was the sweetest girl. Hard working. Ashley was taking classes during the day over at Ohio State to become a nurse."

Jack swiped a hand over his eyes. "She was going to graduate in December...had a job already lined up at the hospital emergency room."

"This would have been December of...?" Derek looked up.

"1999." Jack said.

Hank cleared his throat. "Tell us everything you remember about the night she disappeared."

Jack wiped his eyes again and looked up. "She came in at about seven. Her shift ended when we closed at midnight, but I let her leave a little early because it was a slow night. She worked the tables with the college jocks. They're always a rowdy bunch, hitting on the waitress, loud, obnoxious, think they own the world, but Ashley could handle them—even the ones who had one too many."

Jack fell silent, brooding.

"We need you to elaborate. Every detail about the customers she talked to and her interaction with your other employees."

Jack stared at Hank. "Detective Burke, no disrespect, but all that information is in the report I signed after Ashley disappeared."

"We would like to hear it from you before reading those reports."

"Again, no disrespect, but I'm sixty-six years old and I don't remember much about that night anymore."

Hank sighed. "Okay, tell us what you do remember."

Jack proceeded to recount as much as he could remember.

Derek emerged from the dim interior of the restaurant and out into the blinding noonday sun. He reached into his shirt pocket and hastily slipped on his aviator sunglasses.

Hank grinned. "One of these days, you're going to remember to put the sunglasses on before you leave a building."

"That got us nowhere. Perry was either behind the bar, in the supply room, or his office most of the night. According to him, he barely saw Ashley. And only spoke to her when she asked if she could leave early."

Both men entered Derek's vehicle and shut the doors.

Derek said, "Where to now?"

Hank checked the GPS on his smartphone as Derek pulled forward. "Columbus Police Department to pick up copies of the reports from the night our vic disappeared."

Derek groaned.

Hank grinned. Derek hated reading reports.

Chapter Twenty-Nine

Aaron stood at home plate, the bat clenched in his hands and his ice blue eyes watching the pitcher's movements.

The pitcher ground his cleats into the dirt of the pitcher's mound, gripped the ball behind his back and spat out of the corner of his mouth.

Aaron ignored the decades-old distraction technique. Before he could blink, the ball was headed his way at eighty-five miles an hour.

The loud crack of the bat against the ball was instantly drowned out by the ear-splitting roar of the crowd as thousands of fans jumped to their feet at Wrigley Field. Aaron took off for first base, watching the ball. It flew over the outfielder's head. He rounded first and headed for second, his feet pounding the baseline. The screams faded as his concentration focused on reaching the next base, the one after, and then the most important—home.

He placed a foot on second base then sprinted for third, his heartbeats loud in his ears. He ignored the pain in his knee as he crossed over third. It would be close. The adrenaline pumping through his veins created a natural high hard to beat.

He and the stitched white ball arrived at home plate at the same time. The catcher caught the ball waist-high. Aaron slid his leg just beneath the catch, slamming his foot on the white plate before the catcher could tag him.

The crowd went nuts again. He concentrated on getting his breathing under control as he tried mightily not to limp to the dugout under the intense scrutiny of the Cubs manager.

Sean was the first to grab him, pounding on his back. He grinned as other players smacked various parts of his body. He collapsed on the bench as a trainer handed him a cup of water and a blue ice pack. He threw the water down his throat and wrapped the pack around his knee with a groan.

"My heart stopped in my chest, boyo." Sean plopped down beside Aaron. "You squeaked that one out, sure and ye did. Dinner and beer on me."

"I won't argue with you. A big juicy steak with big fat fries sounds good about now."

The crowd groaned. The batter after him must have gotten an out. He started to rise to take the field for the last half of the ninth inning.

"Stay put Reinhart. I'm putting in a sub." The manager motioned to a player standing at the edge of the dugout.

He sat back down as Sean squeezed his shoulder, grabbed his mitt, and headed to his position at first base. Sean's stats for outs at first base were highest in the league. And he had two solid knees.

Aaron suppressed the feeling of envy as he adjusted the ice pack.

"Hey, Aaron." Peter James, the bat boy, took Sean's vacated spot and handed him another cup of water.

"Sorry about your knee. Are you going to be good until the end of the season?"

"Hope so."

The boy scratched at a bug bite by his elbow and asked casually, "I was curious about the skeleton in the well. Can I ask a couple of questions?" Peter's eager face, topped by a mop of brown hair, looked up at Aaron's face. "Have you heard anything more since it was discovered?"

Aaron couldn't help but smile. Peter was fascinated by mysteries…and murder mysteries in particular. He was always talking to any player who would listen about the books he read and the crime shows he watched on television. But to have Aaron involved in a murder mystery was the icing on the cake. It was actually surprising that Peter hadn't approached him earlier.

"Nope, not a word."

Peter's face fell and then cleared. "Can you describe what it looked like?"

There was a roar from the crowd as a ball hit to center field was caught. Peter looked anxiously over at the manager. He needed to get back to his job.

"I didn't get a good look, but it seemed fairly small and the head wasn't attached."

"A female."

"That would be my guess."

Peter nodded his head. "I've decided to switch my major. I'm going into forensics."

"Peter!"

Peter cringed and then jumped up. "Thanks, Aaron, got to go."

Aaron leaned back against the dugout wall. He closed his eyes and the image of Sophie lying at the bottom of the dry well arose unbidden in his mind. His heart clenched as he shook his head. The players in the dugout did not hear him whisper, "You have to let her go."

He leaned forward and lifted the ice pack off his knee, gingerly moving it back and forth. He sighed as he pressed the ice pack back down.

Chapter Thirty

Hank and Derek sat in Hank's cubicle, poring over reports. Everyone had gone for the day except the dispatcher and the county cops working the night shift. Hank leaned back in his dark gray office chair, tapping an ink pen against his teeth as he scanned one of the witness reports of the night Ashley Keller disappeared. Derek sat in a metal chair against the cubicle wall, his feet propped up on an upside-down trashcan, reading a copy of the same report.

Hank stilled. "Holy Mackerel!"

Derek looked up. "What's wrong?"

"What page are you on?"

"Fifteen."

"Go to twenty-two."

"Man, Hank, did you take a speed reading course?"

"Do you see where it says a customer at the Rib Shack passed Ashley and a man in the parking lot? He said they were arguing and he heard Ashley say, 'Then you should have said something before you started kissing me...before we almost...'

And then the guy said, 'Don't you think I know that? I think about my mistake every day!'"

Derek flipped a few pages. "Hold on; let me find it."

Hank waited, impatiently clicking the top of the pen.

"Okay, I got it...so?"

"Look for the name of the guy she was arguing with."

Hank waited.

Derek's brows pulled together. "Isn't this the same guy...?"

"Yes."

Derek's jaw dropped as he looked up from the report.

"Hold on. Let me find the page for his interview." Hank flipped through a few pages. "Found it. Page twenty-nine."

Both men fell silent as they read the interview.

Hank frowned at the pen in his hand. "This is going to have to be handled very carefully." He looked across at Derek. "I can continue investigating Ashley Keller's timeline for that night, if you want to pursue this new development."

"No, I don't, but it's not like I have a choice."

Derek's cell rang. He listened to the voice on the other line and then answered. "On my way." He shoved his phone in its holster. "My dad's at the emergency room. Fell off the roof."

"Do you need me to come with you?"

Derek paused in the open doorway. "No, they think it's just a broken arm. See you tomorrow."

Hank looked back down at the report. No one would thank them if this played out the way he thought it might. Hank shook his head. *No one would thank them.*

Detective Derek Mason perched on the edge of the sofa. It had to be a hundred and fifty years old if it was day. An antique, in mint condition, it should be proudly displayed in a nineteenth-century era museum somewhere, not holding up his rear end. He smiled as the tiny elderly lady bustled into the parlor with a tea service atop a cart. The tea service was another antique, made of sterling silver.

"Quite a find that tea service. Picked it up at a nice shop called *The Oak Tree* in Petersburg, Virginia." The aged man's voice was laced with pride.

"As I said, I would like to ask you and your wife a few..."

A hand covered with blue veins and paper-thin skin handed Derek a cup of tea in a fragile china cup and then set the sugar and cream on the oval mahogany table within reach.

"Thank you, Ma'am." Derek spooned in a little sugar and stirred until it dissolved.

"Would you like a lemon bar? I made them myself from scratch."

"They look delicious ma'am, but I'm still full from breakfast." He took a sip of the tea and set down the cup. "Just a few questions..."

"You're barking up the wrong tree, detective." The old man's eyes were sharp as a tack.

Derek fought the urge to squirm in his seat. There probably wasn't much those eyes missed, which made him an excellent source of information. Unfortunately, the old man gave the impression that he wouldn't say anything that would put the person they were discussing in a negative light. Derek would need to tread carefully or this interview could be over before it got started.

"Just tell me everything you remember about your neighbor."

Derek turned on the tablet computer and then started to type.

The sun was reaching its mid-point in the sky when Detective Mason pulled into the parking lot at the sheriff's office. After everything he had learned from the people he had interviewed yesterday, he hadn't slept well. His tread was slow as he opened the door and entered the county office. He greeted the receptionist and headed down the hallway to Hank's cubicle. He paused in the doorway—Hank was out. He walked back to the hallway, contemplating the office at the end. The newest, and youngest, of the nine detectives in the office, it seemed as if this case had suddenly taken a jump higher than his pay grade. A little advice on the handling of this suspect would not go amiss. He strode down to the office at the end of the hallway and poked his head in.

"Hey, sheriff, got a minute?"

"Sure, son, take a seat." Jim's smile welcomed the detective.

"I need to talk to you about information we uncovered on the 'skeleton in the well' case."

"Something unexpected...if you're seeking me out." The office chair squeaked as Sheriff Cox adjusted his position.

"Yes, you could say that. Quite unexpected."

Jim folded his hands together on the desk pad. "Go on, son, I'm all ears."

Derek laid out in minute detail every step of the investigation, from the discovery in the well, to the DNA match, the information from the Columbus police reports, and his interviews. When his words finally ground to a halt, the burden he had been hauling around lightened.

He watched as the sheriff seemed to study his folded hands. Derek remained silent and still in his chair, letting Sheriff Cox absorb all the information. As far as he was concerned, the sheriff was one of the best the county had ever had. He was tough, but fair, and beloved by all. Sheriff Cox couldn't care less about politics, always making decisions based on what was in the best interest of the county and those that lived within the borders.

Slowly, he raised his head and Derek blinked. The sheriff's eyes clearly bespoke anguish. Derek clamped down on his tongue before he asked what was wrong.

Jim cleared his throat. "You've done a good job, son. I know you'll treat him with the same courtesy as everyone else that is brought in for questioning. I..."

Sheriff Cox abruptly rose from his desk. "Excuse me."

Derek watched as the sheriff left his office. He hadn't been given a chance to get the advice he needed. He pushed up from the chair and stepped into the hallway.

Hank was walking in his direction and came to a stop two feet away. "What's up?"

Derek filled him in. "Should I call and ask him to come in?"

Hank hesitated a moment. "No. We're taking another road trip."

Derek's eyebrows drew together. "Why?"

"If we call him and ask him to come in, and he's guilty of the crime, he'll have plenty of time to prepare for the interview. I want to see his reaction when we tell him he needs to come down to the sheriff's office for questioning. If he's guilty, he could give something away."

Chapter Thirty-One

Sophie inhaled deeply of the crisp air, enjoying her Saturday morning jog in Brown Deer Park. The trees were achingly beautiful, the vivid red, orange and yellow leaves gently swaying above her head. Her shoes barely made a sound on the trail as she followed its winding path around the park. Her ankle felt strong, but she didn't push it.

"Sophie, you're jogging too fast." Allison labored to keep up.

"You're kidding, right?" Sophie felt as if she were barely moving.

"Yeah. I really want you to speed up."

Sophie laughed. She hadn't felt this totally carefree in…well… when was the last time she felt this way?

"Besides, you tend to forget I'm carrying an extra twenty pounds on my chest. The faster I go, the more likely I am to knock myself out. Then you can figure out how to get me home."

"Exaggerating a bit, don't you think?" Sophie laughed again and then glanced over at Allison. "It's my fault your surgery had to be rescheduled. I'm sorry."

Allison looked down at her breasts. "No biggey. In about a week they'll be a lot smaller. I can't wait."

"I think it's terrific...after all these years of hounding you about how much better you'd feel if you agreed to start jogging with me, you accepted the challenge."

Sophie watched as Allison struggled up the slight incline and then veered off the trail and plunked herself down on the surface of a large rock. Sophie stopped her slow jog and followed.

Allison leaned over and grabbed her stomach. "I think I might puke."

"What? Allison, I never would have suggested this if I knew it would make you sick."

Allison looked up, with a mischievous gleam to her eyes. "Kidding, I needed a break, drill sergeant."

Sophie plopped down next to her. "You don't have to fake being ill. I would have given you a break."

Allison raised one eyebrow. "Changing the subject...yesterday you told me that a woman named Ashley Keller is the most likely match for the skeleton. Why is that?"

Sophie and Allison watched as a male runner sprinted by like he was going downhill— not up.

"I found three missing girls with names that started with an A. Ashley lived the closest to Wisconsin. And when I called and talked to Detective Mason about my hunch, he got all quiet on the phone and then told me he couldn't comment because it was an ongoing investigation and I'm a reporter. Can you believe it? I'm the one who discovered the body."

"Is landing on top of a skeleton the same as discovering it?"

Sophie glared.

Allison continued, "And since when has a cop ever shared information willingly with a reporter? I may not do crime stories, but I know if I asked a cop what color the sky was he would say that was on a need-to-know basis."

Sophie smiled. "Or say, 'what sky?'"

Allison stood up. "I'm not worried about it. You'll get the story… you always do." She glanced up the trail. "How much further?"

"About half a mile."

Allison cupped a hand around her ear and leaned in. "What was that?"

Sophie looked at Allison quizzically.

Allison grinned. "Why are we standing around? There's an iced coffee calling my name."

She took off—Sophie laughing as she caught up with her.

Chapter Thirty-Two

The elevator doors slid open. Hank, deep in thought, hesitated before lifting his foot and stepping into the hallway. He had been with the sheriff's office for twelve years; had brought hundreds of people in for questioning. But this was the first time he had ever been of two minds about a subject being brought in. Yes, the facts of the investigation made him the logical perp. But...

The elevator doors started to slide shut. Hank stepped out and quickened his step to catch up with Derek. He needed to push all personal opinions aside. He had a job to do.

Derek knocked and the door was opened by a well-built man with an easy-going smile. "Detective Burke, Detective Mason, please come in."

Aaron Reinhart opened the condo door wide and took a step back. He shut the door behind the detectives and led them over to the leather couch. He settled into the recliner. "I'm glad you called and asked to stop by while you were in Chicago on business. Has there been a new development?"

Derek lifted the cover on his tablet.

Hank cleared his throat. "There has." He watched Aaron's facial expressions carefully as he made his next statement. "We've identified the victim."

Aaron's face gave nothing away. No nervous tics or tightening of the jaw. Not even a millisecond shift of eye direction—just polite curiosity. But that didn't mean he wasn't guilty of the crime. Many of the guilty Hank had interrogated never gave their guilt away in body movements or facial expressions.

"Who is it?"

"We can't disclose the identity at this time."

"Okay," Aaron frowned. "Why did you want to see me?"

"We need to ask you a few more questions…"

"Not a problem."

"…back at the sheriff's office."

His eyebrows drew together. "Why can't you ask the questions here?"

Hank kept his tone neutral. "Last time we interviewed you, it was informal. As the case progresses, we need interviews to be more…official." He hastened to add. "Mr. Reinhart, we are asking that you voluntarily come in to help us out."

Aaron sighed. "When do you need me to come in?"

"What would be convenient for you in the next few days?"

"Tomorrow. I don't have a game."

"Tomorrow at ten o'clock?"

Aaron nodded, rose from his chair, and showed them to the door, shutting it behind them.

"That was a wasted trip. No signs of guilt," Derek grimaced.

Hank punched the down button on the elevator. "No. But I think tomorrow will be a different story."

Chapter Thirty-Three

Aaron paced the small interrogation room, dragging his fingers back and forth across his scalp. Something wasn't right. He had been escorted into this room by Detective Burke, who said that he and the other detective would only be a few minutes. But that was fifteen minutes ago. He had no reason to feel anxious, but his heart was beating hard. Why was he in this room and not in an office somewhere, being offered coffee? Isn't this where they interrogated suspects to a crime? He was just a witness to seeing the skeleton. He had already told them what he knew. What else was there?

The door opened and he just about jumped out of his skin. Both detectives entered with cups of coffee.

Derek handed one to Aaron. "No need to feel nervous, Mr. Reinhart, just a few questions."

Hank added. "We'll be recording our questions and your answers."

Aaron almost asked why, but he didn't want to drag out this interview any longer than necessary. Let them ask their questions and then he was out of here.

Hank, Derek, and Aaron pulled chairs from around the table in the middle of the room and sat down.

Aaron sipped his hot coffee as Derek stated all the pertinent information about Aaron for the record, and that he had voluntarily presented himself for the interview.

Hank asked the first question. "You stated previously that you were very familiar with the property where the skeleton was discovered because you were the boyfriend of the owner's daughter, Sophie Madison, back in high school. Is that correct?"

"Yes."

"I bet you knew every square inch of that place." Derek's question had a friendly causal tone.

Aaron relaxed a fraction. "Yeah. I helped Sophie's dad harvest the corn before Sophie and I got together."

"And you were at the farm the day she was found because you remembered the gazebo as a special place of meaning for Sophie. And thought she might go there. Correct?"

"Yes."

Hank again. "Any other place on the property that you thought she might have gone?"

"No." Aaron shifted in his chair. "Why are you asking these questions? What do they have to do with the skeleton?"

Derek glanced at Hank and then back to Aaron. "You stated you were leaving the property when you heard the dog bark and then saw the elderly man in the rearview mirror of your car. Correct?"

"Yes."

"Did the old man glance in your direction? Did he see you leaving?"

"No, I don't think so, but you would have to ask him."

For the next twenty minutes, the questioning went over the same ground as the last time he was interviewed.

Aaron heaved a sigh. "Detectives, I've already answered these questions. If there isn't anything new, I need to get back to Chicago."

Hank and Derek shared a look and then Hank pulled a picture out of the file folder in front of him and slid it across the table to Aaron face up. "Do you know this girl?"

Aaron stared at the pretty blonde-haired girl with green eyes. His eyebrows shot up. "It's Ashley Keller. Why do you have a picture of Ashley? She went missing back when I was in school at Ohio State. Have you found her?"

Aaron glanced up.

Hank was glaring at him. "We have. She's the skeleton in the well."

Icy tendrils reached throughout Aaron's body and latched on to vital organs. His heart slowed and stopped for a beat. In its frozen state, his mind couldn't process the information handed to him like a grenade with the pin pulled.

"Mr. Reinhart... are you okay?"

He tried to swivel his head in Derek's direction. The cold disappeared and he was hot. Beads of sweat popped out on his forehead. "Ash..." He took a deep breath and tried to focus on forming the words. "I...wa...was in the...www...ell with...Ash...Ashley's skeleton?"

The detectives wore twin looks of uncertainty. Derek opened his mouth then shut it.

Hank's hand tightened on his cup as he looked at Aaron. Concern infused his words. "Mr. Reinhart, you don't look well. Your face is very pale. Can we get you anything?"

"Where is your restroom?"

"Down the hall on the left."

Aaron grabbed a paper towel from the dispenser in the restroom. He wet it and wiped his sweaty face. Next, he turned on the water in the sink and cupped his hands under the stream. He scooped handfuls of water into his mouth, his throat working furiously. He reached out a hand, water dripping off his fingertips, and turned off the tap. He looked up and stared at his image in the mirror as he wiped his hands with another hand towel. He had been a foot from Ashley's bones in the well. How was that possible?

Aaron's lips thinned. That was why he had been called in for questioning—here at the sheriff's office. It was an interrogation. They suspected that he killed Ashley and dumped her body in the well. Somehow, they had discovered that there was a link between the two of them. *And if they had found out about our argument the night she went missing...* The ice was travelling up his spine again.

Both Hank and Derek were in the hallway as Aaron emerged from the restroom. They straightened up as he approached them.

"I'm...I'm not answering anymore questions today."

Hank stepped forward. "You still don't look well. And your speech...do you need to go to the emergency room?"

"No, I have a speech...im...impediment that tends to return when I'm stressed."

Aaron looked from one detective to the other. "I...I want to make something very clear. I did not kill Ashley Keller."

Hank's tone was neutral. "We'll call and reschedule for another day." He paused for a second. "Continuing to cooperate and answer our questions is in your best interest."

"Goodbye, detectives." Aaron turned on his heel and headed for the exit to the parking lot.

Hank watched him leave as he voiced his earlier thought. "I thought he was having a stroke. It rattled me, to tell the truth."

"You weren't the only one." Derek murmured. "A stammering problem. Wouldn't have guessed that in a million years."

Hank started for his cubicle. "I can't decide if he's telling the truth or a really good actor. He turned white as a ghost and then broke out in a sweat. He seemed to be in total shock. But the circumstantial evidence against him is strong."

Derek shrugged his shoulders. "If he is guilty, it wasn't like he was going to confess today. We'll just have to see what else we can dig up."

Aaron punched a number into his cell as he pulled onto the interstate heading back to Chicago.

"Hey, boyo, what's up?"

"Can you meet me at my condo in three hours?"

"Sure. Why?"

Aaron swerved around unidentifiable road kill in his path. "I'd rather wait and tell you in person."

"I'll be there."

Aaron tapped the icon to end the call. He set his phone in the cup holder. As he traveled the interstate, the road ahead stretching straight for miles and no other distractions, his mind went back to the last conversation he had with Ashley.

He had been in his sophomore year at Ohio State, and he and seven of his baseball teammates had been blowing off steam at Jack's Rib Shack after a particularity grueling practice. The testosterone was palpable around the table, sprinkled with jokes, tall tales, imitations of the coaches, and laughter.

Walking across the back parking lot of Jack's Rib Shack to his jeep, his windbreaker collar pulled up against the chilly night air and trying to avoid the bigger pot holes barely illuminated by the dim lights, Ashley had called his name...

Chapter Thirty-Four

Fall 1999

"Aaron!"

Ashley was rushing towards him. Inwardly, he groaned. She wasn't going to let this go. They had been out on a few dates and, in a moment of weakness, he had almost...Ashley had touched his cheek and looked him in the eyes the way Sophie used to do.

Back in high school, he and his Christian buddies had agreed that "true love waits." In the middle of his runaway passion, shame had washed over him, effectively dousing the lust before he made the biggest mistake of his life. He had apologized, told her how ashamed he was for taking advantage of her. She laughed, said there was nothing to apologize for, she was a big girl and this wasn't her first 'rodeo.' She had tried to draw him back into an embrace. He had backed off and told her he had to leave. He hadn't asked her out again and had declined her invitations to get together, but she wasn't getting the message.

"Hey, Aaron, how did practice go today?" Her blonde hair was pulled back in a ponytail, her necklace with the 'A' initial glinting dully in the parking lot lights.

"It went fine, Ashley."

"It's dead in there now; only Sean, Jon, Mike, and a guy paying his check. Jack said I could go ahead and leave. Do you want to go somewhere and hang out?"

"No, I'm beat and my muscles are sore. I'm going back to the apartment and crash."

Ashley gave him her sweetest smile. "Come on, you can't be that tired. Besides, I give the best massages."

He hated the thought of hurting her, but just looking at Ashley made his gut tighten up. He should have known he wasn't ready to move on from Sophie.

Her smile faded as the silence grew. "Look, Aaron, I need to tell you something. I lied about the 'rodeo' thing. I've only been with one other guy...and it was a mistake. I don't sleep around."

Ashley took a deep breath, her voice desperate. "I love you. There, I said it. It's out in the open. I just want you to give us a chance. We can go as slow as you want."

Aaron shook his head. It was worse than he thought. He had to make her understand. He took his own deep breath. "What happened between us...I never should have...I'm sorry; I just don't feel the same way."

Aaron shoved his hands into the pockets of his jeans. "And since you're being honest with me, I will be honest with you. The few dates we had were fun, but that was all it was for me. I had a very bad break up a little over a year ago. I'm still in love with someone else. It will be a very long time, maybe never, before I can let her go."

Ashley's breathing quickened and her arms stiffened as her hands closed into fists. "Then you should have said something before you started kissing me…before we almost…"

"Don't you think I know that? I think about my mistake every day!"

A man passed by, glancing their way before hurrying to his car.

Ashley's green eyes filled with tears as her face crumpled. "I was a mistake?"

"Oh, no, I didn't…" Aaron took a breath. "Ashley, please listen to me. All of this is my fault. All of it. I'm ashamed of the way I treated you."

Aaron glanced over as a car pulled out of the lot.

Tears were streaming down Ashley's cheeks. "Go…just go away."

He had entered his jeep and left. His last glance of Ashley—standing alone under one of the parking lot lights…sobbing.

Chapter Thirty-Five

Fall 2012

Aaron's fingers jerked the steering wheel, sending him over the line and into the left lane. He quickly turned the wheel, with hands that were shaking, putting the vehicle back in the right lane.

When he left the parking lot at Jack's Rib Shack that night, thirteen years ago, Ashley had been alive. But the next day, he had learned that Ashley was missing. And then the police had come asking questions. He found out that he was the last person to see her that night.

Aaron's eyes widened. The argument with Ashley was in a report with the Columbus police.

That's how the detectives had made the connection.

When Ashley went missing, he had been a "person of interest" because he was the last person to see her alive. But nothing came of it for lack of evidence.

But now there was evidence, circumstantial, but still evidence.

And if they found out what happened when he was seventeen…

Aaron's knuckles turned white on the steering wheel.

He could be in a lot of trouble.

The empty shelves of his refrigerator reminded Aaron that he needed to go to the grocery store. He grabbed the long-necked brown bottle and handed it to Sean. Strange that such a mundane chore had pushed to the forefront of his anxious thoughts.

"Who died, boyo?" Sean's concern showed in his eyes.

Aaron shut the refrigerator door. "Go on in and sit down."

"No. You just handed me a beer. You never have beer in your fridge. Something major's going down." He crossed his muscular arms and leaned back against the black marble counter, the beer bottle clenched in his right hand. "Now. Right now."

"I may be arrested for murder."

Sean's bottle almost crashed on the floor as his fingers started to lose their grip.

Aaron took a healthy swig of beer and headed into the living room. He fell into his recliner, lifting the neck of the bottle for another drink. He ran a finger back and forth over his damp lips. His ice blue eyes tracked Sean as he walked to the couch and slowly sat down.

Sean lifted his dark brown eyes to Aaron's face. "Murder? I don't under… how is that possible?"

Aaron leaned forward, the beer bottle gripped in both hands between his knees. "Do you remember Ashley Keller, the waitress at Jack's Rib Shack?"

Sean's eyebrows knit together. "Yeah, what does she..." Shock contorted his face as Sean connected the dots. "Ashley was murdered?"

Aaron nodded. He stayed silent to give Sean time to absorb the news.

Sean took a breath, thumbed the top off his beer bottle and took a long drink. He lowered the bottle. "But why do you think you'll be accused? That's just crazy, boyo."

Aaron took another sip of beer. "It was Ashley's skeleton that was found in the well with my ex-girlfriend, Sophie."

Sean's jaw dropped open. "What? ...wait. How could Ashley's skeleton be in Sophie's well? That makes no sense... unless..."

Sean's eyes widened.

"Unless I killed her and hid her on my ex-girlfriend's abandoned property."

"Oh, sweet Jesus, mother Mary, and all the saints...that is just not possible. I know you, boyo, like I know myself. You're not capable of murder."

Aaron stared at Sean, his expression bleak. "No, not murder, but I did kill someone. And if the police find out that little piece of information..."

This time Sean did lose the grip on his beer bottle. It clattered on the polished wooden floor, amber liquid pooling and then spreading in an ever-widening circle. He sat the bottle upright on the floor. "Oh man, I'm sorry. I'll clean it up."

Sean jumped up and rushed to the kitchen. He returned and laid a dish towel over the spill and started to mop it up. His hand froze. He looked up, anguish clearly stamped in his features. He let go of the rag and stood, his chest heaving. "No! I know you like my own brothers! You...did...not...kill...anyone! Not Ashley...not ...anyone!"

In contrast, Aaron's voice was quiet, subdued. "Not on purpose, but I was responsible for someone's death."

Sean's arm reached behind him like a blind man; he slowly lowered his body onto the leather couch. "How?"

Aaron explained what had happened the summer he was seventeen... and then he told Sean about the Sheriff Deputies' interrogation yesterday.

Sean grasped his hands together behind his neck, looked down at the floor, and then raised his head. His eyes were full of sorrow. "I'm sorry, boyo."

Aaron set his empty beer bottle on the end table with a hand that was steadier than he felt. "I needed to tell you. What I remember most about the time when Ashley went missing is how you had my back. When the police came to the apartment, and it was obvious that I was a suspect, you told them to back off. That there was no way I was involved."

Aaron's lips gave a hint of a smile, but quickly tightened. "I feel like the walls are closing in around me, sucking out all the air. There is this living, breathing fear...inside me. I tried praying before you came, but..."

"Okay, I'll ask flat out, but I already know the answer...did you kill Ashley?"

Aaron shook his head.

Sean heaved a sigh and rose from the couch. "I'll be there for you, whatever you need."

Aaron looked up. "I know you will."

Sean reached down and grabbed Aaron's arm, pulling him to his feet. "You're coming with me, boyo, to my house for dinner.

Brigid is making my favorite meal, Shepard's Pie. We will talk and laugh and, for a little while, you will forget your troubles."

Aaron smiled despite the band constricting his chest. "I told you I don't like…"

"I know you don't like Irish food. You'll like this, or being accused of murder will be the least of your worries."

Chapter Thirty-Six

Sophie punched the *end* icon on her iPhone, her sea green eyes triumphant. She had been right. Ashley Keller was the victim in the well. She had just finished talking to Ashley's mother. Although advised not to talk to anyone about her daughter, she had opened up under Sophie's persuasive tactics. But the tactics hadn't really been necessary, Sophie had the answer she sought the minute Ashley's mother said she wasn't supposed to talk to anyone. The police had to have been the ones telling Ashley's mother not to give out information on her daughter.

The ringing of phones and multiple conversations around her little work island had never bothered her as she worked the angles for her stories, and they didn't now. In an odd way, the background noises were soothing. She pushed a stray strand of dark hair off of her cheek. Instead of her usual ponytail, her hair was held back by a decorative headband, which allowed the thick waves to flow past her shoulders.

Now that she had confirmation, she could make her next call. She tapped in the number and waited. The call was answered by a female voice. "Walworth County Sheriff's Office."

"Could I speak with Detective Burke, please?"

"Whom may I say is calling?"

"Sophie Madison."

Sophie started when a male voice said, "You're not a physic are you?"

"Excuse me?"

"I had picked up the handset to call you when your call came through."

Sophie smiled. "Great minds, Detective. Why were you calling me?"

"I'd like you to come to the office to answer a few more questions."

"Great minds, indeed. I'd like to ask you a few questions myself."

"Happy to answer what I can."

Ah yes, the famous emphasis on *I can.*

"Thank you, Detective Burke. I can be there around three."

"Works for me. See you then."

Sophie ended the call. She chewed on her lower lip as her index finger tapped the mouse of her computer, causing the little cursor to dance around the text on her screen.

"Coffee?" Hank held up the pot.

"No, getting to be a little late in the day for me." Sophie glanced around the room interspersed with cubicles.

"I should be cutting back…this is my sixth." Hank poured a cup and led the way to his cubicle.

Sophie suppressed any feelings of intimidation that tried to overtake her as she followed the imposing figure in front of her. She hadn't paid attention to how big a man he was when he interviewed her in the hospital. She was like a child following the adult.

"Have a seat."

She sat in the metal chair offered, crossing her jean-clad legs. Her lightly glossed lips turned up at the corners as she gazed at colorful drawings, made by a child, pinned to his cubicle wall. Detective Burke pulled a thick file from a stack at his left elbow. He lifted a photo from the file and pushed it across the desk. Sophie reached for it.

"I assume you know who that is."

Sophie glanced at the picture and then nodded her head. "Ashley Keller. I saw a picture on the internet."

Hank grinned. "You are a clever young lady. When you called the office and asked if the victim was Ms. Keller, I…well… frankly, I was stunned. You identified the skeleton almost as fast as we did."

"And with fewer resources."

Hank gave a belly laugh. "I highly doubt that."

Sophie gave a sheepish grin. "Okay, I have more than a few."

Hank leaned back in his large office chair. "Which is one of the reasons I called you in. I'd like for us to work together."

Sophie slapped her right hand over the upper left side of her chest. "I think I'm having a heart attack."

Hank laughed. "I'm being serious. I think we can help each other out."

"Meaning I give you all my info and you give nothing."

Hank shook his head. "Not true. I will give you *certain* information, as long as I can trust you not to divulge it to anyone. And if you guarantee it will not show up in your paper."

Sophie pursed her lips. "Okay, *if* my paper gets first print on all info you want leaked, and exclusive rights to the story once the killer is caught and identified."

"That could be arranged."

Sophie continued as if Hank hadn't spoken. "And my paper gets to leak the identity of the victim in Friday's paper."

Hank leaned forward. "Wow, not so fast."

Sophie leaned in. "Do you think I'm the only journalist trying to find out the identity of the victim? I guarantee—I'm not. If you want some control on the story, we need to get it out before someone else scoops us."

Hank's eyes pierced Sophie's. "Okay, but only her identity, where she was found, and that she was identified through DNA evidence. No mention of the necklace, or background story on her disappearance. Nothing else. Especially no speculation on how she died. That is, and I quote, 'under investigation'."

"Shouldn't I add a line about any information from the public that might lead to the apprehension of person or persons responsible?"

Hank straightened and took a sip of his coffee. "Okay. And before you ask, I can't give out any info on any persons of interest at this time."

Hardly surprising. Rarely could she get names of suspects from law enforcement. She had to use other resources.

Hank sighed. "I'll take two questions before I ask you my questions."

"Do you have a suspect?"

"I told you…"

"Okay, okay, off the record."

Hank narrowed his eyes. "Can I trust you?"

"Yes."

"We have a lead."

"Male or female?"

Hank picked up his mug. "This is also off the record...male. And now it's my turn."

For half an hour, Hank drilled her with questions, such as: who knew about the farm (everyone in the community) and who had access (anyone), and when was the farm abandoned? By the time he was done, frustration was clearly written on the detective's face. "Thank you, for answering the questions, Ms. Madison. I look forward to reading your article."

Sophie smiled. "Not even a hint of sarcasm. One more question, detective?"

Hank sighed. "Yes, Ms. Madison?"

"Are you're thinking that the perpetrator is someone from the La Grange area who went to Columbus on personal, work related, or *other* business, killed Ashley and stashed her body back here?"

"Like I said before, you are a clever young lady."

Sophie rose from her chair. "I have a good feeling about this case, Detective Burke. We will get justice for Ashley. Thank you for being as candid as you were with me. I think we make a good team."

Sophie held out her slender hand.

Hank's hand seemed to swallow her hand whole. "I'm counting on it. I'm going out on a limb here. You're the first journalist I'm trusting with information I normally keep close to the vest."

Sophie pulled her hand out of Hank's grasp. "You won't be disappointed."

Questions peppered her mind as she left the cubicle and walked out the front door of the building to her replacement vehicle. She had found an unbelievably good deal on a four-year-old sedan. Once inside the car, Sophie turned on her tablet computer and quickly typed in the conversation from memory. As she typed in '*other business,*' something niggled at the back of her mind. She closed her eyes and a word jumped forward— college. Her eyes popped open in alarm. *Aaron.* Thirteen years ago, he was going to school in Columbus at Ohio State. *At the same time Ashley went missing.* What if Detective Burke connected the same dots? She shook her head. Even if he did, the odds were nil to none that Aaron knew Ashley. She was a waitress and Ashley's mother never mentioned that she attended Ohio State.

With a hand that suddenly trembled, Sophie turned the key in the ignition. She took an anxious breath and backed out of the parking space.

Chapter Thirty-Seven

Hank, hair still damp from the shower, poked his head into Derek's cubicle. "Where did you disappear to yesterday?"

"I did some digging on Reinhart...and it's not looking good for one of the star players of the Chicago Cubs."

Derek indicated the open manila file folder on his desk.

Hank started to take a sip of his coffee and then stopped when the hot liquid nearly burnt his tongue. "What's in it?"

"Seems our prime suspect killed someone when he was seventeen."

Hank's hand jerked and hot coffee sloshed over the side of his mug. Brown liquid dripped onto his brown leather shoe. He moved into the cubicle and grabbed a tissue out of the box on Derek's desk and wiped the liquid off his shoe and the mug. He tossed the wadded up tissue into the trash can. He settled in a chair against the cubicle wall, frowning. "Okay, give me the details."

Derek picked up a paper from the file. "He killed Jimmy Madison in July of 1998. It was ruled an accident."

"Wait." Hank's brows pulled together. "Is he related to Sophie Madison?"

"Her father."

Hank's brows shot up. "Whoa. Hang on a minute." He started to say something then shook his head. "Never mind, just give me the facts."

"Reinhart claims that Madison took a swing at him and he pushed him away. When he did, Madison tripped, fell, and died at the hospital from an aneurysm in the brain."

Hank rubbed his shaven chin with the thumb and forefinger of his right hand. "Any witnesses?"

Derek nodded. "The full story is...Madison had suffered a stroke earlier in the day and sexually assaulted his daughter, Sophie. Aaron pulled him off and that's when Madison took the swing at him."

"Accidental death." Hank's eyes bored into Derek's. "Are you thinking what I'm thinking?"

Derek leaned back slightly rocking his office chair. "Another accidental death? Ashley's mother said in her statement that her daughter's car was in the shop the night she went missing and she had dropped her daughter off at work. Ashley told her that she didn't think she would need her mom to pick her up."

Hank's gaze was thoughtful. "Maybe...she planned to get a ride from Reinhart. The witness, who saw them arguing, left the parking lot while they were still standing together. They could have left together in Aaron's car."

Derek tapped the file. "Then they went somewhere else. More arguing..."

Hank blew out a breath. "Speculation. The evidence against him is all circumstantial. We need some hard evidence."

"Or a confession."

Hank took a cautious sip of his coffee. "I think I'll call Mr. Reinhart and have him come in, exert a little pressure. Meanwhile, you keep digging."

Derek nodded.

"I haven't had a chance to tell you, but someone else is helping with the investigating," Hank said.

"Who is it?"

"The ex-girlfriend—Sophie Madison. She figured out who the victim in the well was about the same time we did. I think she'll be a useful source of information. I talked to her yesterday about sharing info."

Derek's eyebrows rose to his hairline. "Have you lost your mind? She's a journalist. You can't trust a journalist as far as you can throw one. And she's Reinhart's ex. She won't share anything that would put suspicion on him."

Hank rose off the chair. "She's determined to find the killer. If it turns out to be Reinhart, my money's on her integrity winning out over an ex-boyfriend."

Derek shook his head as he said, "I wouldn't bet the farm on that happening."

Chapter Thirty-Eight

Sophie laid the newspaper across her desk. It wasn't the top story, but her article had made the front page. The headline read, "Skeleton Discovered in Dry Well Identified." She perused the story for any missed typos and, finding none, sat back in her chair, a satisfied smile on her lips. If the killer lived in the area, the article might make him nervous. And anxiety could lead to a slip-up. Slow footsteps approached her desk. She looked up. Allison was making her way across the room.

Sophie's eyes widened. "What are you doing here? You're supposed to be home resting."

"You try lying around that apartment for a week. I'm bored out of my mind."

"I did—remember." Sophie glanced down at her ankle. "Are you supposed to be driving?"

Allison eased into a chair beside Sophie's desk. "The doctor said one to two weeks. I decided one was enough."

Sophie's lips turned down in the corners. "Allison, don't push this. I was in the hospital room when the doctor said to keep the use of your arms to a minimum even after the drainage tubes were out. And they have only been out a few days."

"Yeah, well I needed a change of scenery."

"Fine, I'll pick you up after work every day and take you sightseeing."

"Sensing a little sarcasm in that comment—but I'll take you up on the offer. My arms are a bit sore from turning the steering wheel." She smiled her thanks.

"And you're not driving home. I'll take you back at lunch. Jason can follow with your car."

"Wait, no, I…"

"Subject closed. Did you see the article I wrote on the skeleton in the well?"

"This morning. You nailed the victim's identity in, what, a couple of months? Give you another two months and you'll have the killer caught and on the court docket."

"I wish."

Allison started to stand up.

"Where are you going?"

She rolled her eyes. "Just to my desk, mother. Want to follow me?"

Sophie's eyes narrowed. "Just don't use your arms."

Sophie turned back to the article, her fingers making drumming noises on the newsprint. Her contact at the Milwaukee Police Department was working on getting her the Columbus Police Department report from the investigation into Ashley's disappearance. But she wasn't good at sitting and waiting.

Sophie opened her desk drawer and removed a yellow sticky note. The online news report had said that Ashley disappeared after leaving work at Jack's Rib Shack. Maybe Ashley's boss knew something. Her lips pursed. What would be the best approach to get answers to her questions? She reached for her cell phone and jerked when it rang. Bryan's name lit across the screen. Her eyes welled as she drew a finger across his name. He had been calling every week since she left the hospital, to check on her. She sighed. She still couldn't bring herself to tell him the truth, which is what he deserved. *Soon, she would tell him soon.*

She waited until the call went to voicemail and then tapped in the number on the sticky.

"Jack's Rib Shack."

"Is this the owner?"

"This is Jack. Can I help you?"

"I hope so. I wanted to ask you a couple of questions about the night Ashley Keller went missing."

Jack's tone went from friendly to cautious. "Who is this?"

Sophie took a breath. "This is Sophie Madison. I'm helping Detective Burke with the investigation into the murder."

"Are you a cop?"

"No."

"Then how are you helping?"

Sophie steeled herself. "I'm a reporter with…"

Jack's tone switched to brusque. "I was told not to speak to reporters."

"You can call the detective; he'll verify that what I'm saying is true."

Jack's impatience came through loud and clear. "Look, Ms. Madison, even if it is true, I told the detectives everything I remember and I don't have time to go over it again. Since you're working with Detective Burke, he can give you my statement."

"I haven't asked, but he probably won't share that information with me."

"I'm sorry, but…"

Sophie played the justice card. "Mr. Perry, I was the one who found her skeleton. I spent three days stuck in a dry well with

Ashley's remains. I want justice for Ashley. I'm not bragging when I tell you I'm an excellent investigator. Wouldn't you like to find her killer as soon as possible?"

The voice coming through the speaker softened. "You found Ashley?"

"Yes."

Jack sighed. "What do you want to know?"

"First—do you know who was the last person to see Ashley alive?"

"His name is Aaron Reinhart."

Sophie's heart stopped for a second and then began to beat wildly. The cell phone slid out of her suddenly numb fingers to the desk. *No, no, no.* Sophie shook her head back and forth.

"Hello... Ms. Madison?" Mr. Perry's voice was barely audible.

It was becoming hard to breathe. Her vision started to gray. The voice speaking out of her iPhone faded. Suddenly bright spots colored the gray of her vision.

"Sophie!"

She jerked. The spots disappeared and the gray dissipated. Allison was standing in front of her desk, a worried frown on her face.

"I..." Sophie pressed the heel of her hand to her forehead.

"Are you sick? You're as white as a ghost."

The room was utterly silent. She looked around. Her co-workers were staring in her direction.

She took a steadying breath. She forced a smile, indicating all was fine with her, and then turned to Allison. "Come on, I'm taking an early lunch." Standing, she shoved her now-silent iPhone into the back pocket of her black pants and grabbed her black leather jacket.

Allison followed her out the door of the building, that fronted State Street, and into pewter laden skies and a light drizzle. "Okay, spill. What happened in there?"

"I'll tell you in the car." Sophie hurried down the block to the parking garage.

She pulled the car fob out of the front pocket of her pants and pressed the button twice. When the locks clicked, she yanked open the door, slid into the driver's seat, and slammed the door. She grabbed her churning stomach with hands that trembled, and rocked back and forth. After a couple of minutes, the passenger door opened.

Allison leaned in. "Sophie, why did you take off like that? You know..." Allison's eyes widened. "Sophie what's wrong? Talk to me!"

Allison slid into the passenger seat. When Sophie didn't respond, Allison squeezed her shoulder.

Sophie groaned as she looked over. "My stomach...I don't feel well."

"Do you need a doctor? I can drive you."

Sophie shook her head, then lowered it onto the steering wheel. "Give me a minute."

Minutes slipped by as the two friends sat in the vehicle.

"It's Aaron."

"What?"

Sophie laid her head back against the headrest. "I just found out that Aaron was the last person to see Ashley Keller before she went missing.

Allison frowned. "Aaron Reinhart? But how could that be? I thought Ashley disappeared in Columbus?"

"Aaron was a student at Ohio State when she disappeared. I don't know the details. I was so upset when the owner of the restaurant said Aaron's name, I almost blacked out. I heard him calling my name but I couldn't respond. He must have hung up on me." Sophie groaned again.

"If you're going to throw up, give me fair warning; it will take me a little longer to get out of the way."

Despite her upset stomach, Sophie laughed—and then immediately started to cry. "He didn't... do it. I...know he didn't kill her."

"Oh, Sophie, please don't cry. I want to hug you, but I can't lift my arms."

A little bit of mirth mixed with the sobs as Sophie turned and buried her face in her friend's shoulder. Allison winced, but laid a hand on her friend's head as she stared through the windshield at the other cars parked in the narrow slots. Her heart ached for her friend. It was obvious that Sophie was still very much in love with Aaron Reinhart.

The entrance door to the *Sentinel* building opened and Noah stepped aside as Sophie and their co-worker, Jason, dashed in out of the cold drizzle. She couldn't stop shivering. Either the temperature had dropped substantially or she was still in shock from the news about Aaron. She rushed to her desk, rolling back the office chair and sitting down. She gave a furtive glance to her right, making sure her boss's door was shut. Sophie's fingers shook as she punched a number into her phone.

"Detective Burke."

"It's Sophie Madison."

"Ms. Madison, what can I do for you?" Detective Burke's tone suggested polite curiosity.

Sophie's quivering fingers gripped her phone tighter. "I know who your suspect is and you're way off base. It isn't Aaron."

Silence.

"Detective?"

"I can't discuss any person or persons of interest."

"Despite the fact that he may have been the last person to see her alive and her skeleton was found in a location he was familiar with...which I admit is suspicious... he didn't kill her. I'm trying to save you valuable time."

"Ms. Madison, if Mr. Reinhart was a person of interest, and I stress *if*, you can hardly be objective because of the relationship you had with him."

Sophie's tone turned grim. "It's because of our relationship that I know he didn't do it. I am now more determined than ever to find the real killer. I won't see Aaron railroaded."

The door to Mr. McNair's office opened. Sophie looked over as he appeared in the doorway. He pointed at Sophie. She held up a finger. "I need a copy of the statement you got from Jack Perry. I need to know every little detail of that night Ashley disappeared from the restaurant."

"I can't..."

"You wanted us to work together. I can't help if I'm given only crumbs. I need at least a full slice of the cake."

Four seconds of silence.

"I'll get back to you." The line disconnected.

Sophie's editor was now bellowing. She shoved her still shaking hands into the pockets of her pants as she rose from her chair.

Chapter Thirty-Nine

Hank escorted Aaron into the interrogation room, told him to have a seat, and set a cup of coffee in front of him. Hank and Derek settled into the chairs on the other side of the table.

Hank opened a file. "I would like to state...

"Excuse me Detective, but I'd like to wait for my lawyer."

Derek and Hank exchanged a glance.

"He should be here any minute." Aaron's mouth quirked up in the right corner.

Hank took a sip of coffee to cover his surprise. *Should have known he would lawyer up.*

Derek cleared his throat. "That really wasn't necessary. You aren't in custody."

There was a knock on the door. Hank pressed his hands on the table and pushed back his chair as Derek rose also. Hank opened the door. A county detective stood in the doorway with another man.

Hank nodded at the detective. "Thanks, Tom." The detective nodded back and left.

Jonathan Richards strode into the interrogation room. He laid his briefcase on the table, adjusted his rimless glasses, and focused on the two detectives. "I'm advising my client not to answer any of your questions." He turned to Aaron, who sat at the table by himself. "You haven't answered any questions?"

Aaron shook his head.

"I'm sorry Detective Burke and Detective Mason, but if you don't have cause to hold or arrest my client, we're leaving."

Hank shifted his gaze to Aaron for a long moment then back to his lawyer. "Not at this time. But I would advise him to cooperate with the investigation."

The lawyer gave the detectives a thin smile as he ushered Aaron out of the room.

Aaron and his lawyer halted beside Aaron's SUV and shook hands.

"I'm sorry you had to drive all this way, Jonathan."

Jonathan dropped Aaron's hand. "Not a problem. I'll be billing the hours to the Cubs." He started to turn and then hesitated. "Have you remembered anything else about Ms. Keller since we met in my office? I don't want to be blindsided by the police or the DA's office. You didn't leave anything out...and you're not hiding any information?"

"No, sir. You know it all." Aaron's gaze was steady.

The lawyer nodded. "Then anything they uncover about you will be circumstantial."

"Do you think they know about what happened when I was seventeen?"

"Undoubtedly. But it has no bearing on this case. Call me if you have any questions or the detectives call you in again for questioning." Jonathan turned and strode briskly to his luxury sedan.

As Aaron and Jonathan were heading out of Walworth County, the phone buzzed on Hank's desk. "Detective Burke."

"Good afternoon, Detective Burke. This is Jonny Johnson. I'm the forensic anthropologist with…"

"Ah, yes, I remember you Mr. Johnson, we met at the dry well on the Madison property. I hope you're calling with the cause of death on the Keller skeleton."

Hank heard Jonny take a drink of something then clear his throat. "I'm sorry it's taken so long, but there was a backlog of cases at the crime lab. I talked to one of the forensic scientists at the crime lab today…and it's as I suspected. Death was most likely due to a hard blow to the upper portion of the face—the upper part of the nose, lower part of the forehead, between the eyes. Without the brain its speculation, of course, but a hard enough blow to the frontal lobe can cause massive hemorrhaging in the brain, followed by death."

"What type of weapon was used?"

"My forensic colleagues at the lab are going with a fist."

"A fist?" Hank's voice rose.

"Yeah, happens more than you think. The official report will be mailed in a about a week, but I wanted to give you a courtesy call because I knew you'd want to know as soon as the results were conclusive."

"How long would it take a person to die by that kind of blow?"

"Depends on how hard the blow was. Could be hours, days, or, in rare cases, death is instantaneous."

"Thank you, Mr. Johnson." Hank replaced the handset. He pushed up from his chair and walked over to Derek's cubicle. "We have probable cause of death in the Keller case."

Derek glanced up from his tablet computer. "Did you ask why it's taken so long?"

"Backlog."

"Okay, what have you got?" Derek looked back at the tablet.

"A fist to the forehead, followed by brain hemorrhaging."

Derek directed his gaze back at Hank. "You'd need some power behind a fist to cause a death like that."

Hank nodded. "I'm having Reinhart's medical records pulled. See if he had any hand injuries around the time Keller went missing.

Chapter Forty

The District Attorney settled into the chair across from Sheriff Cox's desk and crossed his legs. A woodsy scent from the D.A.'s cologne wafted Jim's way. "An arrest warrant has been issued for Aaron Reinhart in the Keller case. On the advice of his lawyer, Reinhart has waived extradition and is allowing our detectives to take him into custody and bring him to Wisconsin. I want your detectives to go pick him up."

"Now wait a minute, Robert…"

"I've got enough to bring him in. He has three strikes against him."

Jim Cox leaned over his folded hands. "All circumstantial."

"There is no smoking gun to be found. She was killed by a fist, a large fist, like Reinhart's. And we now have documented evidence that he had injuries consistent with striking a hard object with his fist the day the victim disappeared."

"The medical report stated…"

Robert Ellison's jaw hardened. "I don't want to belabor the points of this case any further, Jim." He uncrossed his legs.

"He's not the seventeen-year-old kid you remember. Bring him in."

Sheriff Cox stared at the empty chair. A sharp wind whistled outside, drawing his gaze to the large window in his office. The last of the season's dead leaves were being torn from their branches and scattered across the landscape. The deepening gray of the clouds gave the frigid day a gloomy feel—the same as his mood.

Aaron didn't kill that girl. After accidently killing Sophie's father, to protect her, Aaron would have avoided any situation that even suggested he would have to act in a physical manner against another person. He had observed the boy in court that long-ago summer. Aaron had been devastated and riddled with guilt.

The Sheriff sighed as he picked up the phone to call one of the detectives, praying that Aaron had an excellent lawyer.

The door swung inward and Aaron looked at Hank and Derek standing on the other side of the threshold.

Hank took a breath before stating, "Aaron Reinhart, an arrest warrant has been issued in your name for the murder of Ashley Keller. We are here to escort you to the Sheriff's office for booking."

Aaron's heart thumped in his chest as he was read his Miranda rights.

"Do you understand these rights?"

Aaron tried to focus. "Yes."

Footsteps sounded from the living room and a hand gave his shoulder a reassuring squeeze. "I'll meet you at the Sheriff's office."

"Detectives." Mr. Richards gave a deferential nod and left the condo.

"Do we need to handcuff you?"

Aaron shook his head.

"I need a verbal answer."

"No."

Detective Burke reached for Aaron's arm.

Aaron pulled back slightly. "I need to get my cell phone, keys and wallet."

"I'll go with him." Derek followed Aaron into the back of the condo.

Sitting in the back of the county car on the way to the Sheriff's office, Aaron rubbed his hands across his face. How could this have happened? Mr. Richards said all the evidence was circumstantial and they wouldn't arrest him based on that type of evidence. He lifted his hands to the top of his head. He didn't kill Ashley; there couldn't be any hard evidence.

Four hours later, after being fingerprinted, photographed, and answering the processing questions in a daze, Aaron was escorted into the interrogation room to await his lawyer.

Mr. Richards walked through the door, his mouth pulled into a taut line. Jonathan's normally mild gray eyes were the dark gray of a storm-tossed sea. "Are you okay?"

Aaron started to nod his head, but then shook it instead.

"I've been on the phone since I left the condo, trying to get a bail hearing today, but the earliest I could get is tomorrow afternoon. You'll have to spend a night in jail." Jonathan splayed his hands on the metal table. "This should not have happened." He jerked a chair under him and sat down. "Aaron, you're sure you've told me everything?"

"I've been racking my brain since you told me about the arrest warrant. I can't think of anything I've missed."

"Okay, I'll find out what I can. Meanwhile, not a word about the case to anyone."

As he nodded, Aaron glimpsed sympathy in his lawyer's eyes.

"Try not to worry and get some sleep. I'm staying at a local motel. I'll see you tomorrow."

As his lawyer rose to leave, Aaron stared at his folded hands resting atop the cool surface of the gray metal table.

The news leaked out. As Aaron left the jail, after posting a two-hundred-thousand-dollar bond, multiple journalists shouted questions. Mr. Richards, perfectly attired in a three-piece suit, brushed past microphones shoved in their direction, voicing a curt 'no comment' as he led Aaron to his sedan.

"Why can't people keep their mouths shut?" He muttered as he started the car for the trip back to Chicago. "I was hoping we'd have a couple of days before you became national news."

As he turned left out of the parking lot, he glanced over at Aaron's slumped figure. "You need to hunker down in your condo for now. Don't answer the phone or door except for me, family, and your closest friend."

Aaron made no comment.

Jonathan turned his eyes back to the road, allowing Aaron whatever amount of silence he needed.

They were an hour outside of Chicago before Aaron straightened and turned towards Jonathan. "How can I be arrested for a crime I didn't commit?"

Jonathan tapped the brakes as the car in front of him slowed. "Unfortunately, it happens all the time. Look, I know it's nearly impossible, but stop worrying and beating yourself up. It won't help. And I need you rested and sharp for whatever's coming down the road."

He gave a quick sideways glance. "The Cubs hired me right out of law school because I was top of my class in litigation. I'll get you out of this mess. Trust me."

Aaron gave his lawyer a wan smile, leaned his head back against the headrest and closed his eyes.

Chapter Forty-One

Sophie looked up from her computer as the sports editor rushed over to Nate's desk. "Pull up everything you can find on Aaron Reinhart…"

Her hand froze on the mouse.

"He's been arrested for murder."

As if from a distance, Allison gasped. Her hand covered her mouth.

Sophie's breathing thundered in her ears as her vision grayed for the second time in as many weeks. She tried to stand, but her legs wouldn't cooperate. In one fluid motion, she slid beneath her desk as the gray turned to black.

There were voices murmuring around her. In a slit between her eyelids, Sophie surveyed an expanse of white. Forcing her eyelids further apart increased the span of white—a ceiling.

"Hey, she's coming around!" Allison gripped Sophie's hand harder. "Sophie, can you hear me?"

Sophie blinked and turned her head. "What happened?"

"You passed out."

Mr. Andrews, the sports editor, and Mr. McNair hovered nearby. Allison was kneeling beside her. Sophie tried to sit up, but fell back, dizzy.

"I think we should take her to the emergency room," Mr. Andrew said.

"No. Allison, help me sit up."

Allison pulled Sophie upright on the chrome and crimson vinyl couch in the break room. The dizziness was fading. "I'm alright."

"You should get checked out. You did fall into a well this past summer. You're hard-headed as they come, but..." McNair shrugged his shoulders.

Sophie gave a brief smile. "Thanks for the compliment."

McNair squirmed. Compassion and sympathy were not his forte.

"Give me a minute and I'll be back at my desk."

Both men's faces reflected indecision.

"Please."

The men looked at each other, then nodded and left the room.

"Could you get me a water bottle out of the fridge?"

Allison pushed up from her knees.

Sophie grasped the cold bottle, twisting off the top. She took a deep drink. "How long was I out?"

"Ten minutes." Allison crossed her arms. "That's the second time this has happened in less than a month. And you've never passed out before. You have to get checked out by a doctor."

"Have I told you how great that outfit looks with your new B cups?"

And she did look great – stunning actually. After dropping twenty-five pounds around her waist and hips, and four bra sizes, Allison now fit into size six jeans and medium tops. Her shorter haircut brought out the sharp angles of her face.

"Seriously, you think you can distract me by complimenting my new boobs?"

"I didn't faint because of a physical problem..." Sophie turned her gaze away.

Allison uncrossed her arms and eased down onto the couch. "Sophie, I'm worried about you. You're obviously emotionally unstable."

Sophie turned back, quirking an eyebrow.

"No, I didn't mean it the way it sounded. I mean you've been through so much in the last few months, things that would have sent a lesser person to bed for weeks." Allison gripped her hands together. "You've always been *my* rock. Not the other way around. I'm not sure how to help you...how to get rid of the demons or whatever is causing..."

Sophie placed a hand over Allison's hands. "You have been amazing. And you're right; I admit these emotional shocks have taken a toll." She sighed and shook her head. "I can't believe I passed out in front of the whole newsroom. How can I go back in there?"

"There isn't a soul in that room that feels anything other than concern. No one will judge you because they know if they did they would have me to contend with."

Sophie's eyes welled. "You are *my* rock."

Back at her desk, Sophie's thoughts turned to Aaron. *Why did I pass out when I heard he had been arrested?* She sighed. She could deny it all she wanted, but she obviously still had a strong emotional attachment. Her thoughts switched to his murder charge. Logic told her not to get personally involved. If she was to have any chance of healing from the wounds of her past, she needed to stay away from Aaron.

She chewed her lower lip. But...Aaron had dropped everything when she went missing. He wouldn't have given up until he found her. Could she do less, now that he needed her help?

Pray about it, Sophie. God can help.

Sophie sucked in a breath. It was her mother's voice, in her head, like when she was in the well.

God can help.

Sophie had a strong desire to let go of the anger towards God that she had carried all these years. But then she stiffened. God had abandoned her at her greatest hour of need.

"Are you okay? Not going to pass out again?" Nate's eyes reflected his worry. He stood, all five foot of him, in front of her.

"Not likely. My head is still sore from hitting the floor."

Nate gave her a tobacco-stained toothy grin and went back to his desk.

Sophie took in a deep breath and called over to Allison. "Do you have Aaron's cell number?"

Allison looked up and grinned. "No, but I know how I can get it."

The SUV curved around the concrete pillar, coming to a stop before exiting the parking garage. Aaron looked to the right, checking for traffic. A male reporter with a bun atop his head spotted Aaron's vehicle and rushed over.

"Hey, Aaron!" he shouted as he extended his microphone out from his chest.

Aaron turned left and sped away. The glimpse of the reporter camping out near his garage didn't come close to dampening his mood—Sophie wanted to meet with him for dinner. The sound of her voice on the phone had lifted him from the depressive hole he had sunk into. She hadn't said why she wanted to see him, but it was probably linked to his arrest. He shouldn't get his hopes up, but…it was too late.

Aaron parked in front of the *Green Town Tavern* in Waukegan, Illinois. Out on bail, he was not allowed to cross state lines and meet Sophie in Milwaukee. He was early. He smiled at the hostess, then strode over to the bar and ordered a beer. He settled on a tall bar stool, lifted the bottle and looked at the amber liquid. He'd drunk more beer in the last month then he had in the last year. But he wouldn't beat himself up about it and he would stick to one. He took a drink and looked around. It seemed too early for the place to be this crowded. It was a good thing Sophie had made reservations.

"Hey, are you Aaron Reinhart?"

Aaron swiveled to his right. A fiftyish, distinguished-looking man in casual attire was grinning. "I caught one of your games a couple of months ago in Chicago. Three homeruns! I'd like to shake your hand."

A polite smile formed on Aaron's mouth as he shook the man's hand.

"Too bad the Cubs didn't have a great season. My name's Lucas. Mind if I ask a few questions?"

At least it would pass the time as he waited on Sophie.

Twenty-five minutes later, she walked through the door and Aaron's heart stopped. She paused to talk to the hostess. This was not the same girl from the well, with the filthy hair and dirt-encrusted face, or the girl in the hospital bed with the ghostly face and tense demeanor. Aaron stared. How could she be any more beautiful than she had been when they were dating? But...she was.

Sophie turned and headed in his direction, nearly every male eye tracking her movements. She radiated confidence. Her hair hung in loose waves around her shoulders. A green scarf, the exact color of her eyes, haloed her neck.

"Now that's a beautiful woman." Lucas took a sip of his beer.

"Without a doubt," Aaron murmured.

Sophie waved.

"Wow, she waved at me...and is coming this way." Lucus hastily combed fingers through his hair and then cupped a hand over his mouth to test his breath. He lowered it as Sophie walked up.

"Hi, Aaron, our table will be ready in a few minutes."

The man's face fell.

"Sophie, this is Lucas. We've been passing time talking baseball."

Sophie smiled and shook Lucas' hand. "It's a pleasure to meet you."

Lucas lit up like a sunrise. "Do you live here in Waukegan?"

Aaron hid a grin in a sip of his beer.

They had barely settled at their table, put in their drink orders, and perused the menu, when Sophie got to the point of her invitation.

"Aaron, I can't believe you've been arrested." She inhaled and then blew out the breath, talking fast. "I want to help prove your innocence…like you helped me."

Aaron gave an inward sigh at her tone and her words. She hadn't even asked why he failed to come back to visit her at the hospital after saying he would. She wanted to return the favor of him helping her. Nothing personal. She felt she owed him.

"That's not necessary, Sophie. I have an excellent lawyer."

"But you don't have an investigator that can find out the truth about…"

"You don't owe me anything. I don't want you to feel you have to pay me back." His tone had been sharper than he intended. Her eyes reflected her hurt. Aaron's heart clenched. "I'm sorry."

The waiter reappeared with their water and took their orders. As he waded through the tables, Aaron took a breath and started to speak.

"No, Aaron, please…I need to help you."

Aaron looked into her beautiful eyes. "Why?"

Her glossed lips parted as she squared her shoulders. "In the blink of an eye, I shut you out of my life. I know you don't blame me, but…" Sophie slid her eyes away from Aaron's. "I wounded you beyond measure. And you may not believe me, but your pain is my pain."

Aaron reached out and touched the slim fingers Sophie had rested on the table. She jerked, sliding her hand into her lap. Aaron pulled his hand back, wrapping it around his water glass. He ignored the swift pain in his gut. "How do you want to help?"

"By finding the real killer." Sophie pulled a notebook and pen out of her small purse. "Now tell me everything about Ashley Keller, from the moment you met her."

He told her everything except the intimate details of the one night he almost... God forgave him for his temptation, but would he ever forgive himself? Sophie peppered him with dozens of questions as they ate their meal. She finally fell silent. The silence dragged to three minutes as Aaron waited for Sophie to say something.

The waiter removed their plates and asked if they wanted dessert. Sophie shook her head.

"Just the check." Aaron said.

As the waiter walked away, Aaron looked back across the table. "Sophie." No answer. "Sophie."

Her far-off gaze focused on him. "You haven't asked me if I killed her."

"Because I know you didn't. And I don't understand the arrest. The evidence is circumstantial. There has to be something that the DA isn't revealing. I can pressure..."

"I could have."

"Wh...what?"

"It could have been an accident like..." His eyes closed briefly. "...what happened to your father."

Sophie's slightly pink complexion paled. "But...you..."

Aaron sighed. "No, I didn't kill her, accident or otherwise."

Sophie's upper teeth chewed on her lower lip. "We have to find out what they're holding back."

The check arrived and Sophie reached for it.

"No, I've got it."

Sophie slid out of the booth. "Thank you. I'll be in touch."

The imminent loss was excruciating. "Sophie, wait..."

"I'm sorry. I have to go."

Aaron watched Sophie retreat. She had been uncomfortable, fidgety—anxious to leave, once she had the facts of his case. *I don't understand. Why is she unnerved around me?*

Chapter Forty-Two

The crowd yelled as the Green Bay Packers scored a goal late in the third quarter. Cheers resonated from the speakers on his big screen television, but Aaron's mind wasn't on the game. He hit the mute button. The corners of his mouth pulled downward and his brows drew together. He hadn't heard from Sean for days, not since the day he had told him that he had been arrested. And that was not like his friend. In fact, it was the exact opposite of his friend's personality.

Sean should be popping over at least every other day to help Aaron forget about his arrest. He should be insisting they go to the batting cage, or for a run, or a beer—anything to help take Aaron's mind off the looming trial. Why hadn't Sean called and asked to come over to watch the football game with him today? The silence was deafening. Aaron picked up his cell phone from the end table.

"Hello, Aaron."

"Hi, Brigid. Is Sean there?"

"Sure, and he'll just be getting out of the shower."

"I'll hold." Aaron drummed fingers on his thigh as he watched the muted game.

"Hey, boyo."

Aaron's frown deepened. Was it his imagination, or did Sean's tone sound a tad too jovial?

"I wanted to check on you. I haven't heard from you in a few days."

"Sorry, boyo, things have been hectic with Brigid's sister and her three kids visiting. They leave tomorrow."

Aaron let out a relived sigh. "How about a run in the park Thursday?"

"I thought you weren't supposed to leave your condo?"

"I'll deal with the reporters. Staying cooped up is driving me crazy. Can you meet me at ten-thirty?"

A long three seconds of dead air before Sean answered. "Wish I could, Aaron, but I promised Brigid a trip to the Antiques Mall."

Aaron? When was the last time Sean had called him by his first name?

Aaron heard Brigid start to say something and then was suddenly cut off. "I've got to go. I'll call in a couple of days."

Aaron looked down at the silent phone. Sean had never been evasive and abrupt. Something was seriously wrong. He sat the phone on the table. If Sean didn't call back in a couple of days, he would force him to talk about whatever was wrong.

Chapter Forty-Three

Sophie aimed a right hook at the punching bag and followed through with the left. She wasn't very strong…yet, but was slowly improving.

Sophie's trainer, who was holding the bag, craned her neck. "That was better. But your stance is still a little weak."

Sophie adjusted her feet. She had taken up strength training with the punching bag two months ago. Allison had suggested it as a joke to relieve stress, but the idea had merit. Sophie had signed up with a female trainer at the athletic club.

Sweat soaked her black tee shirt and the cotton elastic band across her forehead that prevented perspiration from stinging her eyes. Sophie punched the bag hard. She was getting nowhere with Aaron's case. Detective Burke was so tightlipped she was tempted to go to La Grange and see if someone had sewn his mouth shut. He had sent her a copy of Jack Perry's statement, but refused to comment on whether any new evidence had been obtained since the last time they talked. Her breathing labored, she hit the bag hard again. *What were they keeping so close to the vest?*

"Okay, that's enough for today."

Sophie stood up from her slight crouch. "No, I'm still good."

The trainer started unlacing her gloves. "I won't be responsible for you having a stroke or heart attack from over exertion. It wasn't too long ago you passed out at work."

Sophie's jaw dropped. "How did you know that?"

The trainer bent her head, concentrating on the laces.

Sophie's eyes narrowed. "Allison."

As the trainer pulled off Sophie's right glove, Sophie rehearsed some choice words she was going to have with her friend. But first she was going to finish the conversation she started with the owner of Jack's Rib Shack about the night Ashley disappeared.

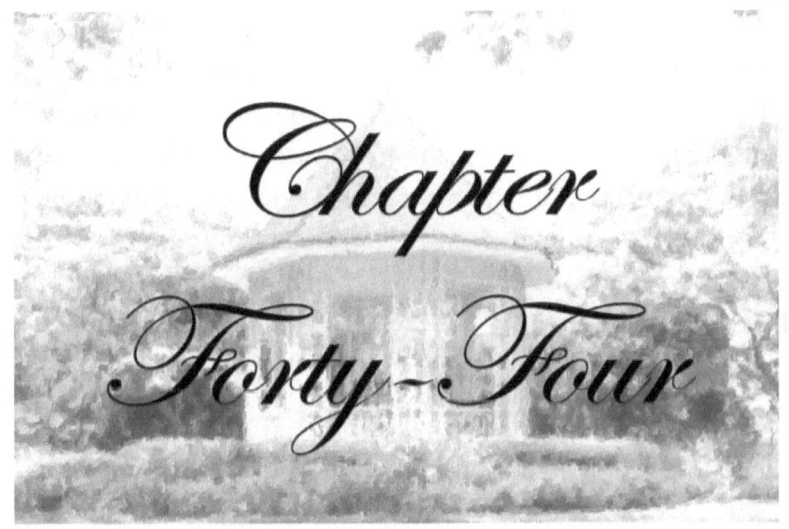

Chapter Forty-Four

Hank glanced up from his computer as Sheriff Cox strode up to his desk. "Got some investigating for you to do on the Keller case."

Jim Cox was one of the most even-tempered men Hank had ever met, but that wasn't in evidence today. "I thought the investigation was finished."

"The DA's office wants Reinhart's vehicle from the night of Ms. Keller's disappearance found and gone over with a fine-tooth comb."

Derek stood in the doorway, a cup of coffee in hand. "Keller case?"

Hank nodded in Derek's direction.

"Wouldn't that be a waste of time? Even if they found her prints among the hundreds of others in the car...so what? They dated." Derek took a sip of his brew.

Jim turned towards Derek. "My mother used to throw a cooked spaghetti noodle at the wall to see if it would stick. If it did, the noodles were done. If the noodle wasn't done, it fell to the floor."

Derek's look of bafflement had Hank stifling a laugh.

"The DA wants as much circumstantial evidence as possible…hoping some of those pieces of evidence, like the spaghetti, will stick in the jurors' minds and get a conviction."

"I'll do my job and so will you, but in my opinion Aaron's being railroaded." Sheriff Cox turned and strode back to his office.

Chapter Forty-Five

The mahogany wall clock bonged ten times. Sunlight passing through the window chased the shadows into corners as Sophie looked up at the clock, raised the oversized paisley-patterned tea cup to her lips with both hands, and took a sip of green tea with honey. She leaned over and set the cup carefully on the French provincial-styled end table and picked up her iPhone. As the number rang she shifted to a more comfortable position on the light gray fabric of her chair and crossed her sock-clad feet on the matching ottoman.

"Jack's Rib Shack."

"Mr. Perry?"

"Yes."

"This is Sophie Madison again. I called you about the investigation into the death of Ashley Keller. I'm sorry about the abrupt end to our conversation a few weeks ago. I…" Sophie took a breath. "To be perfectly honest, I went into shock when you mentioned Aaron's name. He was…ah…is a good friend."

Sophie waited, giving Mr. Perry time to remember their conversation.

"Are you the woman who was in the well with Ashley's bones?"

"Yes."

"Have there been any new leads?"

Sophie's gut clenched. She might as well tell him. He would find out soon enough. "They arrested Aaron Reinhart."

"What? No, not Aaron! I can't believe it." His voice had risen. "He was one of my favorite customers—a real nice guy. He and his friends came to my place a couple of times a week for about a year."

"He didn't kill Ashley, Mr. Perry, and I'm going to prove it by exposing the real killer."

"But they wouldn't have arrested him without evidence."

"All circumstantial. He was in the wrong place at the wrong time."

A sigh came through the phone. "I don't know how I can be of any help. I didn't see anything."

"I'm not concerned with what you didn't see, but what you did. Tell me who was left in the restaurant after Aaron and Ashley left."

"Let's see…a new customer, a male about thirty, who left a few minutes after Aaron, three of the baseball players, and Anne."

Sophie put her phone on speaker as she picked up her spiral notebook and pen.

"When did the baseball players leave?"

"Mike, Jon and Sean left together, about fifteen minutes after Aaron. I was behind the bar when they left and happened to glance out the big front window. I saw Sean split off from the other two and walk around the building towards the back parking lot. Mike and Jon got in a car in the front lot and drove off together." Mr. Perry's recollection jived with the police report.

"Anne was my girlfriend at the time. She stayed to help me clean and lock up."

Sophie jotted the info on the pad. "Did you leave together?"

"Yeah, we were each other's alibi."

Sophie thought for a moment.

"Miss Madison?"

"Oh, sorry, I was absorbing what you said. Did you see Sean come around the building in his car and drive off?"

"No…but he could have left after I finished loading the glasses on the tray and wiping down the table by the window."

Sophie made another note. "Did you hear him drive off at some point?"

There was a pause. "No, not that I recall, but I wasn't listening to hear if he left."

"No one saw Sean leave." Sophie murmured.

"What did you say?"

"Nothing. Thank you, Mr. Perry. If I think of anything else, I'll call. You've been very helpful."

Sophie jumped up and strode to a small mahogany desk a few feet away. She opened a deep pocket drawer and drew out a file from between one of the file dividers. She opened the cover and rifled through the pages until she found the one she wanted: on Sean O'Connor's interview. He stated at the time that he saw no one in the back lot, got in his car and drove off. Sophie pursed her lips. *But if Mr. Perry was wiping down the table at the window, shouldn't he have seen Sean drive off?"*

Sophie stepped back to her chair and picked up her cell phone.

"Hi, Sophie." Aaron's tone was neutral.

"Hi, Aaron. I was wondering if you remember a teammate at Ohio State named Sean O'Connor?"

Sophie heard a stifled laugh. "What's so funny?"

"Hard not to remember. He's my best friend. We were roommates for four years at Ohio State and he plays for the Cubs, too."

Uh, oh. She would have to tread carefully.

"Why are you asking about Sean?"

"I'm...ah, going to interview some of your teammates...looking for leads to the real killer. Could I get his phone number?"

There was a brief hesitation. "Sure...sure. He would be glad to help."

Sophie wrote down the number, thanked Aaron and hung up. She glanced over at the file on her desk. This could get complicated if her suspicions proved correct.

Chapter Forty-Six

The wheels on Aaron's SUV dipped briefly as he entered the driveway and parked beside Sean's white SUV. The house was in Glenview, part of the North Chicago suburbs. He stepped out of his car and closed the door as he stared at the magnificent home. It was over seven thousand square feet, made of white stone and brick. It was Sean's pride and joy.

The son of a pub owner back in Philly, Sean had said he never imagined he would be able to afford a home like this. When he bought it, Brigid grumbled that it was way too big for the two of them. Sean had laughed and said they would fill it with kids, but Brigid's fertility problems had squashed that dream.

Aaron ambled up the walkway to the front door, each exhaled breath misting in the frigid December air. He rang the bell and it echoed through the huge house. The oak door opened and he stared into Brigid's surprised face.

"Aaron! What are you doing here? Sean said...oh, never mind...give me a hug."

Aaron stepped forward and wrapped his arms around the big boned frame of his friend's wife.

Brigid pulled back from the embrace. "I am sorry for your troubles, *a chara*."

"Thank you. Is Sean home?"

"He is. Come in out of the cold." Brigid led Aaron across the tiled floor of the large foyer and past a marble staircase with a wrought iron railing along the left wall.

Once she had him settled on the soft-as-butter, leather couch in the den, she left to find Sean. Aaron glanced around the familiar room. Whenever he passed time in here, he was simply amazed at the tasteful, subtle masculine decorating style Brigid had executed throughout the room. She should have been an interior decorator instead of a nurse.

A large painting depicting the craggy hills of County Cork and the coastline of the Atlantic Ocean hung over the mantle of a black marble fireplace. County Cork was the home of Sean's father before his grandparents moved the family to the United States.

"Hey, boyo, this is a surprise."

Aaron looked up at the greeting.

Sean stood in the framed doorway. Aaron blinked. Creases had formed around Sean's mouth and marched across his forehead. His complexion, normally a healthy ruddy tint, was almost devoid of color. But it was Sean's haunted eyes that had Aaron's hands clench with concern.

Aaron rose off the couch. "You didn't call me back. I came to check on you."

A flash of an unidentifiable emotion shone out of the brown eyes and then disappeared.

"You shouldn't have driven all the way out here. I was going to call you back today." Sean's eyes flicked to the left.

His friend was lying. "Sean, level with me. What's going on?"

Sean shifted his feet and rubbed the side of his face. "Look, now's not a good time to talk. I've got to pick up Corky at the vet."

Aaron resumed his seat on the sofa, placed his hands on his knees and said, in a voice laced with steel, "I'm not leaving until you tell me what's up."

Sean's mask of nonchalance collapsed and was replaced by misery and guilt. He stood in the doorway, mute. Aaron had known Sean for fourteen years. No matter what the problem, Sean had tackled it head on. He grabbed it by the throat, wrestled it to the ground until it cried 'uncle.' He never backed away or admitted defeat. But that was what was reflected on his face—abject defeat.

Sean grabbed his head on both sides and squeezed, his voice laced with agony. "This is a nightmare…and I can't wake up."

Invisible cords pulled tight across Aaron's chest. "What nightmare? Talk to me."

Sean licked his pale lips, looked over his shoulder then back at Aaron. "It's Ashley. But I can't talk…"

Both men jerked at the sound of a loud thud and then two more. Sean raced from the doorway, Aaron on his heels. He barely avoided a fall in the foyer as Brigid's orange cat, Ginger, streaked across his path, hissing. He headed straight for the crumbled form of his wife at the bottom of the stairs.

Sean fell to his knees. "Brigid!'

Brigid groaned as Aaron skidded to a stop a couple of feet away.

Another groan and then Brigid's eyes opened. Sean eased a muscular arm under her shoulders.

"*A runsearc*, my love, my love."

Aaron had his cell phone out. "Should I call an ambulance?"

"No." Brigid struggled to rise.

"Don't move. Something could be broken." Sean tried to hold her down.

"Sean O'Connor, you let me up or you'll be living to regret it."

Sean leveraged Brigid to a seated position. She cautiously moved each of her limbs and rotated her head. Vivid bruises were starting to appear on her arms.

"Nothing's broken. Help me stand." Brigid winced as she rose. A small cut bled at her hairline.

"I'll be taking you to the emergency room—now." Sean's tone brooked no opposition.

Brigid nodded.

Aaron held on to Brigid as Sean raced off for his wallet, keys, and Brigid's purse. After he returned, Aaron held the door as Sean helped his wife out of the house.

"How did you fall, love?"

Brigid grimaced as she stepped down off the portico. "I didn't see Ginger on the stairs. I tripped over her."

"That stupid…." Anger laced Sean's words.

"Not her fault. Though I am a bit miffed at her myself, truth be told."

Aaron helped Sean get Brigid in his car. He gave a thumbs up as Sean backed down the driveway and drove off down the street. He entered his car, turned on the ignition and shifted the gear shift into reverse. His unfinished conversation with Sean was forgotten.

Chapter Forty-Seven

The lamp's glow reflected on the dark panes of the den window as Sean tucked the throw around his wife's shoulders and handed her a cup of Irish coffee. She gave him a wan smile.

"How liberal were you with the whiskey, *Mo chroí*?"

"Enough to lift your spirits, but not too much that you'd be falling down the stairs again."

Brigid grinned up at her husband. "I'll drink to that." She took a sip of the hot liquid and sighed. "I canna believe I was so clumsy."

Sean laid a hand on her riotous red curls. "I'm glad bumps and bruises are all you suffered."

"Aye, I'm glad nothing's broken."

Sean's light banter became serious. "Don't scare me like that again. I would die if I lost you."

'When Irish Eyes are Smiling' sang out from Sean's phone. He lifted it off the end table, his brows drawing together as he read the caller ID.

"Hello?"

"Mr. O'Connor, my name is Sophie Madison. I was wondering if I could speak to you about Aaron."

"Just a moment." Sean looked down at his wife.

"I'll do. Take your call."

He kissed her forehead and left the den, speaking into his iPhone. "Is Aaron alright?"

"Yes. I didn't mean to worry you. Aaron gave me your number. I'd like to ask you a couple of questions about the night Ashley Keller went missing."

Sean came to an abrupt halt in the middle of the foyer.

"I'm hoping to prove he didn't kill her."

Sean cleared his throat. "You're the woman that fell in the well."

"Yes. Has Aaron told you anything about me?"

"A little." Sean moved over to the staircase and sat on the first riser.

"What did he…? Never mind, that's not why I called. Can you give me the details of what you remember from the night Ashley went missing?"

Sean's hand holding the phone trembled slightly as he told Sophie what he remembered.

"So you left the restaurant and went to your vehicle in the back lot. You didn't see anyone."

"That's right."

"Then you got in your vehicle and drove off."

"Yes."

"How many minutes was it from when you walked to the back lot, entered your car, and drove onto the street in front of the restaurant?"

Sean pushed to his feet and ran the fingers of his free hand through his black hair. "Why do you need to know that?"

"Even a seemingly trivial detail could be the clue that cracks this case."

"It couldn't have been more than a couple of minutes."

Silence.

"Ms. Madison?"

"Thank you for talking to me, Mr. O'Connor. I'll be in touch."

Sean pressed the *end* icon to disconnect the call. He swallowed heavily, his gaze drifting furtively to the den.

"He's lying." Sophie made the statement aloud in the packed Mexican restaurant as she ended her call to Sean, set her cell phone on the table and took a sip of water.

"Who's lying?" Allison tossed her tote bag on the booth seat and scooted across from Sophie.

"Sean O'Connor."

Allison eyed her friend. "I know that look. You got a whiff of the scent and are about to start baying as you follow the trail."

Sophie guffawed. "Are you calling me a bloodhound?"

"In the most complimentary way."

The waiter walked over and Allison ordered a white wine. "Come on, share a wine with me."

Sophie shook her head. "Not tonight."

"Okay, spill. You found something on the 'girl in the well' case."

Sophie took another sip of water. "Maybe."

Allison folded her hands on the table. "Well?"

"I'm fairly sure Aaron's best friend, Sean, is lying about when he left the parking lot the night Ashley went missing."

The waiter, a tall, thin man with a receding hairline and dressed in a bright orange shirt and black pants, set Allison's wine on the brightly colored tablecloth. "Ready to order?"

"I'll have quesadillas." Sophie said.

"Chimichangas for me." Allison handed over the menu. "What makes you think he's lying?"

Sophie told her about her conversation with Mr. Perry and then with Sean.

Allison leaned back in the booth. "I agree. If he left right away, the owner would have seen his car through the window. Why lie? What's he hiding?"

"Oh, I don't know—manslaughter—murder?"

"I love your dry wit."

Their meals arrived, plates hot and food steaming.

Allison breathed in appreciatively. "I love Mexican food."

Allison grabbed her knife and fork as Sophie lifted a quesadilla wedge and took a bite.

Sophie chewed and then swallowed. "The problem is going to be proving my suspicion that Sean didn't leave right away."

Sophie took another bite then continued when her mouth was free of food. "Sean is not going to be forthcoming. I need to talk to Aaron. He said they were roommates in college. I need to establish a time line. When did Aaron get back to their dorm or apartment? When did Sean get back?"

Allison raised her wine glass. "Shall we toast to unraveling the puzzle and catching the bad guy?"

Sophie clinked her water glass to Allison's wine glass, then took a sip.

Chapter Forty-Eight

Aaron rose at dawn and strode into the living room, stopping in front of the bay window. He sucked in a breath as the glow of the wintery sun rose over the lake. He tried to empty his mind and take in the beauty of the scene. He couldn't. He closed his eyes and prayed.

"Lord, my life has turned upside down. Forgive me for not turning to you before now for help and guidance. One particular sin, and you know which one, weighs heavily on me and I have not felt deserving of your mercy and grace. I unburden all before you now and ask for your peace that passes all understanding. Thank you for all you do and have done for me in the past."

Aaron opened his eyes. As had happened many times before when he prayed, his spirit lightened and gratitude settled in his heart. He walked into the kitchen to make coffee.

His iPhone vibrated as Aaron brought a forkful of scrambled eggs to his mouth. He set down the fork and picked up the phone, sliding his finger to the right across the screen.

"Good morning, Sophie." His heartbeats quickened.

"I didn't wake you, did I? I know it's early."

"No, I've been up a couple of hours."

"Can I ask a couple of questions about…"

Aaron finished the sentence. "…the night Ashley went missing?" He lifted the fork and shoved the eggs in. No sense in letting his food get cold.

"You must be psychic." Aaron heard the smile in her voice.

"Mind if I eat my breakfast while we talk?"

"No, go right ahead."

Aaron heard a page turning. "I need to establish a time line. When did you and Sean…ah…and the other two teammates return to your dorms?"

"Sean and I had an apartment off campus. Mike and Jon were in the dorm and I don't know when they got back that night."

"Not a problem, I'll talk to them later."

"Sean was already at the apartment when I returned."

Sophie's tone evoked surprise. "What? Mr. Perry told me he left fifteen minutes after you."

Aaron swallowed a bite of toast with honey. "You talked to Jack?"

"Yes. Why did Sean get there first?"

Aaron took a sip of coffee to clear his mouth. "After the argument with Ashley, I was still…well…upset. I went to the gym on campus to work out my anger and frustration. I even messed up my right hand hitting the punching bag bare-knuckled."

"That was dumb. You always wear gloves. First thing my trainer taught me."

Aaron laid the piece of bacon back on the plate. "Trainer?"

"Yeah, I've been training with the bag for about two months now."

Aaron smiled as he picked up the bacon again. "Want to be sparing partners?"

Sophie laughed. "Not in your wildest dreams." Her tone changed back to all business. "How long were you at the gym?"

"About an hour." Silence. "Are you still there?"

"Yes, sorry, just thinking."

"Of what?"

"Nothing. Thanks for your help. I'll talk to you soon."

Aaron shook his head, disconnected the call, and shoved the last of the eggs into his mouth.

Cold sunshine speared through the partially open blinds, patterning the beige carpet of Sean and Brigid's bedroom. Restless, Sean paced back and forth in front of the queen-size canopy bed. He stopped and plopped down on the pale blue comforter. He never, in a million years, thought that Aaron would be arrested for Ashley's death. The guilt had been eating at him and…he had almost told Aaron the truth. If he had, he would have lost everything in this world that mattered to him. He frowned as he reviewed the phone conversation with Aaron's ex-girlfriend.

Sean jumped off the bed and started pacing again. He had to get a handle on this. Push all emotions aside; divert Aaron and Sophie's attention off of him. But how? He started chewing on his lip as he paced. He halted and pivoted to the nightstand to pick up his phone. He punched in the number and Aaron answered on the third ring.

"How you doing, boyo?" Sean made his tone upbeat.

"Not bad, washing up the breakfast dishes. How is Brigid today? Any pain?"

"Some soreness; she's resting in the den downstairs. I wanted to apologize for my behavior."

"Yeah, you had me worried. You looked like death warmed over when I saw you."

"You're right, but I'm fine now. I was torn up about you being arrested. Shock and all. But I've got my fighting mojo back and I'm here for you."

The relief was palatable in Aaron's tone. "Great."

"How about a run? Take some reporters on a merry chase."

Aaron laughed. "Sounds good. But we better make it a slow jog. I don't want to aggravate my knee more than necessary. I'll stop by in a couple of hours."

"See you then."

Sean set the phone back on the nightstand. Ms. Madison wouldn't be as easy to divert. He strode over to his walk-in closet to change into sweats for his run in the park.

Sophie abandoned the article she was working on and rose from her desk to refill her cup with hot water. Back at her desk, she dropped a fresh green tea bag into her cup. She poked it with her finger to make it sink. Her shoulders slumped. The conversation with Aaron earlier hadn't gone as planned. No way to know what time Sean got back to the apartment without asking him point blank. The police in Columbus hadn't asked him. How was she going to find out how long he lingered in the parking lot? And why? Her gut said it had something to do with Ashley.

Nate walked over. "Hey Sophie, can I borrow your stapler?"

"Sure, Nate."

Sophie opened her right drawer. As she reached for the stapler, one of her fingers brushed a sharp-edged object. She pulled her fingers back. Her middle finger had been pricked. A tiny droplet of blood formed. She handed Nate the stapler with her left hand then plucked a tissue from the box and pressed it to the cut. She bent her head to look inside the drawer for whatever had pricked her. She pulled the drawer wider.

A framed photo was pushed up against the back of the drawer. Sophie pulled it out carefully. The tip of a tiny nail stuck out from the right lower corner. Her gaze roamed over the happy couple silhouetted against a mountain. Six months ago, this picture had been proudly displayed on her desk. It was a picture of her and Bryan.

One finger traced the smile on the lips of her handsome ex-fiancé. Sudden guilt washed over her; she hadn't returned his last few calls. When was the last time she talked to him? She took in a deep breath. It was time. She owed him the truth. And once she told him…once he understood…then maybe they could start over.

Aaron's face rose to the front of her mind and her heart skipped a beat. *No.* A relationship with Aaron was impossible. She shook her head to clear her mind of the image.

Sophie dialed Bryan's cell.

"Sophie?"

"Hi, Bryan. I'm sorry I haven't gotten back to you. I've been so busy with trying to find out who killed the girl that was in the well with me. It's no excuse I know, but I am sorry."

"It's okay. I know how oblivious you can be when investigating a story."

Sophie's tone grew soft. "You've always been the most patient, understanding man." She took a breath. "Bryan, could we get together in the next couple of days? I owe you an explanation about my behavior the last time I was at your condo…when I broke our engagement. I'm ready to talk about why I kept postponing our wedding."

The silence went on for a long time. Had they been cut off? "Bryan, are you there?"

Sophie heard a deep sigh. "Sophie, you don't need to explain anything to me."

"Yes, I do. I'm ashamed of myself for how I treated you. You've always bee…"

"Sophie."

Sophie's shoulders tensed at the tone of Brian's voice.

"I'm dating someone. We met at the Governor's Ball last month. I…well…my feelings for her are…strong."

"I'm too late." Sophie whispered.

"What did you say?"

Sophie cleared her throat. "Bryan, I'm glad…you found…that you're happy." Could he hear her anguish?

He had. "Sophie, I'm sorry if I've hurt you. It's the last thing I wanted to do. I've barely talked to you in the last five months. You never indicated that you wanted to get back together."

Tears threatened to fall. "I wish you all the best. Take care, Bryan."

She discontented the call, her gaze drawn back to the picture laying on her desk. A tear slid over a lower eye lid as she placed the picture in the waste can beside her desk.

Chapter Forty-Nine

It was six in the evening when Sophie hung the last of her mama's ornaments on the tree she had picked up the night before from the Christmas tree lot a few blocks away. She stepped back and eyed it critically. As far as she could tell, she had placed the ornaments in the same positions as the last Christmas she had spent with her mama and papa. Her papa had had no interest in Christmas after her mama died, but Sophie had carried on most of her mother's Christmas traditions every year to honor her memory.

Sophie was grateful the ornaments hadn't been destroyed in the fire. Her father had decided to replace the decades old insulation in the attic three days before the fire that destroyed her home. All the ornaments and other holiday decorations had been removed to the barn. She brushed a finger along the smooth surface of her mama's favorite ornament, the clear glass ball with the silver angel hanging by a thin thread inside. She turned her head when the doorbell rang.

"Hey, Allison." Sophie's eyes widened. "Why in the world are you all dressed up for our girl's night in?"

Allison had on a pair of black skinny jeans, a shimmering emerald V-neck sweater, the hem hitting mid-thigh, and black two-inch heels. She also had new highlights streaking her brown hair. Sophie looked down at her own casual attire of worn jeans and black sweater.

"Wow, the tree looks great." Allison pushed past Sophie.

Allison led Sophie into the kitchen and set a brown bag on the round glass table and held up a bottle. "I've got the sushi and wine."

"Don't change the subject. Why are you all dressed up?"

Allison reached in the bag and removed the sushi. "How about a couple of wine glasses, plates and…"

Sophie strode over and lifted the sushi from Allison's hands as she glared at her friend.

"Fine, I might be meeting someone for drinks later." Allison took the sushi back and set it on the table. "Now, go get the glasses."

"With who?"

"Go on, scoot, nosey Nellie."

Sophie turned and, with a good-natured huff, gathered up glasses and plates. After placing them on the table, she returned to the kitchen counter for the salad, two bowls, and utensils. After she and Allison were settled at the table and using the chopsticks to dip the sushi rolls in soy sauce, Sophie asked her question again. "Who?"

"Liam." Allison concentrated on her food.

"Who?"

"Liam. You know, the new reporter."

Sophie's puzzled expression cleared and her eyebrows shot up. "The kid that started last week? The *kid* that graduated college last year? He can't be more than twenty-two." Sophie leaned back in her chair. "You can't be serious."

"He's older than he looks. He is actually twenty-five, with a master's degree."

Sophie shook her head. "Does he know how old you are?"

Allison ignored the question as her eyes lit up. "He has a great sense of humor. We've been talking a lot in the break room. We have similar backgrounds. And the best part...he didn't know me before...before who I am now."

Sophie was puzzled. "Who you are now? You're the same person you've always been."

It was Allison's turn to shake her head. "You know what a disaster dating has been for me. Guys asked me out because of my boobs...period. They didn't care to get to know...me."

Allison took a sip of wine. Sophie wanted to deny what she said, but couldn't because it was true. Each time Allison dated someone new, she had crossed her fingers, hoping for a different outcome. But there wasn't one. By the second date, they were all reaching for her large breasts. Sometimes they didn't even wait for the second date. To her credit, Allison always slapped their hands away and never saw them again—until Ron.

Handsome, charismatic, funny—Ron had really hurt Allison. He took her on dates, pretended to ignore her large breasts, pulled her in, and weakened her defenses. He had waited—waited until she fell hook, line, and sinker in love. A month after she lost her virginity, he decided it was time to move on.

Sophie sighed. "Okay, I will reserve all judgment. Besides, who am I to talk, I pushed the most understanding, loyal, compassionate...."

Allison said a name, covering it up with a cough.

"What did you say?"

"Aaron." Cough.

"I know you didn't say 'Aaron.'"

Allison forked some salad in her mouth, talking as she chewed. "Hey, you were the one describing him."

"I was not. I was describing Bryan."

Allison swallowed. "Oh, my mistake. Aaron's not understanding, loyal, and compassionate."

"I didn't say that."

"What would you say about the man that's still in love with you, would do anything for you. The man you're still in love..."

"I am not!"

Allison's eyes were compassionate. "You are. Don't let this tragedy from the past destroy your future with a man who will love you with every fiber of his being from this life into the next."

Sophie's eyes shone with moisture. "I told you he saw what my father did. And even if he didn't pity me...when I'm around him, I have to struggle hard to keep the images of what he must have seen from solidifying in my mind."

Allison's voice was soft. "Oh, Sophie, I could never even begin to understand the trauma you experienced, but please try to forgive your father...forgive Aaron. But most of all, forgive yourself."

Sophie wiped her eyes with her napkin, took a breath, and squared her shoulders. "I can't talk or think about this now. I need to find Ashley's killer. And I need your opinion."

Sophie took a fortifying drink from her glass. "For the past two weeks, I have chased down every lead possible that could help me figure out when Sean got back to the apartment. I talked to baseball players that were with Sean that night. They went straight back to their dorms. They have alibis. I found the other six students who lived in the other three apartments in Aaron's building. They either didn't see Sean enter the building or don't remember what time it was when he returned.

"I called the businesses around Jack's Rib Shack to see if anyone noticed Sean or Ashley, but they had all closed by the time Aaron and the other players left. I was hoping to uncover a witness the police missed when Ashley disappeared. Nothing. Dead end."

Allison chewed her food, a question in her eyes as she watched Sophie take a bite of salad and follow with a sip of wine.

Sophie took a breath. "What do you think about me being upfront with Aaron about my suspicions of his friend?"

Allison pushed back from the table and crossed a leg. "I don't think he'll listen to you. It's his best friend."

"I agree, but if I can plant a seed of doubt, maybe it will grow and he will ask the hard questions I can't."

"What questions?"

"Did you kill Ashley?" Sophie picked up her last sushi roll and, after dipping it, took a bite.

"Got to say, that's not too subtle." Allison picked up her glass. "But, I think you should share your doubts with Aaron. Even if he gets angry with you for placing suspicion on his friend...so what? You're trying to get him cleared of a murder charge."

Sophie took a sip of wine. "Okay, I will.

Chapter Fifty

Aaron picked up his iPhone and read the name of the caller. It was his lawyer. He hit the mute button on the remote. He took in a breath as he lifted the phone to his ear. None of his calls, so far, had any good news.

"Good morning, Jonathan."

"Morning, Aaron. I promised to keep you abreast of any developments in your case. I've finally got my hands on the forensic report for the skeleton. Good news for you. The cause of death was a blow to the forehead by a large fist."

It took Aaron a few seconds to absorb this new information. "I can't believe anyone would punch Ashley in the face. It's…unbelievable."

"Well, someone did."

"Why is that good news for me?"

"Because I talked to a doctor and he said a blow like that would have damaged the hand of the person landing the blow. You argued with Ashley, but said you didn't touch her and I believe you. We can get your roommate to testify that your hand wasn't injured."

Aaron's body went numb.

"Aaron?"

"I...I...I." Aaron clenched his teeth together and closed his eyes.

Mr. Richard's concern laced his words. "What's wrong?"

Aaron took three deep breaths and then spoke slowly. "It...It was...injured."

"What?"

Aaron fought for control of his words. "I...didn't hit Ashley, but...but I did injure...my hand that same night. I told you...I...I...went to the gym after I left Ashley. I felt pain in my right hand with the first bare-knuckle hit to the punching bag. I lighten up on the punches after that, but by the time I got home the knuckles were swollen twice their size."

Mr. Richards voice was curt. "Did anyone notice the injury to your hand?"

"Sean. He thought I needed to get it checked out. It was hurting quite a bit when I woke up the next day. I took his advice and went to see the doctor to make sure I hadn't broken any bones."

Dead silence.

Aaron's gut clenched. "That's why they arrested me, isn't it? The detectives must have obtained a copy of the medical record."

Aaron's shoulders slumped in the recliner. He really could be convicted of a crime he didn't commit.

"Possibly. The good news is that I will be prepared when the prosecutor enters it as evidence at your trial. We have to track down someone who was at the gym that night and saw you punching the bag. I need you to try and remember anyone who may have seen you with the punching bag, while I track down the gym records of the people who were working out at the same time you were there." Mr. Richard's tone was encouraging. "Aaron, don't get discouraged. I'll be in contact again soon."

The line went dead. Aaron turned his head and stared out the bay window at the calm lake, a tremor passing through the fingers of the hand holding the phone.

The waiter set the glass of sweet ice tea on the table and asked if Sophie wanted to order. She shook her head, explaining she was waiting on someone. She squeezed a lemon wedge between her thumb and finger until the flow of juice stopped. A memory of her mama popped into her mind and she smiled.

From the age of six until her mama died, she would come home from school to find a green-tinted tumbler next to a plate of praline cookies on the kitchen table. Sophie would slide onto the seat and her mama would pluck a lemon wedge from a small plate on the table in front of her and squeeze the juice into Sophie's iced tea.

Sometimes, her mama would pull out a chair and sit with her, telling her stories about growing up on the plantation, while Sophie ate cookies and drank her tea. Her Mama had said that one of her very favorite things to do on hot summer days was to sit on the veranda with a good book and a pitcher of cold sweet tea.

Sophie was jolted back to the present by a blast of cold air. She should have asked for a table away from the door. Aaron removed his jacket and draped it over one of the chairs at the table. He pulled out a chair across from Sophie and sat down.

Sophie greeted Aaron with a smile. "Thanks for driving to Waukegan again. This was something I couldn't talk to you about over the phone."

The waiter magically appeared and took Aaron's drink order. "I should be thanking you. You drove an hour to get here. It only took me thirty minutes."

He looked around the restaurant as he opened his menu.

Sophie fiddled with her napkin-wrapped silverware. "I'm afraid you're not going to like what I have to say."

Aaron glanced around the menu at Sophie and sighed. "Great, more bad news."

Sophie's fingers stilled. "What's the other bad news?"

The waiter returned with Aaron's tea and asked if they were ready to order. Aaron said he would have whatever Sophie was having. She ordered shrimp alfredo for two.

Aaron said, "My lawyer called yesterday. We've made an educated guess on why I was arrested and it's not good."

Sophie tensed. "Why?

"Ashley died from a blow to the forehead."

Sophie's eyebrows drew together. "A blow to the forehead?"

"She was hit in the face by a large fist."

"A fist?" Her jaw dropped open. "But…but why are they sure you did it?"

Aaron sighed. "Remember when I told you about going to the gym and hitting the punching bag with my bare knuckles?"

Sophie sucked in a breath and covered her mouth as Aaron repeated the conversation he had with his lawyer. He saw the fear that had plagued him since yesterday reflected in Sophie's eyes.

"Oh, Aaron, this is horrible!"

"Thanks for the boost of confidence."

"Is there anyone who can testify you were in the gym?"

"I didn't recognize anyone that night. My lawyer is trying to track down the few people who were at the gym when I was working out. But I don't hold out much hope."

"Without a solid alibi of someone actually seeing you punching the bag…" Sophie looked away.

"I could get convicted of a crime I didn't commit."

The waiter placed their meals on the table and asked if there was anything else. Both shook their heads.

Sophie unwrapped her utensils, picked up her fork and then placed it back on the table, her appetite gone. Aaron hadn't even touched his utensils.

She placed her hands on either side of her plate. "We have to assume you won't have an alibi. Which means the only way to make sure you don't go to prison is to find the real killer." Sophie took a breath. "Here comes the part you're not going to like."

Aaron stared, his face inscrutable.

"We have to consider Sean."

Aaron's eyebrows shot up. "What?" He shook his head. "That's absolutely crazy, Sean couldn't hurt a fly, much less punch Ashley in the face."

"He lied to me on the phone."

"What do you mean, he lied to you?"

Sophie told Aaron everything she knew and suspected about Sean the night of the disappearance and what she asked on the phone and how he had answered. Various emotions crossed his face as she talked: disbelief, anger, and incredulity. But the most prevalent was stubborn denial. As soon as she stopped talking, Aaron went on the attack.

"Sophie, your speculation that Sean killed Ashley is so off base it's laughable."

The waiter walked over, his smile turning to concern at the untouched plates. "Is something wrong with the food?"

Sophie shook her head. "I'd like a box."

"One for me, too."

The waiter walked off to get their boxes and the check for the uneaten meals.

"Then why did he lie on the phone? Mr. Perry had a line of sight out of the window for a good ten minutes after Sean left the restaurant. It would have taken Sean less than a minute to get to his car. Less than a minute to start it, back up, and leave the lot. Mr. Perry would have seen him leave."

Aaron leaned forward in his chair. "You don't know that. Jack could have looked away long enough for Sean to drive off."

"So someone came into the parking lot, grabbed Ashley and dragged her off by foot in the five to seven minutes between when you drove off and Sean walked into the back lot?"

"It's possible."

The tiniest flash of doubt crossed Aaron's face.

"Without a sound. No screaming or yelling? No signs of a struggle? Aaron, Ashley had no car. She planned to leave with you. When that didn't happen, she could have asked Sean for a ride home and…maybe she said something about you that made him mad and he hit her. Then he panicked when he realized she was dead."

Aaron sat in stubborn silence.

Sophie's voice reflected her frustration. "What about Ashley's body being found in the well? Sean is the most likely to have picked that spot, knowing…"

"He didn't know about the farm."

"What?" Sophie stammered.

"I never told him about you and me."

The waiter returned with the boxes and Aaron paid the bill, over Sophie's protests.

Sophie picked up the thread of the conversation. "Aaron, is there any way Sean could have found out about the farm?"

Aaron shook his head. "The first time he even heard your name is after you went missing and I said you had been my girlfriend in high school."

Sophie thought furiously. *If Sean didn't know about her childhood home it was possible he didn't kill her. But there was still his lie about leaving the parking lot right away. He could have talked to Ashley.* Sophie frowned. *But why not say so?* She refused to let her only lead to freeing Aaron—go. She unconsciously chewed on her index fingernail, a bad habit from middle school. She dropped her finger, looked up.

"How has Sean been acting since you've been arrested?"

Aaron's voice was cautious. "He was upset for awhile, but now he's fine."

"Upset how?"

Aaron shifted as if he was suddenly uncomfortable in his seat.

"Aaron, please, I know he's your friend, but if you sensed something was off with him, any little thing, you have to tell me."

"I should go."

He started to rise. Sophie grabbed his hand. "Please."

Aaron looked down at her hand holding his and sank back in his seat. He rubbed his forehead with his fingers as if to knead away a headache. "Okay."

Aaron told her about Sean's odd behavior after being told about the arrest. And the conversation he had with Sean at his house.

"How did he look when you saw him in the doorway?"

"Like he hadn't slept in days."

"Did you get a sense about how he was feeling?"

Aaron chewed his lip. "He looked...haunted."

"Aaron, you have to talk to him again."

Aaron pushed his chair back and stood. "No."

He grabbed his jacket off the chair and turned away. Sophie grabbed her coat and clutch, following him out the door, their meals still on their plates, the open take-out boxes empty.

"Aaron, wait." She shivered as she shoved her arms in the sleeves of her coat.

A Christmas carol filled the air as a customer opened the door of the bookstore next door. Aaron turned around, his gaze unreadable.

"I think he's afraid. He started to tell you something about Ashley before his wife's accident."

"Drop it, Sophie." He turned away.

Sophie yelled at his retreating back. "Prove me wrong then! Find out what he started to tell you before he had a couple of days to regroup and act like everything was fine. You want to know. I saw the doubt in your eyes."

Aaron didn't answer. He reached his SUV and slid into the driver's seat. Clutch gripped tightly in her hand, Sophie stomped off to her parked car.

Chapter Fifty-One

Mr. McNair, arms folded, stood in the doorway to his office and swiveled his eyes in Sophie's direction. She picked up the handset to the phone on her desk and pretended to answer it, keeping an eye on her boss. He switched his gaze to Allison and yelled. Sophie replaced the phone as her friend hurried to the editor's office. She picked up her cell phone and started to tap in the number Mr. Perry had given her. It vibrated in her hand. *Aaron.* She took a breath before answering. "Aaron, I'm sorry I yelled at you last…"

"You were right."

"What?"

"I had time to think about what you said and something is off with Sean. Whenever we get together for a run lately it's like…well…this is going to sound weird, but it's like Sean is trying to *act* like Sean. I know that doesn't make sense."

"No, it does. I know exactly what you mean. I've seen people do the same thing when I interview them. They project the person they think I want them to be."

"I'm going over to his house in a few hours for a run. I'll talk to him."

"His guard is going to be up. The only way to get it down is to remind him about what good friends you are. How grateful you are for his support. How he is the most honest, trustworthy...you get my drift. If he feels guilty about something, you have to bring it out."

Aaron sighed heavily. "I hope your suspicions are wrong and he isn't hiding something...I hope we're both wrong."

Aaron hung up. Sophie frowned at the phone for a few seconds before punching in the number she had started to call when Aaron called her. She ducked her head behind her computer as Allison left the editor's office and Mr. McNair again appeared in the doorway. He frowned in Noah's direction. It was uncanny how he seemed to know when his employees weren't working on newspaper business. The unfinished article on her computer stared her in the face.

Normally, she was the dedicated journalist, never making personal calls on company time. But, all she could think about was helping Aaron. She closed her eyes. *He was not going to prison.*

"Hello?"

Sophie's eyes snapped open. "Mrs. Reed? Anne Reed?"

"Yes. Who is this?"

"Sophie Madison. Jack Perry gave me your number. I wanted to ask you a few questions about the night Ashley Keller went missing. Do you mind?"

There was a slight hesitation. "No...I guess that would be okay. It's just a surprise after all this time."

"Yes, I'm sure it is. Did you know that her body was found?"

Mrs. Reed sighed. "Yes, poor girl."

Sophie had memorized Anne's statement and asked a few questions the police asked to check Anne's memory and reliability. Thirteen years was a long time, and memories could fade. But all of Anne's answers matched the police report. Her memory seemed to be as sharp as it had been thirteen years ago. Sophie zeroed in on the one question and answer from the report that had the most potential.

"It's stated in the report that you made a trip to the dumpster behind the restaurant before Jack locked up."

"Yes, I did."

"And there were no cars in the back lot when you went to the dumpster?"

"Just Jack's car. We rode together to the restaurant that day."

"You didn't see anyone around the area?"

"No."

Sophie frowned. What other question could she ask? "Mrs. Reed, did you notice any vehicles on the adjoining properties?"

"Well…"

Sophie straightened in her chair. "Take your time."

"There was an old sedan parked behind the hardware store. The only reason I noticed it was because my daddy had one like it back in the late seventies."

Sophie's heart rate increased, but this could be nothing. "Had you noticed it before…on other nights?"

"No, and I would have because I took the trash out most nights."

"Had there been any other cars parked behind the hardware store at that time of the night?"

"Nope, that's the first one I'd seen parked there, that late at night, since I'd been helping Jack close up."

"Did you see anyone near the car, or maybe a shadow of someone?"

"Didn't notice anyone, but I was only out there for about a minute."

"I didn't see this sedan in your statement."

"Didn't occur to me to mention it. The cops just asked about vehicles in Jack's lot."

"Thank you, Mrs. Reed. If you think of anything else let me know."

Sophie wrote down the information. She would call Aaron and ask about the car Sean had driven at the time. She glanced around the computer in time to see Mr. McNair headed her way. She dropped her phone in a drawer and started typing on her keyboard.

Jonathan Richards hung up the phone. He crossed out the last name on the list. None of the men he had talked to on the phone remembered anyone at the gym using the punching bag the night Aaron was there. He removed his glasses and rubbed his eyes. He would need a miracle to get Aaron acquitted.

The verdict would come down to whether or not the jurors believed the state had proved their case beyond a reasonable doubt. He needed to foster that doubt in the jurors' minds, but the evidence was damning—very damning. The District Attorney had confirmed his supposition: they had the medical records proving Aaron had damaged his right hand the night Ashley went missing.

Jonathan leaned back in his office chair and stared at the ceiling. The DA would paint a vivid picture with the palette of the circumstantial evidence— there would be no room left on the canvas for even the tiniest brushstroke of doubt.

He put his glasses back on and pulled open the deep bottom drawer in his desk. He lifted out the Columbus Police file. He opened the folder and stared at the top page. He had already been over it twice and he would go over it another ten times if that's what it took to find the one small thing that could raise that doubt in the minds of the jurors. If he didn't, his client was going to prison. His eyes flicked back and forth as he read.

Sophie took a cautious sip of the hot tea and then yelped as some of the hot liquid burned her tongue. She placed the mug on her desk as Allison walked over.

"Are you finally ready to go to lunch? It's twelve-thirty already. I want to try that new Thai restaurant."

"I guess." She reached in the drawer for her phone. "I have to call Aaron first and find out what type of car Sean drove in college."

"Why?"

"Mr. Perry's girlfriend saw a seventies sedan parked behind the hardware store next door close to the time Ashley disappeared."

"But I thought Sean parked behind the restaurant."

"I don't know if it means anything. But it's all I have right now."

Allison rolled her eyes. "Whatever… text Aaron."

"Too complicated for a text."

Allison nodded her head knowingly. "Right.'

"Would you stop already with the romantic innuendos?" Sophie fumed as she walked off for some privacy. She punched in Aaron's number.

"Hey, Sophie."

Screaming came through the phone speaker. "What is all that yelling?"

"I'm at Sean's house. He said Corky...that's their six-month old puppy...chewed up Brigid's favorite shoes. He's gone upstairs to calm her down."

"Wow, she sounds really ticked off. If I was that dog, I'd be running for the hills."

"Trust me; I'm staying out of the line of fire. She throws things. Back in college, she kicked a hole in our apartment wall. But Sean will calm her down. That man has the patience of a saint." There was a pause. "That's why I know he didn't punch Ashley in the face."

Sophie's voice turned anxious. "You're still going to talk to him?"

"Yeah, we're going for a run."

"Aaron, I need to ask you something. Did Sean..."

A loud crash came through the phone.

"Sophie, something fell, I have to go and see what happened."

Aaron hadn't disconnected; she could hear footsteps fading away. Aaron must have set down his phone. She ended the call. Hopefully no one had been seriously hurt.

Halfway through her lunch at the Thai restaurant, Sophie remembered that she hadn't been able to ask Aaron about Sean's car. "I have to call Aaron back."

Allison's eyebrows shot up. "Seriously, Sophie...in the middle of lunch?"

"It's important, about the car. It will take only a minute."

"Text him. It's one question." Allison crossed her arms.

"Fine." Sophie's fingers flew over the letters and then hit send. "Okay, happy?"

"Yes. What were we talking about?"

"Liam."

Allison grinned broadly. "My favorite subject."

Her smile was infectious, Sophie smiled back.

Brigid stepped off the last riser of the staircase, still fuming over the loss of her favorite heels. After taking a couple of steps, she paused; an unfamiliar text tone sounded across the foyer. She walked over to an elegant black table graced with a large floral arrangement. Aaron's iPhone lay on the table. He had forgotten to take it with him.

The text tone sounded again. Wondering if the message might be important, Brigid pressed the black button. She froze after glimpsing the brief text. A thousand angry bees buzzed in her brain. *Not possible. This was not possible!*

Brigid took a step backward, and then another. She didn't stop until the heel of her shoe hit the staircase. She lowered her large frame onto the second lowest step. She threw her head back and wailed.

Lowering her head, her whole body shaking, she swallowed bile. *What am I going to do? What am I going to do?*

Brigid's eyes narrowed. That meddlesome journalist had caused this catastrophe. Her head swiveled to the left. She jumped off the riser and stormed into the den, yanking open a drawer in the oak desk. She pulled out a small spiral notebook, opened the cover, and ran a trembling finger down the list of passwords, stopping at *Aaron's iPhone*. He had given the passcode to Sean in case he needed to access information if there was an emergency. Brigid took deep breaths as her blood boiled. *Think!* The text she sent back had to convince Sophie Madison that it was from Aaron.

Twenty minutes later, Brigid had a workable message. She pressed the black button and put in the code. She accessed the last text message. Her lips pulled into a taut line as she reread it.

Aaron, need to know what type of car Sean drove in college. Have a witness that remembers a seventies sedan parked at the hardware store next door to the restaurant around the time Ashley went missing.

Brigid typed in her message. Three minutes later she had a reply. She typed in a new message, and waited. Her jaw dropped when the text appeared.

How can we meet at my house? Didn't think you could cross state lines on bail?

Brigid chewed on her lower lip. She took in a breath and typed in a message about Aaron's lawyer obtaining special permission to cross state lines two days ago.

Her lips pulled into a tight grin when she read the reply. She requested an address. When the phone beeped again, she typed in two words. Finished, she deleted the conversation. She switched the ringer to silent.

She wiped off the phone and set it inside the floral arrangement. That should buy her enough time. Destroying the phone would have been more satisfying, but that could raise questions when it went missing. This way, Aaron might think he dropped it in the arrangement... if he ever found it. She would also have to take care of the texts on Sophie's phone. But that wouldn't be a problem. She rushed back to the den to write Sean a note; she didn't want him becoming concerned about her long absence. If everything went as planned, she would be home in about seven hours...if not...Brigid shook her head. It would work.

Chapter Fifty-Two

Brigid sat in her luxury sedan in the parking lot of the mall, her red hair tucked under a dark blue knit cap, sunglasses covering her eyes. She tapped a number into her iPhone and waited. She wasn't going to make the same mistake twice.

"Yellow cab."

"I need a cab to pick me up at The Glen Tower Center."

Brigid disconnected the call and slid her phone back in her purse.

The cab arrived within five minutes. Even though the temperature was unseasonably mild, in the high fifties, Brigid pulled on a heavy coat with deep pockets. She grabbed her purse and slammed shut the door of her car. She gave the taxi driver the address of a car rental facility. Ten minutes later, the cab stopped in front of a light gray stucco building. Brigid walked through the door and up to the counter.

A young man with large ears looked up. "Can I help you?"

"I would like to rent a car with a roomy trunk, lots of luggage you know, and a quiet motor. I hate listening to the engine while I'm driving."

"We have a hybrid that is very quiet. The trunk is medium sized. We don't have a hybrid with a large trunk."

Which is more important? That nobody hear the car? Or the size of the trunk?

"I'll take that one then." Brigid gave the man a winning smile.

She filled out the paperwork, paid in cash and was handed the key fob. She strode out to the parking lot and found the numbered spot for her hybrid. She settled in the silver sedan, placing her large purse onto the console between the seats. Brigid started the car and then reached into her purse. She pulled out her phone, a package of peanut butter crackers, bottle of water, and a banana. She punched an address into her phone's GPS. Checking her mirrors for anyone behind her, Brigid took a bite out of the banana, backed out of the space, and left the lot.

Chapter Fifty-Three

Aaron halted beside the small lake, breathing hard. He bent over, placing his hands on his knees, trying to ignore the pain in the injured one. Sean stopped beside him, also bending over. When Aaron had his breathing under control, he started stretching his muscles. Sean performed the same stretches then glanced over at Aaron. "Ready to go, boyo?"

"Can we sit for a minute? Need to get off my knee." Aaron walked over to a wrought-iron bench and sat down.

Sean sat beside him, gazing out over the calm waters of the lake.

Aaron wiped sweat off of his face with a small hand towel. "How long you figure we've known each other?"

Sean's brows drew together. "Are you serious?"

"Humor me."

"Let's see, 1998 to 2012. Fourteen years."

"Good years. I couldn't have asked for a better friend. I want you to know that."

Sean shifted on the bench. "Not a problem."

"I'd have a hard time keeping it together over the next few months if I didn't have you to count on."

"Of course." Sean continued to stare across the lake.

"I talked to my lawyer. He gave me some bad news."

Sean finally turned to look at Aaron. "What is it?"

"He found out why I was arrested. Forensics determined that Ashley was killed by a blow to the head."

"Like someone hit her with a bat?"

"No, she was punched in the face with a fist."

Sean could not have looked more stunned if Moby Dick had suddenly arisen from the little lake in front of them. The look was genuine. Sean was not that good of an actor.

"No...no...how could anyone...she was the nicest...I can't believe..." His voice trailed off.

"Do you remember when I got back to the apartment the night of her disappearance, you asked about my injured hand and I told you about hitting the punching bag with my bare knuckles?"

At first, Sean's face showed puzzlement, but then cleared. "Actually, I do remember. It looked pretty bad, I told you to go to the doctor and get it..." His eyes widened. "Did you lie to me? Did you punch Ashley?"

Aaron's eyes held steadfast to Sean's. "No, I didn't lie to you. I didn't touch her."

Sean's gaze drifted back to the lake. "The detectives found out about your hand. That's why you were arrested."

Aaron sighed. "I'm going to prison, Sean. My injured fist is the smoking gun."

Sean's eyes whipped back to Aaron's. "No, you won't. You said your lawyer could get you off."

"That was before he found out about my hand. My lawyer's checking, but I know no one saw me punching the bag at the gym. I'm as good as convicted. It doesn't matter that I didn't kill her."

Sean's hands started to shake. "But…"

Aaron interrupted. "I'm curious about something. When I was at your house the day of Brigid's accident, you were about to tell me something about Ashley. What was it?"

Sean's face paled. "I…it was nothing."

Tears welled in Aaron's eyes as he grasped Sean's shoulder. "Will you do me a favor and call and check on my folks while I'm in prison or if, God forbid, I get the death sentence?"

Sean's body started to shake. He grabbed his head, bent over and started rocking back and forth. "Oh, sweet Jesus, no…this is not happening."

"Sean?"

An anguished whisper. "I can't keep this a secret anymore. The guilt…"

A vise closed around Aaron's guts. "What are you talking about?"

When Sean raised his head, tears streamed down his cheeks. "Ashley…when I came out to the parking lot…she was standing next to my SUV…crying."

Aaron's heart pounded against his chest. "You saw her…after I left?"

Sean nodded miserably.

The pounding increased. "Why haven't you said something?"

Sean wiped his nose on his sleeve. "I couldn't tell anyone." Utter despair covered Sean's face. "I would have lost Brigid if I told anyone what really happened."

Acid churned in Aaron's stomach. "You did kill her."

Sean's wet eyes widened. "No! I didn't kill her. I…we…"

"What?"

Sean's face flushed. "We had sex…in my car…in the parking lot."

Aaron stared at Sean.

Now that he had admitted what happened, the words rushed out in a torrent as Sean relived that long-ago night…

Chapter Fifty-Four

Fall 1999

Sean had been whistling as he came around the corner of the restaurant. His whistling stopped and his pace slowed as he stared at Ashley Keller sobbing next to his car. Two feet away from her shaking body, he stopped. "Ashley?"

The sobs ceased and her eyes focused. "Sean?"

"Ashley, *a chara*, what's troubling you?" He fumbled a clean hankie from the back pocket of his jeans and handed it to her.

She wiped her eyes and nose. "Aaron blew me off. Never wants to see me again."

"I'm sorry." His index finger, with a will of its own, brushed away a strand of hair clinging to her wet eyelashes.

Ashley gave him a trembling smile. "Is there something wrong with me, Sean? Not pretty enough — not sexy enough?"

"You're beautiful to me, inside and out."

The instant the words left his mouth, Sean wished he could take them back. Every time he was around Ashley, his blood would pound. He had been attracted to the pretty, petite waitress from the first moment he saw her smiling at a table of customers. He thought that he loved Brigid, whom he had been dating for two years, but it was becoming harder and harder to hide his attraction to Ashley.

A single tear escaped as Ashley's lips parted. "Thank you."

Sean's finger wasn't steady as he lifted it to her cheek and wiped away the tear. His eyes, which had been looking into hers, were drawn like a magnet to her lips. Ashley placed a hand on his arm to use it as leverage to rise up on her toes. She placed a light kiss on his lips then settled back on her heels. Electricity bolted through him. The invitation was clear in her eyes. A coherent thought broke through the lust: *No don't even think it. What about Brigid?*

For two long seconds, Sean stood frozen. Then he leaned down, wrapped an arm around Ashley and pulled her close. The passion was urgent as he pressed his mouth hard against hers. He reached behind her for the backseat door handle of the SUV. They fell inside.

Sean sat up in the backseat, adjusting his clothes. The shame coursed through him. Once he was decent, he turned to his left. Ashley was staring at him and the tears had returned.

"Sean, I'm sorry. I shouldn't have...I know...how you feel about Brigid. But when you said I was beautiful inside and out..." She flushed. "I was desperate for the hurt to go away." She hung her head, looking miserably at her hands grasped together in her lap.

Sean took a breath and laid his large hand over her small ones. "You don't get to take the blame all on yourself. We both wanted this."

He removed his hand and Ashley looked up, the dim glow of the parking lot light showing her guilt-ridden face.

"Sean, I promise never to tell a soul."

He looked away.

Ashley opened the door and slid out. Sean exited the other side, coming around to the driver's door.

As he opened the door, Ashley pulled on the cuff of his shirt sleeve. "I promise Brigid will never know what happened."

Chapter Fifty-Five

Winter 2012

"I got into the car and drove off." Sean uttered the last sentence barely above a whisper.

Aaron rose off the bench. "You could have told the cops the next day that you had seen Ashley...even if you didn't mention the sex."

Sean looked wretched. "I was scared out of my mind. The girl I had sex with the night before was missing." Sean wiped his face on his sleeve. "You were questioned, but never accused of wrong-doing. There was no need to come forward and blow up my relationship with Brigid. I pushed the whole debacle out of my mind." Sean's eyes implored Aaron to understand.

Aaron's fists were clenched. "But everything changed when her bones were found in the well. Right after I told you those were Ashley's bones in the well, you should have come clean with me."

Sean stood up. "I was afraid of losing Brigid if you told me I had to tell the police."

Aaron's lips drew into a hard line.

"But, you have to believe me… I would never let you go to prison. If the trial started going south and it looked like you wouldn't be acquitted, I had already decided to come clean."

Aaron wrung the hand towel to avoid punching Sean. "What about my career? What about my life? Don't you think getting arrested for murder has probably ruined my career?" Sean's face flushed. "Never mind, don't answer that." Aaron said with disgust.

"You're going to call Detective Burke now and tell him you're coming in to make a statement."

Sean nodded.

Aaron reached in the pocket of his sweats for his phone. He came up empty. He checked the other pocket and then walked around the bench to see if it had slipped out of his pocket. He widened the circle around the bench and then came to a halt. The furrow between his eyebrows cleared as he remembered his conversation earlier with Sophie. His phone was at Sean's house. "Do you have your phone?"

Sean shook his head.

"Then we'll make the call from your house." He headed for the parking lot, Sean dragging his feet behind.

Chapter Fifty-Six

Derek sat in Hank's cubicle, discussing the forensics on the jeep Aaron Reinhart had owned at the time of Stacy Keller's disappearance. It had taken a while to locate the new owner, an avid bear hunter from Maine, who insisted on telling the story of his most amazing hunt when Derek called to talk about his car.

"Bottom line—there is no evidence that Aaron or Ashley had ever been in that jeep. Their prints had been obliterated by a few dozen other prints." Derek took a drink from his bottle of water.

Hank nodded. "Did you inform the sheriff?"

"Headed to his office next."

"He'll consider it good news. He believes Reinhart is being railroaded." Hank reached for the handset as his desk phone rang. "Detective Burke." A pause. "Yes, I recognize your name, Mr. O'Connor. What can I do for you?"

Derek was tossing his plastic bottle towards the trash can when Hank's tone of voice changed. He swiveled in Hank's direction, eyes alert.

"Repeat that, please." Hank's professional tone had an incredulous edge to it. He grabbed a pad of paper and a pen and started writing furiously. "Hold on, let me check my calendar." Hank tapped buttons on his smartphone. "Eleven in the morning will be fine."

Hank disconnected the call, a stunned look on his face. "Looks like the sheriff may be right. That was Sean O'Connor. He told me he has evidence to clear Reinhart."

Derek raised his brows. "What is it?"

"He said he talked to Ashley Keller the night of her disappearance, in the parking lot after Reinhart left."

Derek frowned. "He could be covering for his friend."

Hank shook his head. "You should have heard his voice. Really upset. And coming in and making a statement that he was the last one to see Ashley Keller... that puts the bull's eye square on his chest."

Derek rubbed a hand across the back of his neck. "I don't know. Reinhart could have returned to the parking lot after O'Connor left."

"Going by the police report, I don't think he had enough time. O'Connor said he was with Ashley Keller for at least twenty to twenty-five minutes. Jack Perry saw Reinhart's jeep leave and then O'Connor walked out the door about ten minutes later. That's thirty-five minutes. And even if he lied about going to the gym, I doubt he would have had time to drive back to the restaurant, kill Ashley Keller, stash her body temporarily, and get back to his apartment by the timeline on the police report given by O'Connor."

Derek shook his head. "I can't get past the facts of Reinhart's injured hand and the bones being found in his ex-girlfriend's well."

"You're right there." Hank nodded. "We'll just have to wait and see what O'Connor has to say tomorrow."

Sean sat on the couch with his cell phone in his hands, his body shaking. Aaron stood a few feet away. It would be easy to stay furious with Sean, walk out the door and never look back. But a quiet voice kept repeating six words; *forgive him, as you were forgiven.* But how could he, after what Sean had done to him?

Sean wiped away tears. Aaron's anger dissipated. "If you want, I'll go with you to the sheriff's office tomorrow." Aaron walked over and sat on the couch. "Don't get me wrong, I'm still really angry with you, but you did come clean and you called the sheriff's office. But I need to know… why did you call the sheriff? I couldn't force you to do it. And it would be your word against mine."

Sean wiped his nose with his trembling arm. "Because you were right. I was a coward. And I don't want to be a coward anymore. It's time to do the right thing… no matter what happens."

"Thank you."

Sean gave a shaky sigh. "But I still don't understand something."

"Yeah, where's my phone?"

Sean sputtered a little laugh. He looked at Aaron, puzzlement in his eyes. "If you didn't kill Ashley and I didn't kill her, who put her in the well on Sophie's farm?"

"That is the one-million-dollar question. I didn't tell anyone about Sophie or the farm while I was in college." Aaron shook his head. "It makes absolutely no sense." He stood up. "Where is my phone? I need to call my lawyer. But I can't because his number is in the contacts on my phone. And I still can't believe when you dialed my phone we couldn't hear it ring. I'm sure I had the ringer on."

Aaron ran a hand across his head. "It should have been on the foyer table, where I left it. Do you think Brigid moved it from the foyer table and put it somewhere else?"

"I'll text her. Her note said the hospital needed her to take the shift of someone who had to leave suddenly."

"I'll look around the house." Aaron strode off.

After twenty minutes of searching the house with Sean and no answering text from Brigid, Aaron headed back to the foyer table.

"It was right here." He mumbled as his eyes raked over the surface.

He grabbed the base of the floral arrangement, lifting it off the table to check underneath. It was a lot heavier than it looked. The arrangement started to slip from his hands. Aaron jerked it towards him and something clunked on the table. His phone.

Sean walked over as Aaron set the flowers back on the table. "You found it."

Aaron's eyebrows drew together. "Weird. It was in the flower arrangement, but I could have sworn I laid it on the table." He shrugged. "I don't know. Maybe I tossed it in the flowers when I heard the crash."

Sean gave a ghost of a smile. "You mean when Brigid threw the glass container of potpourri at the wall."

Aaron smiled back. Despite the obvious fears for his future, Sean no longer looked haunted. He looked like a man who had been relieved of a great burden.

"Sean, you know that Brigid will forgive you. You won't lose her." Aaron's smile widened. "You'll have to buy a new car after she takes a sledge hammer to yours…but you won't lose her."

"I'd take losing a car over losing my wife anytime, boyo."

"I'll pick you up in the morning, around eighty-thirty." Aaron turned to leave.

"Aaron."

He turned back. Sean's eyes glistened. "I don't deserve your help. Why aren't you washing your hands of me?"

Aaron's gaze was steady. "Because Jesus didn't wash his hands of me."

Chapter Fifty-Seven

The alarm on Sophie's phone beeped. It was four thirty. She shut it off and reached into her desk drawer for her clutch, sliding the phone inside. She placed her fingers on the mouse and clicked out of all her windows. She shut down her computer and pushed back her chair. Her shoes clicked on the floor as she walked to the break room for her coat. She slung her coat over her arm and turned, almost bumping into Allison.

"What a boring interview," Allison moaned. "I think the woman loved to listen to the sound of her own voice. And now I have to stay and write the article. I'm going to be late for my date with Liam."

Sophie nodded—she had been there. "Sorry... but guess what? I think there's good news on Aaron's case."

Allison's eyes brightened. "What is it?"

"I don't know yet, he's meeting me at my house at five to tell me."

"Meeting at your house, huh?" Allison winked.

"You are incorrigible." Sophie pivoted on her fashionable heel and walked to the door.

Daylight was fading rapidly as Sophie turned down her tree-lined street. It should not be night at five o'clock. She pulled into her driveway, her right index finger pressing the button on the garage opener. She guided her car into the small space and killed the engine. She scoped out the area, eyes alert as she crossed to the screened-in back porch. She had been mugged on her college campus her junior year and was now ultra-aware of her surroundings when she was alone anywhere. She opened the screen door. The rip along the edge of the white-painted wood was getting bigger. *Great. I'll need to fix it soon.*

As soon as she had felt that she had job security, Sophie had started looking to buy a house of her own with the money from the insurance on the burnt farmhouse. This house had been a real bargain and she snatched it up. She had discovered wooden floors in excellent shape under the carpet she ripped up. She had painted the walls in cool grays and blues and replaced the dated appliances and vinyl floor in the kitchen.

Sophie unlocked the backdoor and slipped in, twisting the deadbolt behind her. She slipped the chain lock into place and flipped on the kitchen overhead light before setting her clutch and keys on the kitchen table. She removed her phone from her clutch setting it on the table. Should she offer to cook dinner for Aaron? She shook her head. She didn't want Aaron getting the wrong idea about something that could never be.

The kitchen clock said four-fifty. Sophie rushed to the bedroom to change into jeans and a sweater.

With headlights off, Brigid relied on the street lamplights and the GPS as she glided past mailboxes on Sophie's street. She jerked slightly when her GPS announced that she had arrived. She squinted at the numbers in the dim street light. This was it… 932. She pulled into the driveway and coasted up to the garage. The clerk at the rental place had been right; the hybrid ran as silent as a ghost. Odds were, when questioned in the next few days, none of the neighbors would have noticed this car. Brigid plugged a new address into the GPS and left her phone in the cup holder.

She undid her seat belt and reached into her purse for the hard rubber mallet she had swiped from Sean's wood-working tools. She stuffed it into one of the deep pockets of her coat as she looked at the clock on the dashboard. Five minutes after five—she needed to go. She didn't want Sophie texting Aaron, wondering why he was late. Plus, there was no guarantee he hadn't found the phone. She pressed a button to pop the trunk. Brigid slipped the key fob into her pocket and exited the car, not locking it. She pushed the trunk lid as high as it would go.

A dog barked as Brigid rounded the corner of the house and climbed the three steps to the front door. Adrenaline rushed throughout her body as she closed her fist around the handle of the mallet in her pocket and knocked on the door. Footsteps approached inside, and the door opened. Brigid gasped. Sophie was a stunner. Loads of dark glossy hair, gorgeous blue-green eyes, high cheekbones, trim figure.

"Oh." Sophie took a step back. "I thought you were…"

Brigid took a breath. *Stick to the plan.* Her eyes welled up. "Are you Sophie Madison?"

"Yes. Who are you?"

"My name is Brigid O'Connor. I'm Sean's wife. He told me about you calling the other night." A tear slid down Brigid's cheek. "May I come in and talk to you? I think my husband might have done something…" There was a watery catch in Brigid's throat. "…bad."

Caution and curiosity flicked across Sophie's face. Curiosity apparently won out.

"Sure, come in." Sophie opened the door wider. "I'm actually expecting Aaron any minute."

Hands deep in her pockets, Brigid brushed past Sophie into the living room. She turned to give Sophie an unsteady smile. "I'll wait then and tell you both at the same time."

Sophie hesitated and then returned the smile. "Would you like something to drink? I could make coffee?"

"That would be grand." Brigid blinked back tears.

"Have a seat. Make yourself comfortable. I'll be right back."

Sophie walked into the dining room and through a door to the left. Brigid's face hardened as she followed, her tread silent. She paused in the doorway. Sophie had her head in the refrigerator, pushing items aside. She rose up, shutting the refrigerator door. If she had turned to the right, she would have seen Brigid in the doorway, the rubber mallet in her hand. Instead, she turned left, a container of coffee gripped in her right hand.

Brigid slipped up behind her, raising the mallet above her head. She brought it down with all of her might. With any luck, it would be a death blow. But on the downward arc, a song burst forth from the vicinity of the kitchen table and Sophie turned her head.

Instead of hitting Sophie's skull dead on, the mallet glanced off the left side with a dull thud, knocking Sophie forward into the edge of the sink. The coffee flew out of her hand, hitting a cabinet as she collapsed to the floor. The plastic lid popped off and coffee peppered the floor, sink, counters and Sophie. Brigid swore as she glared at the mess. She needed to see if the blow had been hard enough to kill Sophie, but she couldn't walk through the grounds. Her eyes swept the kitchen as she pulled a pair of latex gloves out of her pocket. There was a dish towel, but that was no good because she would still have to walk in the grinds to get it.

Brigid rushed out of the kitchen to locate a bathroom. She yanked a pewter-colored towel off a rack and ran back to the kitchen. She bent down and brushed coffee grounds out of the path of the back door, from around Sophie, and off her body. She tossed the towel into a corner and then, grunting, she flipped Sophie on her back.

There was a vivid red mark on her temple. With a hand that trembled, Brigid placed two fingers on the side of Sophie's throat. Still alive. She turned and reached for the mallet she had laid on the kitchen floor. Her hand froze inches from the mallet as voices sounded somewhere close by. She held her breath as the voices drew closer.

The doorbell rang. The next minute was agony as she waited to see if the people out front might come around to the back. She held her breath until the voices faded. Her hands were shaking badly, and her mind raced. *Out of here...out of here...got to get out of here...now!* She picked up the mallet and shoved it back in her pocket.

Brigid jumped to her feet and unlocked the back door, swinging it wide. She hurried to the screen door and unlatched it. She rushed back to Sophie. Squatting down, she grabbed both arms and pulled until Sophie was in a seated position. She paused to wipe perspiration from her forehead, which had started to drip into her eyes.

Brigid stuck her head under Sophie's shoulder and leveraged her into position for the fireman carry. She rose up with her over her shoulder. She weighed nothing compared to some of the patients she had to lift at the hospital.

Outside, her heart pounded in her chest as her eyes swept over the houses and street for movement. With hands still shaking, she eased Sophie into the trunk and pressed lightly on the trunk's cover until it gave a soft click. She slid into the driver's seat tossing her latex gloves on the passenger seat. Her fingers froze on the ignition key. *Sophie's phone.* She rushed back into the house, picked up the phone, and shoved it into her pocket. Back in the car, Brigid turned on the ignition and activated her GPS.

She backed down the driveway, the headlights off. As she flipped her headlights back on a couple of minutes later, the shaking started to subside and she took in a deep breath. She voiced a few choice curse words. Her panic had put a wrench into her plans for Aaron's ex. Sophie was supposed to be dead when she went into the trunk. She took a calming breath. *Let it go. She'll be dead soon enough.*

This was the second time Brigid had traveled with someone in the trunk of a car. *Ashley Keller.* Her knuckles turned white on the steering wheel. All of this was that stupid slut's fault. Her eyes narrowed as her mind drifted back thirteen years...

Chapter Fifty-Eight

Fall 1999

Brigid had left the Mercy Hospital School of Nursing in Pittsburg with plenty of time to surprise Sean at Jack's Rib Shack around eight in the evening. But a ten car pile-up on the interstate had delayed her by almost three hours. She was still cussing a blue streak as she blew through a red light a mile from the Rib Shack. She would check there first before going to Sean's apartment.

Slowing down to the speed limit, Brigid slammed the brakes as the entrance to the restaurant appeared. The front lot was empty. Brigid coasted the old sedan to the back lot and spotted Sean's SUV. One of only two cars in the lot. She parked and turned the key. Brigid took a couple of deep breaths.

She opened the door and the interior light came on. She did a quick check of her make-up in the rear view mirror and applied a pale coral lipstick. She stepped out of the car and shut the door. Her heartbeats kicked into overdrive at the thought of seeing Sean. As she started across the back lot toward the front entrance, a slight movement caught her eye. She turned. A silhouette of someone in the backseat of Sean's car. She hurried over.

Two feet from the car, Brigid came to a halt, incomprehension on her face as her brain refused to acknowledge what her eyes were seeing. She stifled a sob, a hand over her mouth. She turned and fled back to her car. She shut the door, weeping bitter tears. She had to get out of here.

Brigid put the gear shift in reverse and backed out of the lot, missing a lamp post by an inch. She backed onto the street and sped off. 'Who was he with? Who was the girl that he was...?' Brigid slammed on the brakes in the middle of the road. She had to know. Flipping an illegal U-turn on the deserted street, she raced back to the restaurant.

As she drew even with the hardware store next door to the restaurant, Brigid yanked the wheel and entered the store parking lot. She cut out the headlights and coasted down a paved path beside the store, coming to a halt in a small rear lot. She continued to cry as she turned at an angle in her seat to watch Sean's car through the driver's side window. Every few seconds she brushed her arm under her running nose.

Now there were two heads in the back seat, moving around, and obviously adjusting clothing. Hiccups seized her. The SUV's back seat door farthest from her opened, but she couldn't see who exited the vehicle. The door closest to her opened and Sean emerged. The hiccups ceased and her eyes welled. He walked around to the other side and paused for a moment before opening the driver side door and getting in. The engine rumbled and the lights came on. Sean backed away from the parking space and left the lot.

Brigid gasped. Ashley Keller stood in the dim light, staring after Sean's car. Her grief morphed into fury. She looked at

Ashley through a red haze, her breathing quick and shallow. She wrenched the car door open and didn't bother to shut it as she crossed the grassy median between the two businesses.

As Brigid approached, Ashley turned. Horror registered on her face. "Oh, my, God…Brigid."

Ashley started talking fast. "Look, it isn't what you think…a mistake. A horrible mistake. Sean loves you."

Breathing hard, Brigid halted an arm's length away from Ashley.

"Brigid, I'm sorry. I…"

Brigid hauled her right arm back, formed her hand into a fist and punched Ashley in the face as hard as she could. Ashley dropped like a rock. Brigid stood over her, fists clenched.

"Take that you, bi…" Something was wrong.

Ashley's eyes were open and unblinking. Icy fingers curled around Brigid's spine. She kneeled down and placed two fingers on Ashley's carotid artery. She pressed for a few seconds, moving her fingers around. There was no pulse. Brigid looked towards the back door of the restaurant. She should call for an ambulance. She started to rise and then froze in place. Ashley was dead, which meant she would be charged with her murder. Her whole body started to shake. Run! She jumped up and started to rush to her car, but stopped a few feet away.

Blood. There was blood on Ashley's forehead. Brigid brought her knuckles close to her eyes. More blood. Her future flashed before her and she moaned. Brigid stiffened as she heard a noise coming from inside the restaurant. She rushed back to Ashley and grabbed her under her shoulders and knees. She staggered under the weight of the body as she stood. She tightened her grip and walked as quickly as she could to her car.

Brigid had reached the trunk of her car when the back door to the restaurant opened. She dropped Ashley's body on the right side of the car, ducking down beside her. It was hard to hear over her labored breathing, but it sounded like someone had opened the dumpster lid and then let it slam shut. She waited. When the restaurant door opened and closed, she peeked around the back end of the vehicle.

The latch to the trunk clicked loudly when Brigid released it. She held her breath. No one came to investigate. Muscles straining, Brigid lifted Ashley and dumped her in the trunk. She shut the lid as softly as she could, ran around to the driver's side, jumped in, and started the engine. She backed around and inched the car past the store and out onto the street. *What do I do now? Where do I take the body?*

Brigid gripped the wheel harder to stop the shaking, and took deep breaths. There were places near her home town where she could dump the body. No. If discovered, Sean could be implicated since it was near where he grew up also. Pennsylvania shouldn't be considered at all, or Ohio because Sean went to Ohio State. But where then?

Despair and fear weighted Brigid down like a heavy cloak. The bright lights of a gas station shone through the inky blackness on the left. Brigid looked at the gas gauge. She needed gas.

She shoved the nozzle into the gas tank, with a hand that still shook, and listened to the gurgle of the gas. Where could she dump the body? She screwed the gas cap back on, took a deep breath, and went inside the gas station to pay.

As Brigid handed over the money, she glanced at the television bolted into the wall above the clerk's head. The highlights of a college football game played earlier in the day was on. University of Wisconsin against Ohio State. Something niggled at her brain. Wisconsin, something about Wisconsin.

"How'd you hurt your hand?"

What? Brigid stared at the clerk.

He pointed. "Your hand?"

Brigid looked at her hand and her gut froze. She looked back at the clerk, her change in his hand.

"I...this guy...at a bar...got fresh. I punched him." She grabbed the change. It might look suspicious to race out of the gas station. She forced herself go slow. A half a mile from the station she pulled into a deserted lot, shaking all over. She held in screams, but she beat her fists on the steering wheel. If only she could kill Ashley all over again. It took thirty minutes until she was under control enough to drive. But drive where? And then it hit her—she knew where to take the body.

She leaned down to the right, reaching under the passenger seat. She pushed up with an old road atlas clutched in her hand.

In the dimness of the interior light, she flipped pages to the driving map of Wisconsin. Her eyes squinted at the map key. There it was...La Grange. She tapped her finger on the small township. This is where she would dump the body. She flipped over to the map of Ohio and traced the route to begin her journey. After laying the atlas open on the seat beside her, Brigid turned the key in the ignition, the engine roaring to life. La Grange would be perfect. Ashley Keller would not ruin her future with Sean O'Connor.

The sky had gone from black to gray as Brigid approached the outskirts of La Grange. It had been difficult staying awake for the long drive across multiple states and she was exhausted. She stopped at a gas station for coffee and a county map. A light mist hung in the air as she turned the sedan onto the driveway of the abandoned Madison farm.

Brigid tried to blink her eyes into focus. She had been on the road for over seven hours since killing Ashley and her eyes were dry and bleary. A field of corn stood on her left, ripe for harvest. There it was: the charred remains of the farmhouse. It looked exactly the same as the picture in the newspaper article she had discovered in the cardboard box.

She had been sitting on Sean's twin bed in the dorm the previous year, waiting for him to get back from class. Twiddling her thumbs, she scanned the room. A corner of a cardboard box stuck out from under Aaron's bed. What was in it? Maybe she could learn more about Sean's roommate. She had pulled the box out, sat down on the floor, and opened the flaps. On top of the contents in the box was a newspaper article about a fire and death on a farm in La Grange, Wisconsin. What connection did it have to Aaron? Five minutes later, Sean's voice echoing down the hall, she shoved everything back in the box and pushed it back under the bed. Later that night she jotted down the address listed in the article in case she wanted to find out more about what happened and why it was important to Aaron. She never had, but she still remembered the address.

She brought the car to a stop even with the charred foundation. She stepped out of the car and turned a slow circle. Where would be the best place to hide a body? The silo was a good possibility. Wait, what was that? Her eyes focused on a large wooden disc laying near the foundation.

A car drove by on the road at the end of the drive. Had she parked the car sufficiently out of sight? Anxiety melded with urgency, which ironically rooted her to the spot unable to decide what to do. She needed to get this over with and get out of here. She ran over to the weathered wooden disc shoving it aside. It covered some kind of well. She started to cough as mold and fungus spores entered her lungs. This would be perfect.

She rushed back to the car, started the engine, rammed it into gear, and backed it up to the well. She jumped out and opened the trunk. An unpleasant odor had her trying to hold her breath between coughs as she lifted Ashley's body out of the trunk and dumped it in the well. She heaved the cover over the well, making sure the fit was perfect, before jumping back in her car, pressing the gas and skidding back onto the driveway.

On the long drive back, Brigid had plenty of time to convince herself that there had been no other option, she had done what she had to do. Crossing the border into Pennsylvania, she forced the entire previous twenty-four hours to the back of her mind. She had a life to live...with Sean. Her mouth formed a hard line...no one would ever stop that from happening.

Chapter Fifty-Nine

Winter 2012

A blast of the horn from an eighteen-wheeler startled Brigid. The memories of killing Ashley, and dumping her body, evaporated. The GPS on her phone announced that the exit for WI-20 was coming up fast. There were no sounds coming from the trunk. If her luck held, Sophie would still be unconscious when she opened the truck and used the mallet on her again. If not…no problem; at the hospital, she had wrestled patients three times Sophie's weight into submission.

A moan escaped through Sophie's lips as she became aware of a horrible pain in her head. A few minutes later, she moaned again. Over her moaning and breathing was a steady, unidentifiable noise. Then a familiar smell…coffee and…some type of cleaning fluid. Something rough and slightly scratchy rubbed her cheek. She needed to see. Sophie struggled to open her eyes. Total…complete… darkness. A panicked bird tried to escape her chest.

The pain inside her skull increased as she tried to lift her head. She gave a long, drawn-out moan and lay still. She shut her eyes. *The well…I'm in the dry well at the farm and it's night.* She opened her eyes and turned her head to seek out the stars in the sky. There were no stars. The ground bounced. Her head hurt more. She frowned. *How can I bounce in the well?*

Sophie shut her eyes again. What was going on? It was hard to think with the pain. She bounced again, harder. She raised a leaden arm and searched the "ground" with her fingers—more of the scratchy material like on her cheek. She reached above her…*metal*. The panicked bird was joined by a few more beating frantically at her chest wall, trying to escape a cage made of her ribs. *Coffin…I'm in a coffin.* She bounced again.

I bounced like this when I was five, lying in the bed of my papa's truck as he drove around the farm checking the cornfields. Sophie turned completely onto her back and lifted both arms, searching. *She was in the trunk of a car.* Tremors cascaded through her body. Her hands formed fists ready to beat on the top of the trunk, make as much noise as possible to attract attention. But before she had moved her fist an inch, she was tossed a few inches into the side of the trunk and then back. The pain caused her to suck in quick, shallow breaths.

Over the road noise drifted the faint jingle of her iPhone ringtone. Which meant whoever had kidnapped her had her phone. Kidnapped her…she had been kidnapped…*Who would…?* Her eyes widened. It had to have been that woman at her door…Sean O'Connor's wife. The pain in her head thudded in time to an imaginary brass drum. She shook her head and moaned again as an ice pick poked her brain. She had opened the door to a big, stocky woman in a knit cap and large coat. What had happened after that?

Sophie's breathing became erratic and the tremors increased. More importantly, where was she being taken and why?

Brigid started and jerked the wheel when the song erupted from her coat pocket. She straightened the car and lifted Sophie's cell phone from her pocket up to face level and pushed the button with her thumb. Two missed calls. From Aaron. She placed the phone back into her pocket. She needed to destroy it immediately.

She glanced down at the lighted face of the phone's GPS. Ten more minutes and she would...a brilliant flash of lightening dead-ahead made her gasp. A booming roll of thunder followed. Suddenly, the car was buffeted by a strong burst of wind. Brigid cursed loudly.

A third peal of thunder rattled the trunk as the vehicle made a left turn. The speed of the car slowed. *Sean's wife must be close to her destination.* Tremors shot through Sophie's body. This would not be a kidnap/ransom situation; Sophie was in the trunk because Sean's wife planned to kill her. Her investigation had come too close to the truth and the woman had decided that she would protect her husband at any cost.

She *had* to escape. Sophie reached her hand out, fumbling in the dark for the latch that closed the trunk. All trunks were supposed to have a release for the very situation she was in— trapped in the trunk of a car. She found the latch. Her fingers continued groping until they closed over the release, a plastic lever that felt like it should be pulled towards her. Should she pull it now?

Sophie took her hand off the lever. If she jumped out of the trunk while the car was moving this fast, she would be injured worse than she already was. She needed to wait until the car slowed to a crawl and then make a run for it. A tremendous boom crashed around her, causing Sophie to jerk and bang her head. Bright spots appeared before her eyes and she moaned with the pain. Her stomach gave a queasy flip. She closed her eyes and took steadying breaths. If she passed out, she was dead.

"Sophie."

Sophie's eyes popped open. *Mama's voice.*

"Pray for God's help, Sophie...now."

It wasn't her mama's sweet, loving tone in her head—it was her 'do as I say with no argument tone.'

"Mama..."

"Now, Sophie."

For twelve years, Sophie had never disobeyed the mother she had loved with all her heart.

"I will, Mama."

Her voice barely above a whisper, Sophie prayed to the God she had rejected. "I'm only talking to you because of my mother. My mama believed in you. She believes you can help me. I don't think you will. You don't care about me at all." Tears welled up and started to trickle down her cheeks. "If you had, you wouldn't have let my mother die or my father…"

The door in Sophie's heart that had been barred and locked to her savior splintered and then shattered into a thousand glistening fragments of glass. Her whispery voice was choked with tears. "Oh, Jesus, I'm scared, please help me. I don't want to die."

Sophie stiffened. The car was slowing down considerably. Her heartbeats pounding loudly in her ears, Sophie gripped her hand around the lever. The vehicle made a right hand turn and moved forward at a crawl. Sophie pulled the lever. A howling wind and cold rain rushed into the trunk. She tried to climb out of the trunk, but the world tilted and spun and she slammed onto a hard wet surface.

Chapter Sixty

The rain beat on her relentlessly as Sophie tried to pull air into her lungs. She curled into the fetal position as multiple fists boxed the inside of her head. She moaned as a wave of nausea hit her and white dots flashed behind her closed eyelids.

Sophie, if you don't get up you will die.

Bile rose up. *Mama?*

Now, Sophie, you have to get up now!

Sophie rolled onto her knees and threw up. She tried to stand on the driveway, but the dizziness had increased and the wind knocked her back to the ground. She could hear her mama's voice in her head shouting. Sophie lay on the broken asphalt, completely disorientated. Her jeans and sweater were soaking wet, her hair plastered to her head and face.

Brigid kept a tight hold on the steering wheel. Strong wind gusts were slamming the car as it crept forward. The bare branches on the trees waved wildly in the brightness of the headlights as she searched for the barn. A flash of lightning illuminated the large, faded-red ruin through the pounding rain. She rotated the knob for the wipers to full speed as she inched towards the opening in the dilapidated structure, one remaining door banging relentlessly against the outer wall.

Rain splashed onto the weed and dirt floor of the roofless portion of the building as Brigid killed the engine under what remained of the barn roof and pocketed the keys. She left the headlights on, pulling the rubber mallet out of her pocket. She opened the driver's door and exited the car. She stepped towards the rear, but halted mid-stride, mouth slack, eyes wide. The trunk was open.

Brigid rushed to the trunk. *Empty.* Her gaze frantically swept the interior of the barn. There was nowhere to hide. It was completely empty except for the car. She dropped to her knees, with the mallet clenched in her fist, and looked under the car. She jumped back to her feet and ran to the doorway of the barn. She looked out into the howling maelstrom, heart hammering in her chest. Sophie could be anywhere. She ran back to the car, opened the door and grabbed her large purse. Digging around, Brigid removed a flashlight. She left the meager shelter of the barn, her knit cap and coat soaked in seconds.

She clicked on the flashlight and trudged through the deluge. The bobbing light fell on a human form struggling to rise in the middle of the cracked asphalt near the road. What luck! She stalked towards her victim, raising the mallet high.

Sophie rolled back to her knees, gritted her teeth, and pushed up with her hands as the wind died down. She grunted as she managed to get her athletic shoe-clad feet under her. Sophie stood in the pouring rain on legs that wobbled and then froze. A horrible apparition appeared before her. Sean's wife's face was a dripping mask of evil satisfaction. A fat headed hammer was held in an upraised fist. Sophie chocked back a sob. Even if she could, there was no time to run or even duck.

As the woman started to swing the hammer at her head, two things happened simultaneously. Sophie's phone burst into song and lightning struck a half-grown tree to the left of Sean's wife. The flash of brilliance blinded Sophie and the loud crack made her ears ring as she dropped like a stone onto her rear end. Her kidnapper was thrown forward, missing Sophie by inches. Sophie's nostrils flared at the stink of ozone. She grabbed her head and moaned.

After multiple attempts, Sophie finally gained her feet again. Sean's wife lay on the ground. Was she breathing? The wind had stopped and the rain had slackened. Sophie's whole body tingled as she ran for the light up ahead...or, tried to run. With the dizziness and pain in her head disabling her, it was more of a weaving shuffle, but Sophie plodded on.

She came to a halt, her eyebrows shooting up to her hairline. She was at the farm. Two barns wavered in front of her. She tried to meld them together by blinking. She glanced behind her, but the woman's form was still on the ground.

She splashed through the mud to the barn. Sophie staggered through the opening. A car was parked in the barn. *The woman's car.* She forced her feet forward to the driver's door. She reached for the door handle, but then moaned as a stronger bout of dizziness and pain dropped her to her knees. She closed her eyes and sucked air rapidly through her teeth.

Minutes Sophie couldn't afford passed as she waited for the dizziness to subside. Slowly, she opened her eyes staring, at the door handle in front of her. *Good... only one door handle.* She gripped the door handle as she leveraged her feet under her. Perspiration popped out on her forehead, her breathing ragged as she pulled on the handle. There was no key in the ignition. She seized the woman's purse, dumping it out on the seat. She frantically searched the items, continuously glancing back at the doorway for the woman.

No keys and no phone. Sophie groaned. They must be on the woman's body. She glanced back and screamed. Sean's wife was standing in the doorway, breathing hard. There was no place to run. There was no other exit. She was trapped.

Chapter Sixty-One

Allison frowned as she placed her phone back in the cup holder. Why didn't Sophie answer? Since the incident in the well, Sophie had promised to keep her cell phone on her, or within grabbing distance of her body. Allison had also made her promise to always answer the calls or texts from her, otherwise she would worry. No exceptions...Sophie had promised. Allison stared down at the phone, willing it to ring or beep with a text. It did not.

At the next light, instead of turning left to meet up with Liam, Allison turned right and sped up. The same uneasiness coursed through her body as the last time she had rushed to Sophie's house. If she interrupted Aaron and Sophie in a passionate embrace then she would apologize, but she wasn't ever again going to assume everything was fine.

Her car bumped up Sophie's driveway and she slammed on the brakes in front of the garage. No car in the driveway. Aaron must have come and gone. She cut the engine, jumped out, and froze in her tracks. The screen and back doors were wide open. Adrenaline pumped through her body as she reached into the car and grabbed her phone out of the cup holder and dialed 911. She didn't care if she was overreacting.

"911, what is your emergency?"

"I need the police to come out to 932 Wind Terrace Lane." As she spoke, Allison hurried around the car and headed to the porch steps. "I've arrived at my friend's house and something's wrong."

"Who am I speaking with?"

"Allison Summers." Allison rushed up the steps. "Both the screen and back door are wide open. And my friend keeps both locked when she is at home."

"Ms. Summers, is your friend at home?"

"I'm checking now." Allison froze in the doorway of the kitchen, and gasped.

"Ms. Summers, what's wrong?"

Allison tore her gaze from the mess in the kitchen and shouted as loud as she could. "Sophie!"

The dispatcher raised her voice. "Ms. Summers."

Allison charged through the kitchen and into the dining and living area as she shouted into the phone. "I need someone here now. Something has happened to Sophie."

She ignored the voice on the phone as she rushed up the stairs to the second level, shouting for Sophie. She wasn't in the house. Allison reversed direction and ran out the back door to the garage. Sophie's car was there, which made Allison's fear a living, breathing thing.

Finger shaking, she disconnected the call with the dispatcher and stood in the darkness beside the garage. She pulled up the find-a-friend app on the iPhone she had bought after Sophie left the hospital. Sophie knew she had the app, but didn't know how many times a month Allison checked that her best friend was safe.

After a few agonizing seconds, the locater blue dot stopped atop an unfamiliar street name. With a finger she could barely control, she pulled up her contact list and found Aaron's number. She tapped the phone icon. *Come on...come on!*

"Hello?"

"Aaron, this is Allison. Is Sophie with you?" *Please say yes.*

"No. Why would you think she was with me?" Aaron's puzzled tone was a knife through Allison's heart.

"Oh, no. Please, God, no." Allison burst into tears.

Puzzlement changed to alarm. "What's wrong?"

"It's... Sophie, she's... missing again."

Aaron's voice turned to steel. "Tell me what you know."

Between sobs, Allison related the last few minutes.

"You're right, something's wrong. She would never voluntarily leave her house with the doors wide open. The mess in the kitchen sounds like she struggled with someone."

Tears streamed down Allison's cheeks. "It's your friend, Sean, isn't it? Sophie found out about his old sedan parked at the hardware store the night Ashley went missing. He went after her didn't he?"

"What...wait...what did you say? An old sedan? Sean didn't own an old sedan in college, he drove a ...Oh, no...it can't be."

Allison stopped sobbing. "What's wrong?"

"We have to find Sophie...now." Aaron's voice was choked with emotion.

"Aaron, I know where she is, or where her phone is."

"Where?"

Allison swiped it up as sirens sounded down the street. "Territorial Road. The police are almost here."

"I have to call the sheriff. I know who has her and where she's taken her."

"Where?"

"Her farm."

"Who…?"

Aaron had hung up. Allison looked up as the police cruiser turned into the driveway.

A band of steel constricted Aaron's chest, making it hard to breath as he searched in his wallet for the card with the number to the sheriff's office. Instead of the front desk, he got a busy signal. He stared at the phone. He tried the number again, with the same results. He dialed 911.

"State your emergency."

"A friend has been kidnapped and I can't reach the sheriff's office in Walworth County, Wisconsin."

"Your name, sir."

Aaron refrained from yelling out his frustration. "Aaron Reinhart. Please call the Walworth County sheriff and tell him to go to W7645 Territorial Road right now, before she kills Sophie."

She couldn't be dead. Not when they had finally reconnected.

"Who is in danger?"

Aaron had never felt so helpless. He would have jumped in his car and broken the law by crossing the state line if thought he could save Sophie, but the farm was almost three hours away. Whatever was happening to Sophie was happening *now*.

"Mr. Reinhart?"

"Sophie Madison has been kidnapped by Brigid O'Connor. Brigid plans to murder Sophie, if she hasn't already. If you can't reach the sheriff, please call the closest law enforcement...now, before it's too late."

Aaron hung up.

He punched in 411 on his phone as he paced back and forth in front of the large bay window. He requested a number. He listened, disconnected, and then tapped in another number. The Wisconsin State Police came on the line. He relayed the information on Sophie. To their credit, they took the call seriously and said they would alert local law enforcement to investigate his allegation. He told them that the Milwaukee police were at Sophie's house, but he didn't know the address. Aaron pushed the disconnect button. He stared out into the black night, tears running down his cheeks and his hand clenched in an impotent fist around his cell phone. *Lord, Jesus, please don't let Brigid take Sophie away from me.*

Chapter Sixty-Two

A streak of lightning back-lit the enraged woman in the barn's doorway. Sophie's insides quivered. Sean's wife pulled something out of a pocket in her coat. *My iPhone!* Sophie's eyes tracked the phone as it fell to the ground, bouncing once in the wet dirt. Before she could blink, Sean's wife destroyed it with the hammer in one swift, fluid motion.

"Now, there'll be no more interruptions."

A crack of thunder sounded in the distance.

Sophie licked suddenly dry lips. "Please, let me go and I won't press charges. I know you're just trying to protect your husband."

Sean's wife gave a maniacal laugh. "Protect my husband. I don't have to protect my husband. He didn't kill Ashley. He fell under the spell of that whore. She…never mind."

The woman started to walk towards her. Sophie rushed around the front of the vehicle putting the car between them. Brigid halted. A few moments passed as Sophie assessed the situation.

Sophie broke the silence. "Look, Mrs. O'Connor, like I said before, I won't press charges. We'll get an excellent lawyer for your husband."

The woman pulled up even with Sophie on the other side of the car, emphasizing her words. "I told you he didn't kill Ashley."

"Look, we both know that he did kill..."

"I killed Ashley." The woman had the audacity to smile.

Sophie felt the blood drain from her face as ice encased her spine. There would be no negotiating, no talking Sean's wife out of the act of murder again.

"You poor thing. You're as white as a ghost. Mrs. O'Connor is rather formal, don't you think? Call me Brigid."

Sophie struggled to move when Sean's wife suddenly rushed around the back of the car and reached out a hand to grab her. Brigid missed her by inches as Sophie hurried to the driver's side. The pain in her head kicked up a notch and the barn swam out of focus. If she could get outside, there were places she could hide. She couldn't keep going in circles. It would make the vertigo worse. And then she was dead.

"You don't look good. How's the head? I would have killed you at your house if it hadn't been for your phone."

Brigid was trying to distract her for another end-run around the car. This time Brigid would catch her; she had one chance to get away. Sophie was now closer to the doorway than Brigid. She had been a runner most of her life; she could out run Sean's wife. She took two deep breaths. She pivoted and sprinted for the door.

Heavy footsteps splashed behind her as she charged through the doorway into the light rain. She screamed. Brigid had a fistful of her wet hair and yanked her to the muddy ground. Sophie's eyes widened through the rainwater as Brigid hefted the hammer for the second and final time.

Halfway through the downward swing of the hammer, Sophie's vision was blocked for a split second by a cream-colored blur. The grip on her hair released. Incensed growling and the furious snapping of strong jaws ripped the air. As sirens sounded in the distance, Sophie tried to rise, but the pain and vertigo returned with a vengeance and she fell back to the ground, the inky black clouds above fading into nothingness.

Chapter Sixty-Three

In his fifteen years as Sheriff, Jim Cox couldn't remember a scene as bizarre as the one that greeted him when his county car careened through the rain and mud up to the barn on the Madison farm and he stomped on the brakes. A female lay on the ground, legs bent and arms flung out from her sides. Inside the barn, a yellow Lab was viciously tearing into a bulky woman who was trying to hit the animal with a large rubber mallet. Running across the bare cornfields was an old man, in long johns and mud boots, brandishing a shotgun.

Jim jumped out of his vehicle as another county car, sirens blaring, slid to a stop beside him. He pressed the button on his two-way hand-held radio and told the dispatcher to get an ambulance out to W7645 Territorial Road. He ran to the woman on the ground. *Please, Lord, don't let that be Sophie.* Hank and Derek rushed past him into the barn. Jim squatted, his body tensing. It was Sophie. He placed two fingers to her neck and sighed. She was alive. Jim pulled his arms out of his jacket sleeves and laid the coat over Sophie's torso, careful not to move her in any way.

Inside…the barn was chaos. The woman was cursing. Hank and Derek were shouting instructions at each other on the best way to subdue the dog. The old man arrived in the glare of the headlights and whistled. The dog dropped to four feet, fur bristling and throat growling.

"Cooper, down!"

The Lab backed up and dropped to his belly, never taking his eyes off the woman. Hank and Derek rushed the woman as she tried to open the car door. She swung the mallet at their heads. Both detectives ducked and Hank pulled his weapon.

"Drop it! Now!"

The gun in Hank's hand gave the woman pause. Her chest heaved as she took in deep breaths, eyes darting back and forth between the two men. Jim had never seen anyone more furious in his life. Her face was the color of a ripe beet and her body was coiled like a tightened spring. The woman looked like she might toss the mallet at Hank's head despite the gun aimed at her heart. But then the mallet dropped onto the dirt.

"On the ground! Now!"

The woman slowly dropped to hands and knees and then lay prone in the weeds and mud. Derek pulled out zip ties and cautiously approached.

Hank steadied his weapon. "Don't move a muscle."

Derek pulled one arm, and then the other, behind her back and secured her hands. He grabbed an arm and then lifted her, none too gently, to her feet. "You are under arrest for the kidnapping and assault of Sophie Madison."

Jim watched the dog as the woman was read her Miranda rights. Cooper never moved a muscle.

"Do you understand your rights as I explained them to you?"

Brigid O'Connor glared.

"Do you understand your rights?"

Brigid spat out the word, "Yes."

Hank returned his gun to the holster and stepped forward to search the woman for any other weapons. With a nod to Derek, Hank fell in step as they escorted her to the county vehicle.

Jim's gaze switched from the detectives to Territorial Road. *Where was that ambulance?* A car door slammed and Derek returned with an evidence bag for the mallet.

"Sherriff, do you want me to stay here?" Derek paused by Jim.

"No, son, I'll see you back at the office. You boys did a good job here tonight."

Derek nodded and then retrieved the mallet with a gloved hand. "CSI boys shouldn't be too long."

Sheriff Cox turned back to Sophie, checking the pulse in her neck again.

The old man called out, "Cooper, up."

The yellow Lab bounded to his feet and padded over to Sophie. He leaned down over her head and whined. Jim's knees protested as he rose to his feet, water dripping off the brim of his hat. The ambulance sirens were finally audible. He walked over to the wiry old man with a head of thin white hair plastered to his scalp.

"Cooper is one fine dog, Howard. I haven't got a clue what happened here, but I don't think I'm off base when I say your dog has most likely saved this young lady's life twice."

Howard's gaze shifted to Cooper, who had lain down next to Sophie, gently licking her cheek. "It's the strangest thing, Sherriff. Never seen anything like the instincts he has for this girl. He was barking and scratching at the door, fit to be tied. It's almost like someone told him where she was and what he needed to do." Howard's gnarled hand adjusted its grip on the shotgun. "Strangest thing."

The rain stopped as the ambulance pulled up to the barn. Jim gave a brief upward glance at the slivery half-moon peeping through the dark clouds as he waited for the EMT's to triage Sophie.

Chapter Sixty-Four

The scent of a multitude of flowers filled the air. It was lovely. Sophie breathed in deeply. There was a voice—urgent. She breathed deep again. The voice became louder. She frowned and moved her head a fraction of an inch.

There was pain. Not a lot, but there. She moaned. The voice grew insistent. She needed to tell it to stop and leave her alone. She opened her mouth a crack. Nothing came out.

"Sophie."

There was something familiar about that word. That's...*my name.* She lifted her eyelids enough to let in a sliver of light.

"That's it, Sophie, open your eyes."

There was something familiar about that voice. She gave the briefest of smiles.

The voice became excited. "Did you see that? She smiled!"

She lifted the heavy lids higher but everything was a haloed blur. There was a strong grip on her hand. The fuzziness started to solidify into a face. Someone familiar. *Who?*

The person said, "It's me, Allison."

Sophie frowned. *Allison?* Oh! Allison!

"Allison?" she whispered.

"Yes, yes…it's me. I'm right here."

Sophie moved her head on the pillow so she could see her friend better. Her smile was back. "Allison."

Allison's eyes glistened with moisture. "You're back. You came back to me."

The nurse in the coral pink scrubs halted in the doorway to the waiting room and nodded in Allison's direction. Allison rose from the chair, squeezing the hand of the man who sat beside her. She strode to Sophie's room in the Neuro Care Unit at Froedtert Hospital in Milwaukee. She paused in the doorway. The light was dim. A wintery blast shook the frosted window. Since the passing of Sophie's aunt, and with Bryan out of the picture for good, Allison was the closest thing to family Sophie had.

Allison had been warned not to volunteer any information on the ordeal Sophie had experienced. Sophie had suffered brain trauma—a fractured skull and concussion. She had been in a medically-induced coma for two weeks to give her injury time to heal. Sophie had been allowed to wake up this morning. But after smiling at Allison, she had fallen asleep. She had been woken at intervals throughout the day and was awake now.

Each time Allison had been in to see her, Sophie had been dazed, confused. But she had recognized Allison. Allison took a deep breath and walked as quietly as possible to the chair beside the bed. She lowered herself onto the cushion as Sophie turned her head in her direction.

Sophie smiled. "Allison."

"Hey, sleepyhead. How you feeling?"

"Tired."

The doctors had explained that this was normal for her type of injury. "I brought you something."

Allison held up a stuffed plush owl.

Sophie's eyes lit up. She reached up a hand. "My favorite animal."

One of the many bands around Allison's heart loosened as she handed over the bird. *She remembers.* "We need to start planning that trip to Alaska we're always talking about, to see the great snowy owls."

Sophie's brows pulled together.

"Never mind." Allison's tone was light.

"The doctor was here."

"Was he?"

"I asked why I was in the hospital."

Allison's gut clinched. "What did he say?"

"He said I hurt my head...but I don't remember how that happened." Sophie frowned.

Allison squeezed her hand. "No worries...you will."

"Allison?"

"Yes, love."

"I've had the strangest dreams while I was sleeping."

The doctor had not told Sophie about the medically-induced coma yet. Allison had been researching head trauma and MICs; some patients experienced dreams. "What were they about?"

Sophie's face grew thoughtful. "Heaven...I think. The most amazing images and colors, but not like here—more dazzling, brilliant. It seemed real, like I was there, walking amongst the colors and ...people, but I couldn't see them clearly. I know that sounds strange. I felt such peace..."

Allison continued to hold Sophie's hand as she listened to her talk about the dreams she had experienced while in the coma. Sophie's tone began to soften and her speech pattern slowed. Her eyelids drooped and she fell asleep. Allison let go of her hand and stood. She planted a kiss on Sophie's cheek. She left the room and walked back to the waiting room. "She's asleep if you want to go sit with her."

Aaron smiled his thanks as he rose and walked to Sophie's room. He settled into the chair Allison had vacated. He folded Sophie's hand in both of his. He closed his eyes and whispered in a voice choked with emotion. "God, I can't thank you enough for...for bringing Sophie... back. Please... he...help her brain to heal quickly... and give her peace from the or...ordeal she went through." The next three words came out on a soft sigh. "I love you, Sophie."

Aaron pressed his wet cheek against Sophie's.

Chapter Sixty-Five

A week later, Allison exited the elevator and headed for Sophie's room with a bakery bag of chocolate éclairs clinched in one hand. They were Sophie's favorite pastry. She sighed as she strode past the waiting room. Aaron had gone back to Chicago the day after Sophie woke up.

For two weeks, he had sat at her bedside, holding her hand, telling her what she meant to him and to her friends…how much everyone missed her. When he told Allison, the day Sophie woke up, that he wouldn't be back, she had argued, threatened, pleaded, and begged for him to stay. But he was adamant. Sophie had a brain injury—he wouldn't risk upsetting her now that she was awake. The day she woke up was the day he said goodbye.

The door to Sophie's room was closed. Allison had raised a hand to knock, when it opened suddenly and Sophie's neurologist stepped past. He turned to Allison. "I'm not happy about it, but I have given permission for Ms. Madison to learn the details of her injury. Try not to upset her."

Allison swallowed. "I won't, doctor."

He nodded before striding to the room next door. Allison entered the room. Sophie sat up in bed, a determined look on her face. "I don't want to talk about the weather, my co-workers' antics, Mr. McNair's tirades, the latest recipe find, or Liam. I want to know what happened to me."

"Okay... I brought you éclairs." Allison set them on the tray table. "Have you had your walk down the hallway yet?"

"Allison." Sophie crossed her arms.

Allison sighed. "Okay, but I will stop the second you get upset."

"I'm fine. My head barely hurts and there's no dizziness when I walked up and down the hallway."

Allison sat in the cushioned wooden chair. "What do you remember?"

By the look on Sophie's face, she had been thinking about that question.

"The last thing I remember is having lunch with you at the new Thai restaurant."

"Do you remember texting Aaron?"

Sophie's brows furrowed, then cleared. "Yes, I do remember." Her eyes widened. "Ashley's murder. I totally forgot about it."

"Do you remember what you texted to Aaron?"

Sophie slowly nodded. "It was about whether Sean O'Connor owned an old sedan in college."

"Sean didn't, but his wife, Brigid O'Connor, did."

Allison told Sophie how a murder in Columbus, Ohio, thirteen years ago, led to her abduction and attempted murder three weeks prior. She ended her tale with Sophie's trip to the hospital in Milwaukee. To her credit, Sophie took her doctor's advice and stayed calm throughout. At times, as Allison talked, her eyes widened or her lips thinned, but she didn't express any anger or have any emotional outbursts.

"I don't remember any of this."

"The detectives will not be happy to hear that. They've been clamoring to interview you since you woke up a week ago."

"Sean O'Connor's wife killed Ashley?"

"Allegedly. She's hasn't spoken a word since being arrested. But Aaron and I are convinced she killed Ashley...and that it was her sedan parked near the scene of the crime that night, behind the hardware store."

Sophie's eyebrows drew together. "How did she find out I knew about her car?"

Allison leaned forward. "Now this is a guess, but Aaron left his cell phone at Sean's house when he and Sean went for a run. We think Brigid read your text and decided you were too close to the truth and had to be eliminated."

"We?"

"Aaron and I."

Sophie smiled. "When did you two get so buddy-buddy?"

"Here at the hospital."

"What? Aaron is..." Sophie's voice faltered.

"Aaron was allowed to cross state lines and visit you in the hospital after his lawyer convinced the District Attorney that Aaron was not a flight risk and he would assume all responsibly for his client. But I think the real reason the DA caved was because of Brigid O'Connor's arrest."

Allison voice softened. "Sophie... Aaron was here in the hospital from sunup to sundown the two weeks you were in your coma."

Sophie's eyes widened.

"The nurses told me he sat by your beside for hours at a time, holding your hand. When I came to visit you after work, or on the weekends, he was always in your room. We would sit together in your room and talk about how much you meant to us." Allison sighed. "Sophie, he saved your life. When Aaron couldn't get a hold of the sheriff's office because the phones were down, he called the state police and they contacted the sheriff by radio."

Sophie drew a hand to her mouth, tears forming in her eyes.

Allison's soft brown eyes locked with Sophie's sea-green ones as she said quietly, "Sophie, he loves you so much."

The tears fell as Sophie stared silently back at her friend.

Chapter Sixty-Six

Aaron looked through the peep hole. He took a deep breath and opened the door. It had been a month since Aaron had seen Sean, and he looked like the walking dead. His face was haggard—gaunt. But his eyes were the worst. Empty, no life in their depths.

A fellow ball player had called Aaron that morning and told him that Sean had met with the Cub's manager and lawyers. To protect their reputation, the Chicago Cubs needed to sever their relationship with Sean and the sensationalism of his wife's crimes. Sean had agreed to the dissolution of his contract.

Why hadn't the Cubs done the same after he had been arrested?

Jonathan Richards had called a few days ago to inform Aaron that the District Attorney had dropped all charges. Brigid O'Connor had finally confessed to killing Ashley Keller.

"I understand if you don't invite me in, but I had to come and say how sorry I am…for what I did, for what Brigid…" Moisture formed in Sean's eyes as he cleared his throat. "For what Brigid did to Sophie."

Aaron opened the door wider. "Come in."

Sean walked through the doorway and stopped.

Aaron walked around him to the living room. "Have a seat."

Sean sat on the loveseat, hands trembling.

"Do you want anything to drink?"

Sean shook his head as he wiped his nose.

"Sean, I'm sorry for your pain. What you have to deal with must be unbearable."

Sean nodded, clenching his hands together. He looked up. "Brigid's lawyer is trying to get a plea deal. If she pleads guilty to voluntary manslaughter, her prison time for killing Ashley, and the kidnapping and aggravated assault of Sophie, can be served concurrently."

"Did she tell you why she killed Ashley?"

Sean nodded miserably. "She drove to Columbus for a surprise visit. When she pulled into the parking lot at Jack's, she saw Ashley and me having sex in my car. She drove to the hardware store and waited until I left, then confronted Ashley. She…" Sean chocked back a sob. "You know her temper. She didn't mean to kill her when she punched her in the face."

Aaron had deduced as much. But there was one question whose answer still eluded him. "How did she know to choose Sophie's farm to hide the body?"

Sean cleared his throat again. "She snooped through the cardboard box you kept under your bed in the dorm."

Aaron nodded. "She read the article about the farm being abandoned after the fire and Mr. Madison's death."

"She remembered the article when she was trying to find somewhere to dump Ashley's body."

"Did she tell you what happened at Sophie's house, and the farm, before the sheriff got there?"

Sean shook his head. "Brigid insisted I be present when her lawyer interviewed her about Ashley's death, but asked me to leave when the lawyer started asking questions about Sophie." He wiped the underside of his nose with the sleeve of his shirt and then sighed. "I think she had justified in her mind what happened with Ashley and she wanted me to know that she never intended to kill her. But she didn't want to witness my reaction when I heard the details of what happened the night she tried to kill Sophie."

Aaron shook his head, pulled in a breath and then let it out. "You both did what you did because you were afraid of losing each other."

Sean stood. "And that, boyo, is something I will regret for the rest of my life."

Aaron was suddenly awash with nostalgia of the first time Sean had addressed him as 'boyo' in their freshman dorm in college. His heart ached with the loss of Sean's friendship. After the last few weeks of letting anger consume him, Aaron had finally asked God to help him to forgive Sean and Brigid. The anger had dissipated, but the bond of friendship had been broken beyond repair.

"Sean, I've already forgiven you. If you trust in Jesus and lay your sins at the foot of the cross, you will be forgiven and relieved of the horrible burden you carry. I prayed to God to help me live with the burden of pain, guilt, and sin after I killed Sophie's father. And he answered my prayer."

There was a brief flicker of hope in Sean's eyes. "I'd forgotten what happened to you when you were seventeen." His voice faltered. "I...I haven't been to Catholic mass in a long time." He drew in a breath. "But I'll go Sunday... and I'll pray for Brigid and me."

Aaron walked to the door and opened it for Sean. "I wish you the best and I will keep praying for you and Brigid."

The moisture was back in Sean's eyes. "You, too, boyo."

Aaron pushed the door shut and dug out his phone from the pocket of his jeans. Allison had called yesterday. Sophie was being released from the hospital today and Allison wanted him to call Sophie…begged him to call her. If only he could go to her, touch her face, and comfort her as he had in the hospital. But she had made it clear, on more than one occasion, that she no longer had feelings for him.

Aaron had said goodbye to Sean forever. He needed to do the same for Sophie. He put the phone back in his jean pocket.

Chapter Sixty-Seven

Moonlight shone through the slats in the window blind, casting pearl-colored lines across Sophie's comforter as she awoke with a start, nightshirt soaked and body trembling. *Another nightmare.* Every night, for the past week, since being released from the hospital, she had dreamed she was being stalked through a horrible storm by a hulking shape with no face holding a sledge hammer in both hands. She pulled the soaked shirt over her head and tossed it to the floor. She pulled the comforter up to her neck, shivering. Slowly the shivering left her as she took deep, even breaths.

The psychiatrist at the hospital had warned her that she would likely experience bad dreams because of the horrific events she had been through. He said she may or may not remember what happened to her the night she was kidnapped. Some patients experienced fragmented memories; some never gained their memories back. Only a very few remembered everything.

Sophie lowered the comforter and took a last calming breath. Did the nightmares stem from what she had been told or from her subconscious? Either way, she couldn't let these night terrors change her life—like the events of the summer she was seventeen. She sucked in a breath.

Aaron.

She closed her eyes, an imaginary finger tracing the contours of his face. Her heartbeats quickened. Allison's voice whispered, *'He loves you so much, Sophie.'* She opened her eyes and flung off the comforter, stepping to the dresser. She pulled another night shirt over her head and headed down the stairs to the living room.

Sophie turned a lamp on and walked over to the built-in bookcase. She pulled out a book with the title 'How to Become a Better Writer.' She placed a hand lovingly on the paper jacket cover. She had thought the book had been lost in the fire that consumed the farmhouse, but Aaron had found it the next day in the gazebo and returned it to her aunt, while she was still in the hospital.

She opened the book, her fingers gently flipping pages. They stilled mid-way through the book. A pressed flower lay on the page. She lifted it to her nose. She breathed in, but no scent remained upon the dried petals of the rose Aaron had given her the day they had walked hand and hand through the field of the Burbage farm for a picnic. It was the evening Aaron had kissed her for the second time. The sweet pressure of his lips had had time moving in slow motion and Sophie wishing the kiss would never end.

She returned the flower to the book and the book to the bookshelf. She clicked off the light and made her way back to her bedroom.

Chapter Sixty-Eight

A nurse in scrubs bearing the Chicago Cub's logo flicked a finger against the IV bag. The slow drip resumed. She shook her head and muttered, "Modern technology."

She turned with a bright smile towards her patient. "There you go. Anything else? More water in your pitcher?"

Aaron nodded. "By the way, can I have your nurses' scrubs? I'll be the envy of everyone on the team."

Nurse Lori laughed. "I special ordered them. We get a lot of you boys from the Cubs for orthopedic surgery at Weiss Hospital."

She grabbed the water pitcher off the tray. "Back in a sec."

Aaron returned to the musing he had been doing before the nurse arrived. Sophie had called him an hour ago. At the sound of her voice, his traitorous heart leapt.

Sophie was having a tough time. She had nightmares and anxiety attacks every few days, but had agreed to see a therapist. For the last month, Allison had been phoning him every other day on Sophie's progress. But the conversations had finally become too unbearable and he had told Allison yesterday morning that he and Sophie led separate lives and it was time to sever all ties. He had thanked her for the flowers and told her gently, but firmly, that she was welcome to call anytime, but he didn't want her to mention Sophie's name.

And then out of the blue, Sophie had called this morning. It had been an awkward conversation. She asked how his surgery went, and when he could go home. Thanked him for visiting her in the hospital. All the correct, polite things you say to someone you know, but aren't particularly close to. By the end, his heart had turned into a lead weight. Before she hung up, Sophie had said his name, then paused as if to say something else, only to abruptly say good bye and hang up.

He pushed himself further up in the bed, gritting his teeth at the stab of pain in his knee. He was being released tomorrow. After his knee healed, he could look forward to grueling sessions of physical therapy. Aaron sighed as he looked out the window at the fat snowflakes floating down. *Sophie.*

Cold March sunlight streamed through the kitchen window. Sophie, hands on her hips, stood next to the table, tapping her foot. *Where are my running shoes?* It was Saturday and her neurologist had cleared her to start running again—slowly. The frown creases smoothed out. *I left them in the trunk of the car.* She slipped on a pair of clogs and hit the button on the garage door opener. She pressed a button on the car key fob and the trunk popped opened. Sure enough, her gym bag with the shoes and a running outfit sat right where she had put it sometime back in December.

Sophie leaned into the small trunk and was slammed with vertigo. She grabbed the bottom edge of the trunk as images bombarded her. *Wet, cracked asphalt...a bright flash of light... a woman, soaking wet, holding a fat-headed hammer in her hand. Wet strands of hair whipping across her face...a loud crack...and the smell of coffee.*

Sophie gripped the trunk edge tighter and struggled to breathe as darkness pressed in all around her...*In the darkness of the trunk, her mother's voice.*

Sophie closed her eyes. Her mother had told her to pray. Her eyes popped open. *She had prayed for God to help her and...*Sophie slowly stood up, the vertigo dissipating, tremors coursing through her body. *He had answered her prayer.*

She staggered over to the cold porch steps and slumped onto the top step. Her eyes filled as she craned her head upwards and whispered, "God?"

Warmth infused her body even as she started to shake. She leaned over and wept.

Sophie wiped her eyes and nose with her sleeve. Her breaths misted in the air as she climbed to her feet and entered the kitchen. She sat down heavily in a chair, picked up her iPhone and tapped in a number as she took in a shaky breath.

"Hey, Sophie."

"Can you come over?"

"What's wrong? You sound upset." Allison's tone was laced with concern.

"I remember what happened to me. All my memories are back."

"I'll be right over."

Sophie set the phone on the glass table. Why wasn't she dead? Sean's wife attempted to kill her three times and should have succeeded. But Brigid O'Connor's plans had been thwarted by the ringtone on Sophie's phone, a bolt of lightning, and a dog. These three random acts were not coincidences. There was only one reason she survived…God answered her prayer. Bowing her head and closing her eyes, Sophie offered up another prayer.

Chapter Sixty-Nine

Family, friends, and fans were yelling and cheering as the twelve-year-old young man with a prosthetic leg ran for the base. Aaron was coaching at first base and high-fived the pre-teen as he arrived. The boy's grin went ear-to-ear. The next batter up was an eight-year-old boy with Down syndrome. The retired pitcher for the Milwaukee Brewers moved in closer and lobed the ball. The boy knocked it a couple of feet and took off running. He jumped on the square white bag and shook a fist.

Aaron grinned. It was a perfect day to hold a charity event for disabled youngsters at Whitewater High School. The April showers had held off and the temperature was a balmy seventy degrees. He had been unable to train with the Cubs this spring while his knee recovered and had decided to volunteer for the event when his mom called and told him about it.

His best friend from high school, Jason Burbage, one of the announcers, gave him a thumbs up when their gaze connected. It was the first day in months that Aaron could truly say he was enjoying himself. He had shaken hands and hugged people he knew from his senior year in high school. Only one person was missing, but he pushed her to furthest reaches of his mind.

It was the ninth inning and the last batter rolled up to home base in his wheelchair. His grip on the bat was firm and his face a mask of furious concentration. There was a loud crack when the ball met the bat. It sailed over the pitcher's head. The crowd went nuts as the young man pumped the wheels of the chair like a piston to first base and then rounded it for second.

Another young man, missing an arm, chased after the ball in the outfield. He scooped it up like a professional and tossed it out of his glove to second base. But by the time the ball was headed for home, boy and wheelchair had crossed over the base. Jason announced that the game was over, but could barely be heard over the shouts and screams. People poured out of the stands, congratulating the young ballplayers. Mothers were wiping away tears as they hugged their handicapped children.

"You've got some competition coming up." Aaron's mom was wiping away her own tears.

Aaron grinned. "That I do, Mom...that I do." He waved at his dad, who was standing by the bleachers. "Thanks for picking me up and bringing me here today."

"Are you ready to go to Jessica's for dinner with the Burbages?"

"Whenever you are." Using the crutch to help take the weight off of his knee, he followed his mom, the brace on his knee forcing a stiff-legged gait.

As he reached his father near the stands, Aaron glanced up and halted mid-step. He blinked to make sure he wasn't hallucinating or projecting what he wanted to see. But she was still there, sitting on the top row of the bleachers, wisps of hair caressing her cheeks in the breeze. *Sophie.* His breath caught in his throat. She looked exactly as she had in high school. Her hair was pulled back in a ponytail and she was wearing a yellow sundress, similar to one she had worn quite a lot during the summer of their senior year.

Time stopped and the clock turned backward. He was seventeen again, heart thudding against his rib cage with a love that could never be extinguished.

"Aaron, what are you staring...oh."

Sophie waved and rose from the bleacher.

"Come on, David." Aaron's mother grabbed her husband's arm. "Have Sophie bring you to the restaurant." She walked off with Aaron's dad.

David looked back over his shoulder at his son, who had not moved a muscle. "What's going on?"

"Isn't it obvious?" She wiped another tear from her eye.

Aaron focused on Sophie, carefully making her way down from the bleachers. She walked the few steps to where Aaron was standing.

A few more dark hairs pulled loose from her ponytail in the breeze. His mind flashed back to Sophie swinging on the tire swing at the farm, wisps of hair fanning her face. His fingers lifted and smoothed the strands back behind Sophie's small ear.

She sighed and pressed her face against his palm. The gesture quickened his heartbeats.

"Aaron," she whispered.

"Sophie," he murmured back.

She grasped his fingers with her own, sending an immediate warmth coursing through his body.

"Will you come with me to my mother's gazebo? I have some things I need to tell you."

Aaron nodded. He adjusted his crutch and, mindful of his knee, they slowly made their way to Sophie's car.

Sophie and Aaron sat down on a peeling bench in the gazebo. Sophie pulled away a little. Was she struggling with how to begin? He laid a hand over her hands pressed tightly together in her lap. She turned, her smile trembling at the corners.

"Sophie, if this is too uncomfortable for you, we…"

"No…it's just…" Sophie squared her shoulders, took a breath, and began by telling Aaron what transpired on the day her father died, before Aaron arrived at the farm. Then she told him about the fourteen years they had been apart—how driven and focused she had been in college and with her career—trying to stay one step ahead of the bad memories and the devastating loss of the boy she loved.

Tears ran down Aaron's cheeks as Sophie's words finally whispered to a halt and she covered her face, weeping.

When her crying stopped, Aaron ran a sleeve across his face and spoke in a tone full of remorse, "I'm sorry. It's all my fault. If I hadn't been late…you wouldn't have…your father wouldn't have…"

Sophie dropped her hands and shook her head. "No, if it's anyone's fault, it's mine. My refusal to see a therapist and face my fears…pushing you…out of my mind and out of my life, as if you never existed." Her lower lip trembled. "Can you forgive me?"

"Can you forgive me?"

"There is nothing to forgive," they said in unison and then smiled a bit.

Sophie's eyes were twin blue-green pools, strong emotion shinning in the depths. "Aaron, I want what we had before...I want...you."

Aaron sighed heavily and looked down at their entwined hands. "But I don't want you to be reminded of...I don't ever want to hurt..."

"Will you marry me?"

Aaron's head jerked up. "What?"

A mischievous sparkle arose from the depths of the twin pools. "It's a simple question, milord. Requiring only a 'yes' or a 'no.'"

Aaron rose carefully to his feet, pulling Sophie with him. He brushed a strand of hair away from her eye. "Milady, it would be my honor."

He then lowered his head and kissed her with all the pent up emotion of fourteen years of separation.

When he lifted his head, Sophie brushed quivering fingers across his cheek. "I love you, forever and always."

Aaron lifted his hand and grasped hers. "Forever and always."

Muted conversations and quiet laughter traveled on the light breeze across the still waters of the pond. The small, white chairs placed in neat rows in front of the gazebo were filling with women in their Sunday best and men in jackets and ties. The lowering sun glinted off the prisms placed artfully among the wildflowers and bows decorating the gazebo. The gazebo, repaired and repainted, glowed a pristine white.

In the back seat of a large SUV, Sophie watched the arriving guests. Her heart swelled. Her heavenly Father had given her the strength to let go of the last thread of emotional trauma that tied her to the past—the thread that had kept her from living the life she was meant to live with the man she loved. She laughed.

"What's funny?"

Sophie looked over at Allison. "The look on Aaron's face when I asked him to marry me."

"He couldn't have looked more stunned than I did when you told me you had asked him. I almost fainted dead away. You didn't even tell me you were going to see him. You said he was your past...period."

"I thought he was—but I was wrong." Sophie looked back out at the guests.

Allison leaned over and smoothed out a small wrinkle in Sophie's sleeveless, tea-length tulle and appliqué lace white gown. She and Sophie had visited ten stores before finding the perfect dress. Sophie looked absolutely beautiful in it. "Sophie?"

Sophie turned back.

"I haven't had a chance to tell you, with all the preparations, but I went to mass last Sunday for the first time in over ten years. Liam went with me."

Sophie's eyes widened.

Allison picked up Sophie's hand. "You've been so happy...so full of joy since renewing your relationship with God...I realized I've missed...him."

Sophie squeezed her hand. "Me, too." She reached a hand up and lightly ran it down the back of her head. "How's my hair?"

Allison's eyes roamed over the loose dark curls that flowed past Sophie's shoulders. The glossy tresses were held back by a headband of petite white wildflowers. "Perfect."

Sophie's head turned again as music entered the car. Aaron's eighty-year-old maternal grandmother, dressed in a periwinkle blue dress, was carefully escorted to a seat in the front row. Next, Aaron's mother, in pale pink, was escorted to her seat. A car door opened and Aaron and his father emerged from a vehicle identical to her SUV. Her eyes welled as her heartbeats quickened. Aaron, resplendent in a dove gray suit and lavender tie, walked through the wildflowers to the front of the gazebo.

The door on Allison's side opened and David Reinhart—an older version of Aaron, with gray instead of blonde hair—held out his hand to her. She gave Sophie a quick peck on the cheek and exited the vehicle. She looked stunning in a short-sleeved, calf-length lavender dress, her hair pulled back in a French knot. Allison slipped her hand through the crook in David's arm as they strolled to the front of the gazebo, separating as they approached Aaron.

"Ms. Madison." Mr. McNair had his right hand out to help her out of the backseat.

Sophie had nearly burst into tears when Mr. McNair had approached her at work and said it would be an honor to escort her down the aisle at her wedding. Raising her hand to be grasped by her escort, she smiled at the genuine happiness for her that had transformed her boss's face. Who knew that underneath that gruff, intimidating exterior, beat a tender heart?

She rose from the vehicle and Mr. McNair shut the door. Sophie gripped Mr. McNair's crooked elbow and walked towards the aisle of wildflowers.

A soft bark sounded from the back row, on the left. Cooper sat on his haunches beside his owner, his tail sweeping wildflowers back and forth. As Sophie came even with the yellow Lab she paused to bend over and give Cooper a loving pat on the head. As she reached the midway point of the aisle, she spotted Sheriff Cox and Detectives Burke and Mason. She gave them a grateful smile before turning her eyes back to the love of her life.

As she approached Aaron, a single tear escaped from her left eye and slid slowly down her cheek. *Thank you, God, for showing me the way back to Aaron.*

Mr. McNair and Sophie came to a stop in front of Aaron. The music ended and a young man stepped forward. The taped intro to 'When God Made You' began and the singer raised the microphone.

More tears fell as Aaron held out his hand and Mr. McNair stepped back. She grasped Aaron's fingers and they both turned to climb the two steps into the gazebo, followed by Allison and David. They halted in front of Pastor Anthony as the lyrics and music Aaron had chosen especially for her flowed around them.

Her aquamarine eyes smiled through her tears into Aaron's blue ones as soft crying erupted behind them. Aaron raised her hand and kissed the knuckles.

The music ended and the Pastor cleared his throat. "It is my great pleasure this evening to unite Aaron Reinhart and Sophie Madison in holy matrimony."

With the pounding of her heart loud in her ears, Sophie barely heard the words of the pastor as he talked about the sanctity of marriage. The pastor's flow of words came to a halt and a woman in her early forties took the microphone from the young man and sang the song Sophie had chosen. A song about losing her way and God setting her back on the path to Aaron— 'Bless the Broken Road.'

Tissues appeared from clutches and pockets as Sophie softly kissed Aaron's knuckles. The pastor produced two handkerchiefs and handed one to Sophie and one to Aaron as the last notes of the song faded. "I bring two to every wedding."

The guests laughed as Aaron and Sophie wiped their faces.

Pastor Anthony looked out over the guests. "Aaron and Sophie have written their own vows. Sophie has asked to give hers first."

Sophie took a shaky breath and gripped Aaron's hands tightly. "Fourteen years ago, I died and an actress was born. I played my part well, pretending emotions I could no longer feel. And I would have lived the rest of my life as a thespian on the stage, had it not been for an accidental fall into a well. A face, your face, full of love, gazed down at me in that well and for the first time in fourteen years I felt...the stirrings of something I thought long dead."

Aaron squeezed her hands as she took another breath. "Those feelings were accompanied by bad memories—as you know." Aaron nodded. "And you...and you..." Sophie chocked back a sob. "You loved me so much, you walked away for the second time."

She quickly swiped her eyes and nose with the handkerchief. "God showed me how to let go of the past and embrace a future with you. Thank you for gifting me with your unconditional love. I vow to be worthy of that love for the rest of our lives."

Sophie smiled tremendously up at Aaron. "I love you."

The pastor glanced at Aaron.

Aaron rubbed the top of Sophie's right hand with his thumb. "Sophie, I have loved you since the moment I saw you in the doorway of our English class in high school. I even loved you when you *pretended* to want nothing to do with me." Sophie smiled. "I vow to be your companion, friend, confidant, baseball player...," Sophie laughed, "...and safe harbor for as long as we both shall live. There is no sacrifice that I would not make for you. I love you now and forever."

More tears welled as Sophie eyes were drawn to movement over Aaron's right shoulder. Shimmering amongst the wildflowers by the pond was the image of a dark-haired woman in a flowing white dress, blowing her a kiss. She blinked and the vision disappeared. Sophie turned her wet eyes back to Aaron.

Genevieve approved.

Acknowledgements

The main setting of this book is based on trips to the Midwest during my childhood. I have many fond memories of visiting relatives in the farmlands of Wisconsin. Sophie's farm is based on my cousin Shirley's farm in La Grange. Her husband, Dean, was beyond helpful on all aspects of a farm, including planting and harvesting corn, and the function of a dry well.

A large portion of the novel centered on law enforcement investigating the discovery of a skeleton found in the dry well on Sophie's farm. Career Officer Scott Worley read every scene involving the investigation, making corrections on procedure where needed.

Randy Rowlett, judge, lawyer, and member of my church sent detailed emails full of invaluable information for writing scenes involving Aaron's lawyer and other legal procedures.

Most writers know your novel is not complete without a methodical, critical read through by your beta readers. They are wonderful at ferreting out those writings mistakes all authors make. Their critique was invaluable.

As with my other novels, I give all glory for my writing gift to my father in Heaven.